They were coming. . . .

Charlotte knelt down, peering into the darkness of the hollow log.

"Honey, it's okay," she said, "I'm here with your father, come on out!"

Paul made it up the slope and peered over her shoulder. "Darryl, can you hear me? Come out, son, please!"

Charlotte could hear movement in the woods behind them, getting closer by the second. She turned back to the log and pleaded, "Darryl, listen to me! You've got to come out now! There isn't much time!"

Footsteps . . . almost on top of them.

Paul howled at the darkness, "DARRYL YOU COME OUT OF THERE THIS INSTANT!"

Charlotte had started to say something . . . when she heard the dry-husk sound of gunmetal snapping behind her.

"Get down!" she cried, barely grabbing a piece of Paul's shoulder and yanking him to the ground.

And then the woods erupted behind them.

Praise for Jay Bonansinga's thrillers:

**"Bonansinga sets a new record
for breakneck pacing."
—*Publishers Weekly***

"Serious entertainment."—*The Times* (London)

Bloodhound

Jay Bonansinga

AN ONYX BOOK

ONYX
Published by New American Library, a division of
Penguin Putnam Inc., 375 Hudson Street,
New York, New York 10014, U.S.A.
Penguin Books Ltd, 27 Wrights Lane,
London W8 5TZ, England
Penguin Books Australia Ltd, Ringwood,
Victoria, Australia
Penguin Books Canada Ltd, 10 Alcorn Avenue,
Toronto, Ontario, Canada M4V 3B2
Penguin Books (N.Z.) Ltd, 182–190 Wairau Road,
Auckland 10, New Zealand

Penguin Books Ltd, Registered Offices:
Harmondsworth, Middlesex, England

First published by Onyx, an imprint of New American Library,
a division of Penguin Putnam Inc.

First Printing, September 1999
10 9 8 7 6 5 4 3 2 1

For Joey

ACKNOWLEDGMENTS

A special thanks to Jeanne Bonansinga, Joe Pittman, Jennifer Robinson, Bob Mecoy, Peter Miller, Ben Adams, Norm Kelly, Dave Johnson, Officer John Buckley, Dr. Robert DiDomenico, Dr. Harry Jaffe, Julie Stewart, David Quinn, Harlan Ellison, Ed Gorman, Michael Stein, Jim Wilson, Bruce Clorefene, Mort Castle, Don VanderSluis, and Bruce Ingram.

Also lending inspiration and background were the life works of Dorothy Allison and David Morehouse.

A special acknowledgment goes out to the writings of Harlan Ellison, especially his masterwork, *Mefisto in Onyx*, without which I could not have created this story.

PART 1

THE COIN

"The mind is a dangerous weapon,
even to the possessor . . ."
—MONTAIGNE

1

Opening a Circuit

"I brought something with me," the mousey woman said, rooting around in her purse. "I don't know if you can use it . . . but Paulie used to carry it around with him . . . a good luck charm . . . you know."

She pulled the coin from her purse and set it on the dining table.

It was the color of old pewter, tarnished and oxidized with age. It had a dull gleam to it. And a weightiness. Looked as though it had been burnished by the caress of countless greedy fingers, countless transactions. It was an old Susan B. Anthony silver dollar.

The psychic looked at it carefully, but made no effort to pick it up. "That's fine, honey," the psychic said, "but first I need to know a little more about you and your boyfriend. How it all happened."

There was a pause, and the mousey woman took a deep breath, glancing wistfully off at the windows.

Across the table, Charlotte Vickers, the area's leading police psychic, waited patiently. Charlotte was a soft woman in her late thirties, with peaches-and-cream skin, raven hair, and pale blue eyes that shimmered perpetually with emotion. She was still dressed in her quilted silk robe and slippers, and was just now sipping the morning's first cup of Earl Grey. Charlotte had her mother's physique, a body that ad men used to call "full-figured" and her father used to say was the spitting image of Jane Russell. But unfortunately, the fleshy glamour-girl look went out sometime back, around the heyday of the hula hoop, and now Charlotte had to perform minor miracles with the blush-on and eye shadow. Especially as she crept toward the forty side of thirty. She had started sticking cartoons of circus fat ladies and corpulent barnyard animals on her refrigerator.

Only minutes ago, Charlotte had been awakened out of a deep sleep by the mousey woman's knock on the front door, and things were still rather blurry. The facts were as follows: The mousey woman had introduced herself as Natalie Fortunato, a local woman who had read about Charlotte in the newspaper, and she was here this morning as a last resort. She was desperate to find her missing boyfriend, and it now seemed that someone of Charlotte's métier was her last hope.

Charlotte had been reluctant at first—she was officially retired from missing person work—but her big, soft heart had gotten the better of her. She had invited the little gal inside, and now the two of them sat at Charlotte's enormous oak dining table, a sterling silver tea service spread out in front of them, the Seth Thomas clock ticking steadily in the background.

"His name is Paul," the mousey woman began. "And we'd been going out for three years before he . . . you know . . ."

"Vanished?" Charlotte said, blowing on her tea.

Natalie nodded. "It was so sudden . . . Things had been going so well, you know . . . I still can't believe it."

Charlotte sipped her tea, then said, "How long ago did he vanish, honey?"

"Eleven months, seven days, and fourteen hours."

"I see." Charlotte felt a splinter of sympathetic emotion stab at her temple. She shook it off. There was something eating at her, something about this woman. Something familiar. "Can you tell me the circumstances?"

"I was supposed to meet him at his office," the little woman said bitterly, staring at the tea service as though it were a basket of dead kittens. "He was in the accounting business, you know, but he wasn't boring or anything, he was fun—you know?—and we were supposed to have a picnic that day at Oak Street Beach." She paused for a moment, wiping the corner of her eye with the back of her hand.

Charlotte watched the mousey woman for a moment. The little gal was barely over five feet tall, with tanned, wiry arms and almond eyes that darted about on currents of electricity. She looked like an anorexic Chihuahua on fen-phen. Somewhere in her late thirties, she had chromium blond hair pulled back in a tight bun—a vein of black roots beginning to show—and she wore the kind of discount high-fashion garb that just broke Charlotte's heart. A denim skirt with little sunflower appliqués, a denim top, an imitation leather vest.

"But when I showed up at his office," she went on, "the door was open, and the coffee machine was on, but Paulie was gone. Just . . . gone."

"What do you think happened?" Charlotte asked. "Do you think he was kidnapped?"

Natalie shrugged. "I don't know why in the world anybody would want to kidnap Paulie. I mean, his family was dirt poor, and Paulie was probably still paying off his college loans. Besides, if he was kidnapped, wouldn't somebody send a ransom note, something like that?"

Charlotte nodded and sipped her tea, thinking, then she said, "I guess you went to the police, right?"

Natalie scowled as though tasting something bad. "Those guys don't give a good goddamn about finding Paulie—pardon my French. I filled out all their forms

and answered all their questions, and far as I can tell,
they haven't done one thing."

There was a torturous pause as Natalie Fortunato
chewed her lip, the words hanging in the air like a
bad odor. The light shimmered off the little lady's
eyes, her tears welling, glistening. Finally one broke
free and tracked down her cheek, dripping on the
table. Charlotte felt her stomach tighten. This was just
plain unfair.

Natalie was sniffing back her tears now, gazing
around the room.

To most visitors, Charlotte's place seemed surprisingly simple: a prairie-style nest of early American
folk art and Colonial-repro furniture. No crystals, no
pyramids, no candles, no holy water . . . none of the
typical accouterments one might expect to see in a
psychic's lair. The home was very practical, very cozy.
The heart of the bungalow was a combination living
room–dining area, bordered along the front by a
comfy sectional sofa drowning in pillows and antique
stuffed animals. The fulcrum point was the massive
nineteenth-century dining table around which Natalie
and Charlotte now sat. It was the place where Charlotte conducted most of her consultations—usually
four or five private referrals per week. These sessions
provided enough income to pay the bills, but not much
more. Charlotte had to be careful about how many
consultations she conducted; they took so much out
of her. Plus the clients had to be carefully screened;
she could not risk getting involved with anything
nasty—it could virtually rip her brain out of her skull
by the roots.

And she experienced enough of *that* action on her
police cases.

"Palmistry?" Natalie was saying, wiping her eyes
with a napkin, gazing off at something on the wall.

"Pardon me, honey?"

Natalie pointed toward the bookcase. "Says Palm-istry. Those books. You read palms?"

"Oh . . . yeah, yeah, I'm sorry, honey, yes, I do read palms." Charlotte smiled. The wall behind her was lined with bookcases brimming with textbooks and manuals on tarot cards, astrology, and other New Agey practices. But mostly there were books on palm-istry. Well-thumbed copies of *The Big Book of Palm Reading, Revealing Hands,* and a portentous-looking, leather-bound number called *Palmascope.*

Aside from her two years of junior college, Char-lotte's formal education had mostly been self-adminis-tered, and palmistry had become her specialty. She liked the intimacy of it, the warmth, the touch. There was always something very soothing about cradling a person's hand and "reading" the fissures and fault lines of that person's destiny. But mostly it was a safe way for Charlotte to "tune" her feelings to an individ-ual's frequency without actually opening a circuit.

Opening a circuit was how Charlotte had come to think of her talent (never clairvoyance or mind-read-ing), and there was indeed something *electrical* about it. Something in the neurons, or the synapses, or the neuro-chemical reactions that happened in Charlotte's noggin. Something like that. Charlotte didn't spend too much time qualifying it. It was hard enough just living with it, because sometimes a circuit would open on its own, unbidden, just from the slightest touch. And then the images would crackle across Charlotte's mindscreen, uninvited, lurid and garish. All from the accidental grope of a doorknob or telephone receiver or light switch. It was mostly visual, but often other sensory information would jolt into her head as well. Ephemeral thought-banners, feelings, sensations from someone else's brain that were happening right at that moment. It could be maddening. And that's why Char-lotte had developed an internal switch. Like the pop of a jaw, or the click of a double-jointed bone, she could usually open the head circuit at will, or keep it closed off if she were feeling the least bit reluctant.

Like this morning.

The truth was, plugging in to a person's head was like breaking in to a strange house in the pitch dark of night without a floor plan. There were strange smells, mazes of hallways, odd vibrations, and God-only-knows-what-else lurking in the crawl spaces. It was an experience Charlotte made every effort to avoid.

But sometimes—like this morning—it seemed inevitable.

"I'll tell you the truth, honey," Charlotte added softly. "I prefer reading palms to locating missing persons."

"I'll pay you whatever you need. The seventy-five dollars is nothing to me. I'll pay you ten times that."

"It's not the money."

The mousey woman swallowed hard. "Then what else can I offer you?"

Charlotte sighed and sipped her tea. Again she was stricken with the feeling that she had seen this little gal somewhere before. Maybe on television? Could that be possible? Could this mousey little thing in the TJ Maxx denim be famous? Charlotte wasn't a big TV-watcher; she mostly liked the late-night shows. Insomniac Theater. Anything to fill the terrible silence at three o'clock in the morning.

The coin sat there on the tabletop like a dull silver stain.

"Please, Miss Vickers, I'm begging you," Natalie softly pleaded.

Charlotte looked at the coin.

Natalie muttered, "Please."

Charlotte picked up the coin, closed her fist around it, and opened the circuit—

(—a thousand miles away—)

—and Charlotte flinched slightly, and swallowed air, and cleared her throat. It happened sometimes: A spontaneous jolt of energy off an object before Charlotte was completely ready, coalescing in her mind as pure cognition. Like static electricity crackling in her brain. This particular coin was charged with it.

Charlotte looked down at the tarnished silver dollar in her hand.

It was practically vibrating.

"Miss Vickers? You all right? You feel something?" Natalie was staring at her.

"I'm fine, honey," Charlotte managed to say, and then uttered softly, "but I think we hit pay dirt."

2

Shards

It took less than a half an hour to get a general idea of the man's location.

The sensation was a little bit like gobbling an ice cream cone too quickly, or sucking down a milk shake too fast: that momentary vise grip at the top of the nasal passages, so excruciating and sharp it brings tears to the eyes, and once in a while even makes the nose bleed. Charlotte was feeling that pain right now as she sat in the dining room, still in her robe, holding the Susan B. Anthony in her hands, the sunlight slanting in through dust motes.

She kept rubbing the coin, her heart thumping, her eyes pressed closed—

(—*bright light . . . bright blue light . . . up in the trees . . . the sky . . . through the pine boughs . . . like bright blue shards of broken glass*—)

Charlotte shuddered, taking another deep breath, wiping away a curlicue of dark hair that had become matted to her sweaty forehead. It was shaping up to be a hot one today—maybe even record-breaking hot for June in Chicago—and Charlotte was laboring furiously, all her powers of concentration focused on the open circuit between her hand and the coin. Across the table, Natalie Fortunato was chewing her fingernails, watching, wide-eyed and jittery.

Charlotte closed her eyes again, and let the distant feelings flow into her on invisible current—

—and Natalie watched Charlotte's eyes dancing and flitting beneath her lids—

—as the involuntary REM jolted down Charlotte's cerebral cortex—

(moving down a sun-dappled dirt trail behind the cabin, the forest so dark and thick it seems to swallow up the light, there's a continual burbling sound off to the left, the glitter of sunlight on a stream peeking through the blue spruce and aspens, and now I'm walking over turf that's almost like a soft carpet, the moist pine needles and leaves, the air crisp with Ponderosa pine. Smells so goddamn great around here, with the wildflowers—what do they call them?—Indian paintbrush? Smells fresh, like a fresh start—yeah, that's it— A FRESH START!—)

Charlotte blinked again, the pain interrupting the flow of sensation.

The psychic current was amazingly visceral this time, more visceral than any other missing person case Charlotte had ever encountered. She could feel the spongy carpet of pine needles on the soles of her bare feet, as though the very carpet beneath the table had momentarily transformed. She could smell the mountain air, so clean and crisp it hurt her lungs. Or maybe that was the altitude. It felt as though her little bungalow had levitated up into the clouds.

Natalie was transfixed by it all, watching, waiting. Every few moments Charlotte would murmur something to herself—something low and inarticulate—and Natalie would practically jump out of her skin. This little woman was so tightly wound, so tense, so edgy, Charlotte was starting to worry that the woman might actually have a nervous breakdown right here in Charlotte's living room. Especially when the little lady learned just exactly what the coin was saying about her boyfriend.

But Charlotte wanted to be sure before she said anything.

Squeezing the coin one last time, Charlotte closed her eyes and opened the circuit—

—into a missing man's brain—

(—*peering through the foliage, the undergrowth like a tapestry of green, I see a deer. It's a big twelve-point buck with a mangy hide and big fiery eyes, and it makes my heart race, and it's so beautiful, and all of a sudden I'm thinking, I did the right thing. Coming out here. I'm over the past now, I'm over it, because I've got a wife who loves me now, and my two precious boys, and they've all been troupers about the move, and I'm over the pain and heartache of Chicago, and I'm over being guilty about what I did, 'cause I got a brand new life now—*)

Charlotte cringed, the shooting pain cutting off the transmission.

Natalie stirred: "What is it? What is it?"

"Sometimes there's a sharp pain or two," Charlotte muttered breathlessly.

"Any clues yet? Anything at all?"

"I'm not sure," Charlotte said.

"What do you mean, you're not sure? You said we struck pay dirt. You said you needed to concentrate for a few minutes. You've been working on the thing for how long—forty-five minutes?"

"Take it easy, honey," Charlotte said, trying to ignore the ice cream headache that was splitting her skull in two. She had reached critical mass, and she needed an aspirin, and she needed a cold rag on her forehead, and she needed to get up and walk around for a while. But all of that would have to wait because she now knew all about the missing man. She knew he was somewhere a thousand miles west of Chicago, probably Colorado. Charlotte wasn't sure of the exact location yet, but the details probably didn't matter much anymore. Charlotte knew that the man named Paul Lattamore was married now—probably with a couple of stepchildren—and he was very happy to be away from Chicago. As a matter of fact, it was becoming clear that the man had vanished of his own accord. From the feelings of having a "fresh start" and "good riddance to Calumet City," it was painfully obvious that Lattamore had *wanted* to disappear.

So how was Charlotte going to break this news to this little wreck of a woman?

"Did you see something?" Natalie's voice was stretched thin with nerves. "Is he okay? Is he alive?"

"Yes, honey, I'm pretty sure he's okay, and he's definitely alive, *definitely*."

"Where is he? Was he kidnapped?"

Charlotte rubbed the bridge of her nose. "That's where it gets complicated."

"Why? Where is he?"

Charlotte looked at her. "I think he's in Colorado."

Natalie froze for a moment. *"Colorado?!"*

"Yes, honey, I think that's where he is. I think he's living in Colorado—"

"Goddamnit! Where?!" The mousey woman's voice had suddenly spiked an octave. She was leaning forward now, elbows on the table, her face a collection of jagged, broken angles, her eyes narrowed down to slits, a row of tiny lower teeth showing a feral sort of grimace. "What city?—Jesus Christ! Why Colorado?"

"Honey, it's not gonna do you any good getting all bent outta shape," Charlotte said. "Let's take this one step at a time. The good news is, your boyfriend's alive and well."

"I asked you what city in Colorado." Natalie was boring her gaze into Charlotte now.

"If you just listen to the rest of what I have to say—"

"Are you gonna tell me?!"

"I know you're upset, but if you just let me explain, I think you'll understand."

"Understand what?"

Charlotte took a breath, searching for the proper words. This wasn't going to be easy. "Honey, when I locate a person—a living person—I sometimes get a sense of their state of mind. What they happen to be feeling."

"So what's he *feeling* exactly?" Natalie said, and the emphasis that she put on the word *feeling* was like biting down on a shard of ice. The little gal was obviously seething with intense anger and pain and grief and confusion. Eleven months, seven days, and twenty-two hours of anger, pain, grief, and confusion, to be precise.

Charlotte took a long moment before she finally replied very softly but with enough resolve to make her point loudly and clearly: "He wasn't kidnapped, honey."

There was another pause, as Natalie glowered, veins pulsing in her temple.

Charlotte sighed. "Honey, I know this is terribly painful, but the thing is, Paul Lattamore is living a new life a long way away from here."

The mousey woman looked at her and said, "What do you mean, a new life?"

Charlotte realized that it was time to tell the truth. "He's married, Natalie. With kids. He has a new family now."

There was another awkward pause then, and Charlotte braced herself for the storm.

Natalie looked away, covering her mouth with her hand, and for a moment it looked as though she might begin to cry, or maybe even scream, or perhaps overturn the dining table, but then the strangest thing happened. Her eyes seemed to crystallize, her gaze turning into a laser beam, burning into the carpet, and from the looks of her face, that beige carpet was an abomination of nature. Again, Charlotte felt that vague feeling that she had seen Natalie's picture before in a magazine or a newspaper.

Natalie's voice was suddenly lower, flatter than before: "I need to know where he is in Colorado."

Charlotte said, "I don't know for sure, honey, I didn't get the specifics . . . but don't you think it kinda doesn't matter?"

Natalie looked up at Charlotte with eyes like acetylene torches. "What kind of fucking psychic are you?"

Charlotte felt goose bumps crawl up her back, the feeling of pure liquid hate radiating off the little gal. Charlotte said, "Honey, listen, I'm sorry it was bad news but—"

"Stop calling me 'honey' and stop calling me 'sweetheart' and stop with the bullshit."

There was another stretch of tense silence, and Charlotte could feel the rage filling the room like smoke, and she could feel her stomach tightening, her throat seizing up. She had expected a strong reaction, but nothing like this. The anger was seeping out of the Fortunato woman's pores, the lines deepening around her face until her flesh looked like an etching, her eyes like two little black diamonds pulsing with heat. She seemed to have aged fifteen years over the last minute.

Charlotte took a breath and said very softly, "I know you're upset, and I don't blame you, but you've gotta understand, I just get general impressions at first. And besides, I didn't think you needed to know his exact—"

The skinny little woman lunged across the table at Charlotte.

A bony hand clutched at Charlotte's throat—

—and a flashbulb popped in Charlotte's mind.

It happened so abruptly, so violently, that Charlotte

was barely aware that both teacups had skittered off
the edge of the table and careened to the floor, because now a deluge of feelings was streaming into
Charlotte from the tips of the mousey woman's fingers, and Charlotte was frozen to her chair as though
she were being electrocuted, and the feelings that were
pouring into her were chaotic and unorganized, a cacophony of hate and humiliation, devouring her like
black flames—

—and then Charlotte managed to yank herself away,
nearly tipping over backward in her chair.

The mousey woman stood over her, growling, "I
ask you to find out where he is, and all you can tell
me is *Colorado*?"

Charlotte was standing up now, backing away from
the little woman, rubbing her neck. "You're upset,
and you don't know what you're saying . . . and I
think you should go. Please. Now. Please go."

Natalie went over and scooped up her purse. She
turned and looked at Charlotte for another brief moment—and it looked as though Natalie might say
something else—and then she dug in her purse and
pulled out a few wrinkled twenty-dollar bills. She
threw them at Charlotte, and the bills fluttered to the
floor. Then Natalie turned, stomped across the living
room, and stormed out the front door.

Charlotte went over to the door and watched the
wiry little woman marching down the sidewalk.

Heading toward an obscenely huge Cadillac.

A huge Cadillac?

(*—snap!-CLANG!—*)

(*—the pump on a 12-gauge shotgun—*)

Charlotte slammed her door with a resounding
thump!—and then pressed her back against the door,
heart racing, mouth going dry. The revelation was a
dry pop in her skull, a firecracker going off in her

head. Her ears were ringing. She felt as though she were about to vomit.

She remembered where she had seen Natalie Fortunato.

A huge Cadillac.

The tiny tiles of a Rubik's Cube puzzle were clicking into place in Charlotte's head.

It was worse than Charlotte had imagined.

3

Cold Sweat

Paul Lattamore heard the noises sometime in the wee hours, and before he knew what was happening, he was sitting up in bed, covered in a sheen of clammy perspiration, his heart hammering furiously in his chest. A rangy man with ruddy, freckled skin and a thick head of sandy hair, he looked much younger than his forty-five years would suggest. Dressed in his customary sleeping attire of sweatpants and T-shirt, he blinked away the fire dots and swallowed the sour taste of fear as his eyes adjusted to the darkness. The tiny bedroom was just as he had left it before turning in, the shitty little veneer dresser in one corner, the spider plant hanging near the window—the medusa knot of tendrils hanging down, throwing shadow webs of moonlight across the opposite wall—and Sandy lying next to him, sweet Sandy, still smelling of the sex they had shared a couple of hours ago. The curve of her back was rising and falling gently under the covers, and Paul silently thanked Christ he hadn't awakened her again.

The sad fact was, Paul Lattamore was growing accustomed to waking up in a cold sweat in the middle of the night.

It went with the territory.

Somewhere downstairs the scratching noises continued, a faint, rhythmic tattoo like an icicle scraping glass, and Paul felt the skin on the backs of his arms and legs rashing with gooseflesh. He had felt so cocky earlier that day, dozing in his hammock, so smug in his little mountain paradise, and then the feeling had come like a bolt out of the blue, like a shock wave in his brain, and he was thinking tumor, and he was thinking stroke, and all the old fear and cold sweats had returned with a vengeance, and now his mind was filling with all sorts of images—a glass cutter on the sliding glass doors down in the kitchen, a stainless steel instrument picking at the front door's dead bolt—and he wondered if *this* was the uninvited visitor he had been bracing himself for these last twelve months. Was *this* the old fucker with the black, hooded robe and scythe, old Mister Death coming to claim his children?—children—*children!* A new surge of panic rose up in Paul's brain like a deadly jack-in-the-box. The kids were sleeping in the room across the hall, oblivious to the fact that somebody was downstairs trying to get into the house and do them all harm.

Paul padded barefoot across the room to the closet where he kept a Taurus .38-caliber snubbie. Nestled inside a plastic file case pushed against the back wall, it was one of the guns that the federal marshal had recommended off the record as the best bet for home defense. Paul kept it in the bedroom because it was probably the most idiot-proof of all his weapons. It was lightweight, easy to load, and mechanically very simple, and God knew, Paul Lattamore needed the most user-friendly weapon he could get. He was no gangster, after all—he was just a goddamn accountant. Standing on his tiptoes, he dug the revolver out of the case and quickly opened the cylinder. There were five rounds in the gun—Winchester 38-special hollow-points, another recommendation from Federal Marshal Vincent—the sixth chamber empty for safety purposes. Paul snapped the cylinder closed.

The sound rang out across the stillness, the air shattering like broken glass.

"Paul—?"

Sandy's voice came from behind him, hardly a whisper, but charged with sleepy panic. Paul turned and gazed at his wife, who was sitting up against the headboard. Paul whispered, "Stay calm, sweetie—"

"Paul—?"

"It's probably nothing."

"Omigod," she uttered, her fingers touching her teeth, her eyes wide and hot.

"It's nothing—stay here—"

"Paul, the kids—"

"Stay here, Sandy."

"But what about the drill? The drill, Paul—we're supposed to follow—"

"Everything's gonna be fine," he said, moving toward the door, the scratching noises skittering faintly downstairs in the dark. Paul put his hand on the doorknob, turned it silently, then glanced back at his wife. "Keep the door locked, and stay by the cordless," he whispered. "If you hear anything suspicious, anything at all, call the WITSEC emergency number. They'll have somebody here in a flash."

Paul stepped out into the hallway, the bedroom door latching closed behind him. He went over to the boys' door, carefully opened it, latched it from the inside, then pulled it closed. *Locked.* The glimpse he had just gotten of the two youngsters sprawled in their bunks—six-year-old Timmy in his Tasmanian Devil pajamas, nine-year-old Darryl in his lucky White Sox T-shirt—was burned like a flash frame across Paul's dark-blind retinas. How could he have put these boys in such jeopardy? It was a question that Paul had asked himself again and again, and the answer was always the same: Because Paul Lattamore was a stooge, a ruse. He had done this to his family because of plain old greed, because of ego, and mostly because Paul Lattamore was a chickenshit. And now, moving through the darkness of his cheap, little Colorado two-story, moving toward the staircase with a loaded weapon in his sweaty grasp, he was trying to channel all this self-hatred into something approaching courage.

(In his mind, a voice was screaming: *Why the hell choose a house that's so goddamn isolated? What's so great about three acres of remote forested property, eight thousand feet above sea level—where even during the summer the night winds will freeze your gonads off—when all you really need is a neighbor who might help you out of a jam?*)

He descended the steps as quietly as possibly, his ears hypersensitized to foreign sounds, his head cocked. The scratching noises had momentarily ceased, but Paul could still see the shadows of pines dancing out on the kitchen tile, coming through the sliding glass doors. Something was moving out there, moving along the foundation.

Paul thumbed the hammer back, gripping the gun with both hands.

Moving toward the kitchen, his feet ice-cold even through his thick wool socks, Paul felt the sensory overload washing over him: the distant burble of the creek that ran across his property line, the faint odors of mildew, traces of dinner—Sandy had cooked Middle Eastern for supper, and the house still smelled vaguely of nutmeg and curry—and even the cool, molded, beavertail grip of the .38 in his hand. Paul was trying to remember Marshal Vincent's crash course in defensive shooting: the tripod posture, elbows locked, left palm cupped, ready to absorb with his shoulder, breathing through the shot, breathing, breathing . . .

He entered the kitchen.

The pebbled tile was so cold it was like walking

on a skating rink, and the shadows swirled across the laminate cabinets, across the front of the fridge. In his panic-charged peripheral vision Paul could see the snapshots of his sons dressed in Little League gear stuck to the fridge door with pinecone magnets, and the sight of them gave Paul a strange kind of jolt—a mixture of shame and fight instinct that made him sharp, sharp as a razor, aiming the snubbie way out front with both hands—

The scratching noise again, behind him, to his left!

Paul pivoted suddenly, swinging the .38 toward the sound, locking onto the target outside the sliding glass near the plastic garbage pail, his brain registering the target a single micro-instant before the blast, hesitating, hesitating—a bony blur of fur out there burrowing into the bottom of the pail—sending the information back down to Paul's trigger finger, and all at once Paul realized what it was. He let up on the trigger, swung the barrel away, and let out a long sigh. His spine was throbbing with pain, his shoulder muscles spasming from the sustained tension.

He swallowed the sour-sweet taste of fear, walked over to the sliding door, and gave the glass a little kick. "Get outta here, you mangy piece of shit!"

The coyote glanced up at Paul with dumb brown eyes, sniffing the glass. Then Paul kicked the glass again, and the creature reared backward, ears pinned, whining indignantly a couple of times. Then it turned and ambled back into the shadows beyond the cement porch. Paul felt his body winding down in stages, relaxing, his muscles aching.

He went over to the fridge and fished around in the freezer for the bottle of vodka.

Sitting on a stool at the kitchen counter, swallowing big gulps of icy fire, Paul found himself thinking back over the last year and the ordeal he had put his family through.

The Lattamore family vanished from the face of the earth on a Thursday morning last July, a stunt which turned out to be one of our government's more inspired institutional magic tricks. It started around 11 A.M. when a couple of plainclothes federal marshals showed up at the Lattamores' home in Cicero, a blue-collar enclave on the west side of Chicago. The marshals wore Levi's and polo shirts, and they drove a nondescript Chevy Blazer, and they loaded the entire family into the vehicle—husband, wife, two boys, and one suitcase per person—and then they drove to O'Hare. The family was then escorted on board an unmarked military aircraft and flown to the WITSEC Orientation Center somewhere outside Washington, D.C.

WITSEC was an acronym for the Federal Witness Security Program, which had become known to most civilians as the witness protection program.

The Lattamores spent two weeks at the "safe site," a concrete purgatory that housed a walled dormitory within a walled compound. They never saw the outside of the facility—they were brought in via windowless vans and windowless garages—and the inside of their dorm was a sterile labyrinth of carpeted corridors and automatic doors. Under constant surveillance, secured by networks of electronic security systems and closed-circuit cameras, the safe site was where the Lattamores learned to shed their old skins and start their new lives.

It was an arduous process. Each member of the family underwent medical and dental exams, psychological testing, and even a battery of vocational inventories. The marshals provided groceries, incidental supplies, even CDs and videos for the boys. Each day—while the kids watched Jim Carrey movies—Paul and Sandy would study brochures and newspapers from various regions of the country. They were given the choice of where they would be relocated, just as they were allowed to choose their new last name. Paul thought it would be best to keep their original *first* names, especially for the kids. But Paul never dreamed how difficult the whole redocumentation process would be on the boys. They bickered and fought constantly, and they cried themselves to sleep each night. Little Timmy insisted on choosing his new last name, but Paul was forced to veto the six-year-old's choice of Schwarzenegger. Finally, after much trial and error, the Lattamores were transformed into the Staffords.

Grand Lake, Colorado, was chosen as the Staffords' new hometown—their "neutral site," in the parlance of the program—probably because it fulfilled many of the family's requirements. It was rustic and beautiful and offered countless outdoor activities for the kids. It was a small town with small town values and very little crime, yet it still featured enough action from the tourist trade to provide myriad employment opportunities. Plus, it seemed as though every other native was a transplanted Midwesterner of one sort or another. Again, it was Paul's modus operandi to avoid the necessity of lying as much as possible. There was then less risk of a kid making a slip at school, or Sandy making a faux pas at a backyard barbecue.

But now that the Staffords had lived in their new skin for almost a year, Paul was learning that the hardest part had nothing to do with new identities or documentation or home defense or even the constant drone of fear just under the surface of every waking moment. The hardest part was living with his family's collective pain. The hardest part was getting his wife and kids to trust him again—

The sound of footsteps across the front room shattered Paul's memories.

He looked up and saw Sandy standing on the threshold of the kitchen.

In the moonlight she looked sepulchral, her flesh ashen white, her eyes luminous. The very sight of her made something deep inside Paul break apart. It wasn't just the fear on her face; it was the bone-deep anguish in her eyes, the way her mouth hung slack, the way her shoulders slumped, her fists like little tight white balls. She was barely able to get the words out: "What was it?—Paul?—The noise—"

Paul went over to her, took her in his arms, and held her desperately tight. "False alarm, San, I'm sorry . . . I'm so sorry, I'm so goddamn sorry . . ."

The tears were coming before Paul even knew what was happening, and he started weeping uncontrollably, and he held his wife and cried like a little lost child into the nape of her neck, and pretty soon Sandy was stroking his back, comforting him, holding him as tightly as he held her. And the questions that had been haunting Paul these last few months were surfacing again in his mind like ghosts. How had he screwed up his life so badly? How had it all come unraveled? Wasn't it only two years ago that he was leading a relatively normal life back in Chicago, serving his middle-class clientele as an ordinary little private CPA, working out of his ordinary little storefront on North LaSalle Street? What in God's name had Paul been thinking when he had taken that first under-the-table project for John Fabionne? John "the Fist" Fabionne! What did Paul think would come of it? Doing money laundering deals for the most infamous mob boss in Chicago history?! But now it was too late. Now Paul was a government informer, a frightened rat who was too scared to take his lumps and go to jail for even a couple of years. Now Paul was standing in the cool darkness, clinging to his long-suffering wife, wondering if the ghosts of his past would ever stop waking him in the wee hours.

But mostly Paul was wondering if one particular ghost was going to fulfill her promise.

Paul could remember the last day he'd laid eyes on her like it was five minutes ago. It was overcast, patches of fog. Outside the courthouse, as the federal marshals led John out the back loading dock, down a ramp, and into a waiting armored van, he saw her. She had been standing across the cordons by the curb, dressed in black as though mourning her father's death, and just before Paul had ducked inside the van, he caught a glimpse of Niccoletta Fabionne, her ferretlike face under her veil, her tiny pearl teeth showing in the gray light. She looked as though she were growling. Then Paul heard her gravelly voice calling to him—the hard R's of her Cicero accent making one last impression.

"We'll find you, Lattamore, somehow, someday . . ."

Nearly twelve months later, Paul Lattamore was still having dreams about that voice, jumping at the slightest sound of an intruder, wondering each time if Niccoletta Fabionne had found a way to keep her promise.

4

The Woman Who Died
Seventeen Times

The heat was taking its toll on the city. The buildings down in the loop were baking in the silver, hazy sun. Sidewalks were glaring white hot, reflecting angrily back into the eyes of harried executives as they scuttled from one air-conditioned obelisk to another, their suits and long dresses matted to their weary bodies. Noises seemed harsher than usual, the clamor of a jackhammer or the hiss of a tar truck assaulting the nerves. And even Lake Michigan seemed to have evaporated, leaving behind a barren gray salt flat all the way to Benton Harbor.

Up north, along the byzantine side streets, fire hydrants fizzed and frothed for the kids. Old-timers sat out on their porches, wiping their necks with handkerchiefs, looking wilted and beaten. And the chirring of locusts, galvanized by the brutal temperatures, competed with the ubiquitous drone of traffic. It was a miserable day any way you sliced it, but it was even worse if you had business with the police.

Charlotte was just now coming to this realization as she sat sweating inside her Ford Taurus, trying to decide whether or not to go inside the precinct house. She was parked in front of the Area Thirteen Police Headquarters, a low-slung building bordered by spindly maple trees and cement planters. The front entrance was a thick, double-glass door, and was constantly in motion, disgorging and accepting both uniformed officers and nervous, disgruntled civilians at an alarming pace. But Charlotte simply couldn't bring herself to go inside.

Her reasons were varied. On one hand, she knew the smart thing to do was to go to the police immediately, reporting everything that had occurred with the Fortunato woman that morning. Considering Charlotte's history with the department, they certainly would take her seriously. But on the other hand, Charlotte was worried about talking to the wrong cop. She had heard rumors over the years that the Fabionne family—and other factions like them—had more than a few of Chicago's finest in their pockets. What if Charlotte got a crooked detective? Plus, many cops vehemently resented the presence of psychics. In fact, some of them outright hated people like Charlotte. It seemed no matter how successful a psychic became, the old-school cops just didn't buy into it. The FBI agents were worse. They considered psychics part of the Dark Ages, a superstitious scam that was anathema to the modern, high-tech investigator.

And this was precisely why Charlotte was presently sitting in her little oven of a car, paralyzed with indecision, a pearl of sweat stinging her eye.

She looked at her reflection in the rearview and saw that her mascara was running, and beads of perspiration had gathered above her lip. She was wearing a powder blue cotton jumper over a lightweight T-shirt, and cute little espadrille sandals. She was braless, too . . . although she wasn't sure why. She had told herself it was the heat. But when you're as bosomy as Charlotte, you don't go au naturel lightly. Had she planned on distracting the cops with her décolletage? Or was it some deeper urge to stay in touch with her own earth-mother femininity in the face of this dangerous game she was playing?

How had she gotten herself into this thing? Charlotte had never asked for this horrible gift. She never prayed for this terrible talent. She never expected to live the life of a freak-show performer. She had always wanted to be a nurse. Or a teacher. Or a counselor. Or maybe even a doctor. To make a difference somehow.

Even back when she was a child.

Born and raised in farm-belt country, she had grown up a typical country girl. Autumn, she de-tasseled corn and worked at the local nursing home. Springtime, she helped her father work at the local grain elevator. Summers, she worked as a lifeguard at a nearby public pool. She was an only child, but she always had plenty of friends. And she was popular. Most of all, she had a big heart. She had a talent for connecting with people. Maybe too much of a talent.

The psychic ability came in her teens. The first encounter came as she was shaking the hand of a favorite teacher—Mrs. Coolidge—and she felt the black currents of a suicidal depression flowing out of the woman's pores. A week later, the teacher was found dead in her apartment after swallowing an entire bottle of sleeping pills. Charlotte was heartbroken, and angry, and mostly frightened. She started getting signals off strangers in grocery stores and restaurants. She would brush by somebody and get hit with a surge of sensations—like a shortwave radio being tuned to distant stations—and the program was usually tawdry, or obscene, or ugly, or just downright embarrassing.

The truth was, Charlotte never really wanted to know what was in other people's minds.

The gift started devouring Charlotte from the inside. She started avoiding friends and relatives, for fear of learning how Uncle Harry *really* felt about the babysitter, or what Billy Marsten was *really* thinking in Algebra class as he stared at Charlotte's breasts. She started eating like a stevedore to deaden the stress. She gained weight, and she lost friends, and she became a virtual hermit. By the time she had enrolled in a small junior college outside Chicago, she knew that she would never be able to lead a normal life.

A year later, she did her first missing person case. It was somewhat of an epiphany. Up to that point she had been repressing her skills. Stuffing them down inside her. Trying to lead a normal life, working normal jobs, living in the spaces between the psychic bolts. Then she helped a neighbor locate a missing pet, and word got out, and the dam burst. For the first time in Charlotte's life, she realized her talent might actually benefit others.

The first job came from a downstate sheriff's investigator. It was the dead of winter. A family had been in a car wreck, and their infant son had been thrown down a snowy precipice, vanishing in the wild. After handling the baby's car seat, Charlotte located the infant fifty yards south of the crash site, a frozen little porcelain doll caught in the branches of a tree. They gave Charlotte a letter of commendation from the governor, and a ticket home, and Charlotte suffered from nightmares for six weeks. And this was how her "gift" would ultimately work: She would experience the pain of the victims and their families over and over again. A year later, it was an elderly man with Alzheimer's disease who had wandered off and drowned in a sewage treatment pond. After that, a teenage girl raped and beaten and left for the vermin in a highway ditch. And on and on. The experts called it *retrocognition,* but Charlotte knew it by its real name: *dying . . . again and again.*

Seventeen cases in sixteen years, seventeen times Charlotte Vickers had died.

And now she was wondering whether number eighteen would be the final death.

Her own.

"Hey! Lady!" A loud voice startled Charlotte from behind. "Shit or get off the pot!"

She turned and saw a cab hovering off her left rear quarter panel, idling noisily, waiting to see if she was leaving. Charlotte reached outside and waved him on. The cabbie squealed his tires and shot away. Charlotte just shook her head wearily to herself.

Another typical male.

She grabbed her purse, opened her door, and got out. Smoothing the wrinkles in her jumper, licking her finger and wiping the runny mascara from the corner of her eye, she took a deep breath and then made her way up the narrow walk toward the entrance. As she was approaching the door, a pair of beefy plainclothes cops were leaving.

"My hand to God, Levy," the older cop was saying, blustering through the door and past Charlotte. Thinning flattop, big belly poking out the front of his sport coat. "Guy's twisted like a pretzel, wedged between the fuckin' subway car and the wall."

"Goner," the younger cop was murmuring, picking his teeth with a toothpick.

"How's that?"

The younger cop tossed his toothpick, noticing Charlotte's breasts, muttering softly: "Minute you move the poor bastard, all his internal organs gonna collapse."

The older cop wasn't listening anymore. He, too, had noticed Charlotte's zaftig figure, and was making a concerted effort to grow eyes in the back of his head. Both their gazes lingered on Charlotte's bustline as they sauntered slowly toward the street, and Charlotte could hear the crackle of testosterone in her midbrain like a hectic beehive. The backs of her arms prickled with gooseflesh despite the heat, and she felt dizzy, nauseous, unsteady.

She turned back to the entrance and grasped the cold door handle.

She inhaled suddenly—

(—an envelope stuffed with small bills, bribe money being slipped under a desk blotter—)

—and she reeled for a moment, steadying herself against the door. Her mind swam. What was going on? Was she manufacturing these paranoid delusions now? Or was it another fragment of the truth . . . like a pebble in her shoe? Bribe money, cops on the take, detectives in John Fabionne's pocket. Charlotte shook the bees from her brain, grasping the door handle, swallowing back the panic, trying to get her bearings. *Calm down, girlfriend,* she told herself. *Just go inside the damn station and get it over with already.* But she couldn't motivate her legs, couldn't make herself move.

"Excuse me, miss—" The voice came from the dim light inside the glass door, startling Charlotte.

"Sorry," she uttered, backing out of the way.

"Excuse me," the elderly man said, then waddled out the door, his cane scraping the tile threshold.

The little man trundled down the walk and vanished into the heat rays.

Charlotte stood there for a moment, a single bead of sweat tracking down her back. The realization was a hard, black cinder in the pit of her stomach: She would not go to the police. She would solve this her own way.

But how?

How?

She glanced off toward the north, toward the tops of ancient, swaying elms that had stood sentry over this neighborhood since before the Chicago Fire. Wrigley Field was beyond those trees, and Loyola University, and Northwestern, and the B'hai Temple, and all the postwar bungalows, painted ladies, and scabrous brick two-flats that lined the shaded streets.

And Junior.

Of course, Junior was up there as well.

Charlotte started toward her car, wondering why she hadn't thought of Junior in the first place.

5

Best Pain Guy in the Business

The howls rose up into the humid afternoon, a horrible cacophony of noise, carrying across the fences and wild shrubs and clotheslines of the north side neighborhood. The noise sounded as though someone were torturing a tubercular mezzo-soprano. In reality, though, one of the voices was coming from Junior Parrick's tenor saxophone, an instrument Junior never bothered to learn how to play very well. The other was emanating from Monty, a very old, very feeble, very loud Newfoundland.

The dog was the least objectionable of the two voices.

"Keep it going, Monty, I'm digging your groove . . . yeah, I'm digging it, Daddy!" Junior Parrick was urging on his pet from his lawn chair, his sax between his legs. The faint sizzle of an old Parliament Funkadelic record could be heard filtering through the screen door behind them. That patented George Clinton thump—*Whap!-Whappa!—Whap-whap-whap!* And oh, what a strange sight it was: man and dog, grooving to seventies funk music on a makeshift brick patio crowded with broken pottery, hubcaps, and surreal lawn ornaments. Monty continued yammering loudly to the tune, spittle flying, while Junior threw his head back and kept time tapping his Birkenstocks.

Junior was a fireplug of a man with a hard, barrel-shaped gut that jutted out of an oily leather vest, ham-hock forearms, and squat little bull legs. The guys back in his platoon used to call him "Stove," probably because, since the time Junior Parrick was old enough to get a hard-on, his body had resembled a potbellied stove. And now that he was crawling toward fifty years old, the pot had gotten more belly on it than ever. Only his boyish face belied his age. And his clothes. He was stuck in the sixties, with the fringe and the moccasins and the beads and the Grateful Dead T-shirts. And he could get away with it, too. There was something eternally youthful and puckish about Junior, with his head full of thick, curly gray hair, his round cheeks, still as rosy as the day he got his first Red Ryder air gun for Christmas, and his long-lashed, gray eyes still twinkling with mischief. And God help us, but he was still into his god-awful sculpture, music, and painting.

Anything to occupy the hours, help him forget his lost days in the army.

"Parrick!" The distant voice was barely audible above the howling. It came from across the back fence: a neighbor named Bill Reese. A stressed-out salesman with three kids. "Give us a break!"

"Hiya, Bill!" Junior called back.

"Parrick, please!"

"Whattya think, Bill?!"

"What?! What do I think about what?!"

"Monty's instrument!" Junior bellowed. "He's really coming into his own!"

In the distance, through the power lines and trees, Bill Reese's head was poking out through the sliding glass doors of his patio. "Parrick, the noise! I'm begging you! The kids are doing their homework!"

Junior waved. "I agree, Bill! I think it works, too! Thank you!"

Bill Reese shook his head, then vanished back into his house.

Junior grinned, then got out of his chair and went over to the dog.

"Enough, Monty, that's enough." Junior scratched the dog's chin, and the dog yapped a couple of times, then fell silent. Inside the house, the record came to an end. And in that sudden silence came an unexpected sound.

The front doorbell was buzzing.

"Who the hell?" Junior murmured to the dog. Then he led Monty over to a stake and clipped his collar to a rusty chain. Monty immediately flopped to the ground and started chewing on a favorite tennis shoe.

Then Junior went inside and answered the door.

"How ya doing, Junie?" Charlotte Vickers was standing on the porch.

Junior was stricken silent.

It wasn't the woman's Rubenesque figure, damp from perspiration and nerves, standing there on the cracked cement stoop, looking desperate and edgy. It wasn't the incredible curve of her face, or the way the light played off the cascade of the wondrous curls around her shoulders. It wasn't even the flutter in Junior's gut, the same flutter that washed over him every time he saw Charlotte.

It was the look in Charlotte's eyes, all shimmery with terror.

"Hiya, Ace," Junior finally managed. "How the hell are you?"

"I need to talk, Junie."

"What's the matter? You look like you swallowed a shit sandwich."

She looked up at him with those glimmering eyes. "I got myself in a mess, Junie."

He gently took her hand. "Get your butt in here."

"Who found who?" Digger Mussolino was confused. Less than an hour ago he had gotten an emergency phone call summoning him to the Fabionne estate. But now that he had shown up, and was standing in the home's magnificent vestibule, things were murkier than ever.

"The psychic, you idiot, *the psychic!*" Natalie yelled at him from across the foyer. Her eyes were red from either anger or tears or both, and the front of her appliquéd denim vest had dark wet spots where she had dribbled wine. "I told you, I was gonna get that psychic from Lincoln Park—the lady, helps the cops— I told you."

"The locator?"

"Yes, for Chrissake, the locator, the locator—she found that motherfuckin' snitch."

"She found the accountant?"

Natalie rolled her eyes. "No. She found Bozo the Clown—Jesus-Mary-and-Joseph, who the fuck you think I'm talking about?—yes, the accountant. I don't know how that bitch did it, but she did it. Says the rat's holed up in Colorado."

"Colorado?—Colorado?—*Jesus.*" Digger Mussolino gazed off toward the massive living room, where giant Raphael murals flanked the fireplace, and imposing Italian sculpture mingled among the period furniture. The place looked like the Medici Chapel, and being inside the home had always made Digger feel strangely ennobled to be a ranking member of the Fabionne clan.

Not that Digger had an inferiority complex or anything. Very few things made Digger Mussolino feel inferior. Tipping the scales at nearly three hundred pounds, he was impervious to most external threats. His immense neck was creased and wrinkled like elephant hide, and his broad shoulders strained the seams of his black sharkskin suit. Today he was wearing his thirteen-hundred-dollar black lizard boots and a black fedora tilted back at a jaunty, Damon Runyan–esque angle.

His muscles were hardened from over twenty years of unloading contraband off the backs of freight liners and working over recalcitrant juice-loan customers. But now that Digger had made it to the top of the Fabionne crime family—recently attaining the status of full capo—he had learned how to use the more subtle tools of his arsenal: vocal inflections, the twitch of a cheek, the gesture of a meaty hand. At the end of the day, though, when force was necessary, Digger was fucking Jupiter: the biggest planet in the solar system—a gravitational field that would end any dispute faster than you could say "deep tissue damage."

Right now he was standing in the foyer of the Fabionne house, feeling a little sheepish. But then again, the grand foyer of the Fabionne home would have made William Randolph Hearst a little sheepish. It was a masterpiece of transplanted materials, from the gilded Genoan mirror tile to the gold-plated chandelier from Milan. The old man sure knew how to disguise his wealth; from the outside, his daughter's place looked like any run-of-the-mill northshore mansion, but inside it was a regular palace.

The Fabionnes ran one of the most powerful Midwestern factions of the Gandolpho family, which was based out of Brooklyn, New York. The Gandolphos held a major position on the main council of families, and Digger had built a solid reputation over the years as one of the most effective button men in the Midwest. But then, a little over a year ago, the whole house of cards had come tumbling down. All because of that little prick Lattamore, the fucking little bean counter.

Natalie's father—"Big John" to his minions, "the Fist" to everybody else—had been using a series of small, private accountants on a rotating basis over the years, laundering the bulk of the family's juice-loan, off-track betting, porno, and prostitution money into legitimate investments. Every few years, Fabionne would come to the conclusion that the current accountant knew too much and had to be whacked. The job was usually assigned to Digger and his crew, and was usually carried out with a minimum of muss and fuss. A simple take-down in a dark parking lot after hours—always making it look like a robbery, some nigger from the neighborhood—and then the Don could get a good night's sleep again. But everything went wrong when Big John started going on golf outings with Lattamore, taking the guy and his wife out to dinner, taking a shine to the guy. Digger knew it was a bad idea from the get-go, but what's a capo to do? It wasn't like Digger was going to tell the Fist what to do. And when that little prick accountant started getting nervous—crisis of conscience, all that bullshit—Digger saw the writing on the wall. By the time Big John had decided to get rid of Lattamore, it was too late. The little rat had already gone to the feds.

Which meant, for almost a year, Digger had been forced to deal with the humiliation of answering to Fabionne's nutcase daughter Niccoletta—or Natalie, as she liked to call herself—the word coming down directly from the federal penitentiary in Marion, Illinois, where Big John was doing his time. All orders came through the daughter. But maybe now that they'd found the accountant, Digger could make things right again—for the boss, for the family, for everybody.

And maybe, just maybe, the boss would reward Digger with a leadership role.

"Give me the town and the address," Digger said gravely, pulling a small spiral-bound notebook from his pocket. "We'll take care of the situation right away."

Natalie looked at him as though she were looking at a dog turd. "Did I say I had the address?"

"You said she found the guy, you said Colorado."

"I said the psychic lady *found* the guy, I didn't say she got us a fucking address."

Digger was nonplussed for a moment. "What did she say?"

Digger listened as Natalie told him everything that Charlotte Vickers had said about Lattamore's current location.

A cold current of anger started coursing through Digger's veins. Not because he hated the accountant, but because Digger felt as though he were being played for a fool. What kind of a moron did the Fortunato broad take him for? Digger knew that the cops rarely used psychics, no matter how stumped they were. And the feds never used them. Digger wasn't even sure he believed it was possible to locate somebody via psychic channels. But the mousey little woman wouldn't stop ranting about it.

Nodding his head, pretending to listen, Digger reached into his pocket, pulled out a slim, black graphite cigarette case, and with meticulously buffed fingernails selected a Dunhill menthol. He sparked his cigarette with a gold-plated lighter, taking a luxurious drag and thinking about croaking that little rat-fink accountant. This was all part of Digger's "thing"—the European cigarettes, the tough-guy lingo, the manicure, the suit, the fedora, the laissez-faire way in which Digger thought about murder—the whole gangster trip. The wise-guy attitude, the look, the walk, the cadence of his speech—all of it was so very studied, mannered. *La Cosa Nostra* meant "our thing" in Italian, but this thing was mostly Digger's thing. Most of it came from the movies—some of it from books, but who reads anymore?—and Digger Mussolino had used it all to become a walking special effect. He was pure

Central Casting, a living, breathing version of life imitating art. Digger was Warner Bros. in the 1940s, and Digger was Mario Puzo, and Digger was David Mamet, and Digger was Scorsese and Tarantino, and right now Digger was starting to itch to make some more of that gangster stuff happen.

"We got good people out west," Digger said finally, after Natalie had paused to take a breath. "We could find that cocksucker in a couple weeks—a month, tops."

Natalie closed her eyes, and for a moment she looked like she was counting backward from ten. "Goddamnit, that's not good enough," she growled. Then, all at once, she spun toward the mirrored wall behind her and kicked the bottom panel hard with the toe of her fashion boot. The glass cracked, blossoming spider veins. "That's not good enough!"

"What can I do? Tell me," Digger implored, staring at the broken tile, thinking to himself, *Seven goddamn years of bad luck.*

"She knows, I'm sure of it."

"The address?"

"Yes, the address, goddamnit—*she knows*!"

Digger looked at her. "What do you want me to do, Miss Fortunato?"

Natalie was breathing hard now. "What do I want you to *do*?"

"Yes, what I'm saying is, whatever it is—whatever you want me to do—I'll do."

Natalie bit her upper lip, her face flushed and hectic now. "What I want you to do, Digger, is pay the psychic a visit."

Digger nodded. "I understand."

"Get her to reveal the address, whatever else she knows. Is that clear?"

"Clear as a bell."

"But listen to me, Digger, understand something. I

don't want you to just rush in there like a bull in a china shop, you understand what I'm saying?"

Digger nodded again. "I understand exactly what you're saying, Miss Fortunato."

"What am I saying?"

"You want me to practice a little psychology."

"That's correct, Digger."

"You want me to finesse it out of her."

Natalie swallowed hard, her right eye twitching, and she swallowed again and looked as though she were swallowing thumbtacks. She moved closer to Digger, and Digger could smell all sorts of odors coming off the woman: two-day-old cologne, stale cigarette smoke, and something musky that Digger couldn't identify. "I want to make this very clear, so there's no confusion." Natalie was speaking very softly now, eye twitching. "I want you to get somebody to work on the psychic, somebody who specializes . . . Do you understand what I'm saying?"

Digger said, "Yeah, absolutely, you want me to farm this thing out."

"I want you to supervise it, but I want you to get somebody good, I want the best pain guy in the business."

Digger nodded confidently. He didn't even have to think very hard about who he would go to. There was really only one guy. One true pro. "I got it, Miss Fortunato. Don't you give it another thought. I'll get right on it, and I'll get back to you in a day or two."

Natalie looked at him sourly. "Don't give it a thought?—with Pop in the slam, eatin' oatmeal every morning?—you're telling me not to *think* about it?" She spun toward another mirror tile and kicked it good. "That's all I think about! Now get outta here! Go!"

By the time Digger had made his way outside, he had lost count of all the years of bad luck that were being racked up.

6

Margin of Error

They sat in the kitchen in the rear of the apartment, a tidy little room with parquet floors and lots of windows. Junior poured them each a glass of sun tea, and Charlotte ran through the sequence of events. It took her nearly twenty minutes. She left nothing out. She related every last detail, down to the precise words spoken. And Junior listened very carefully, saying very little, sipping his tea. Finally, when Charlotte was done, Junior nodded and gulped down the last of his tea.

Then he set down his empty glass and said, "You haven't told anybody else about this?"

"Not a soul."

"And you came directly here from the police station?"

"That's right."

"And all the Fortunato lady knows is Colorado?"

Charlotte thought about it for a moment. "Yeah . . . I suppose that's true."

"Did you tell her anything more specific?"

Charlotte thought back to the session, the wiry fingers on her throat. "No, not really."

"You didn't tell her what part of Colorado—the plains, the mountains?"

"I didn't know myself."

Junior looked at her. "You never got a fix on it?"

"I didn't even dig for it—once I realized the man

was married, living with his family—I didn't see a need to press the matter."

"And you're pretty sure about Colorado and everything? I mean . . . in terms of . . . margin of error?"

She gave him a look. "I'm sure, Junie, and don't start."

He grinned wanly. "Just asking."

"Junie, please. The last thing I need right now is a skeptic."

Junior raised his hands in mock surrender. "Just making sure."

It was an ongoing source of good-natured teasing between the two of them. Junior was the debunker, the practical one. Charlotte was the flake, the visionary. And neither one of them let the other one forget it. In fact, since the day Junior won first prize in a Christmas raffle down at the V-A hospital where he worked—one free psychic consultation with Charlotte—he had been ambivalent about the whole phenomenon. Sure, he realized there were things in this world that science simply could not explain. Hell, he saw some things in the 'Nam that would have made Rod Serling's head spin. But then again, he was a realist. He didn't trust anything he couldn't hold in his hand, measure, photograph, or cut up and smoke in a bong.

The only exception was Charlotte Vickers.

Junior believed wholeheartedly in Charlotte Vickers.

In fact, from the moment he had laid eyes on her, a year and a half ago, he had been bug-fuck crazy in love. For months, he had tried to play it cool. He started coming over to her place for weekly consultations; and by God, she was able to glean some amazing insights into his life just by caressing his palm with those incredibly soft hands. She knew about his tough childhood, his experiences over in Southeast Asia, his loneliness, even his nightmares. There *was* something very special about this lady. But unfortunately, every time Junior hinted at turning their relationship into something more than pals, he got the same speech about Charlotte's life being too complicated, too messed up. It was maddening. And the worst part— the part that made Junior the craziest—was the uncertainty. How far inside Junior's mind had Charlotte already traveled? How much did she know about him? She claimed that she would never purposely invade a person's mind for her own benefit. But still, Junior wondered . . .

"You probably know what I'm thinking right now, right?" Junior said.

"Very funny."

"I'm serious."

"It doesn't work like that, Junie, and you know it."

Junior sighed. "Okay. Look. I gotta tell ya, I think the best thing to do is call the FBI."

"I already told you—"

"I know, I know, you don't think feds will believe you. Lemme ask you a question."

"What?"

"You truly believe these scumbags can get to Lattamore?"

Charlotte told him she did.

Junior shrugged. "Then the fastest way to protect the guy is to call the field office in Colorado."

Charlotte looked at him. "I'm telling you, Junie, you don't know how much these FBI jokers hate the whole idea of a psychic."

"So what? It doesn't matter. Once you call them, they're obligated to move Lattamore, or at least send a car out to wherever he is."

"It won't get that far, Junie. Believe me. They'll consider a psychic an affront to their professionalism."

"Sounds like egomania to me."

"Whatever you want to call it, they'll spit in my face."

Junior sighed. "I don't know what else you can do."

There was an awkward pause, and Charlotte anxiously bit her lip, gazing past Junior toward the window. Junior had started to say something else, when he saw something glinting in Charlotte's eyes. Something sharp and desperate. Junior felt a pang of dread in his gut. "Don't tell me," he said then. "You're thinking of doing something heroic."

Charlotte looked at him, and her gaze felt like a laser scalpel. "The man has a family, Junie. Lattamore—he's got kids."

"Don't even think about it."

"I have to try, Junie. I have to."

"Try *what,* fer Chrissake?"

"Try finding him."

"What?!"

"I have to, Junie. This is my fault. My problem. I have to fix it." She took a deep breath, then rose from the table. She went over to the counter and grabbed her purse. "I gotta go, Junie. I gotta take care of this thing."

"Whoa! Hold on just a minute there, Tonto!" Junior was up now. He went over to the counter. "Where are you going exactly?"

"My house."

"I'm not sure that's a good idea."

She looked at him. "What are you talking about?"

"Your house. Going back there right now is not a good idea. These guys know where you live, Charlotte."

There was a jagged pause. "But I— They won't— I don't think they'd come back."

"How do you know?"

Charlotte let out a pained breath, as though some-

one had kicked her in the stomach. She started pacing.
"Oh my God, what have I done? What have I done?"

"Easy there, partner." Junior felt horrible, watching
the pain on her face. "We'll figure this thing out.
Don't you worry. You can stay here tonight. We'll
come up with something. I promise."

She was still pacing. "This is my fault, Junie. I have
to fix this thing myself."

"Now you're talking nonsense—"

"No, no, it's my problem, nobody else's. I have to
find the Lattamore family. Warn them."

"Charlotte—"

"I can do it, Junie. I can. All I have to do is—"

And then she stopped, her hand raised in the air,
trembling faintly.

"What is it?" Junior was staring at her.

Charlotte's eyes were big and wet, her lips quivering. Sheer terror on her face. "Oh my God," she
uttered, her voice strangled.

"What? What?"

She looked at him with those liquid eyes. "My God,
Junie, the coin . . ."

"The what?"

"The coin, the silver dollar that belonged to Lattamore." Charlotte looked as though she were running
a fever. "It's still in my house."

"So what? Leave it there."

"No, no, Junie, you don't get it. The coin is the
only way to find Lattamore." Charlotte started backing toward the door as though sleepwalking. "I have
to get it, I have to get that coin before somebody
else does."

"Charlotte, calm down—"

"I have to get it, Junie—I have to!"

Charlotte turned and got halfway through the door
before Junior grasped her arm, trying to pull her back
inside, but Charlotte was a steam engine now, all the

fear and guilt and pressure urging her forward. "Lemme go, Junie!" she cried, and then wriggled out of his grasp.

She hit the front steps running.

"Charlotte!" Junior lingered in the doorway for a moment, watching her rush headlong down the steps toward the street. Then he turned and hustled back across the apartment to the futon by the window.

The strongbox was hidden under a shipping blanket. Junior dug it out, quickly opened it, and pulled out a stainless steel Smith & Wesson .357 magnum—Model 65—from its foam cutout. It was one of Junior's three handguns. He also had a .22-caliber Ruger semiautomatic and a SIG-Sauer .380 auto-load. In his closet was an Ithaca 10-gauge Roadblocker shotgun. Junior had been a gun nut ever since he was a kid, and not even his experiences as a sniper in 'Nam could squelch his love of weaponry. Maybe it went back to his dad's influence, or maybe it was something else, something buried deep in his psyche . . . but right now it didn't matter. Right now he just needed to pack a little protection.

He quickly clicked open the .357's cylinder, inserted a speed loader, and injected six rounds. Then he snapped the mechanism home and stuffed the gun into a small rucksack.

For one brief instant, Junior wondered how much extra ammunition he should bring.

7

The Hollow Man

"Who is this guy anyway? This St. Louie dude."

"Do your homework, Tiny. The name is St. Louis, *Lou St. Louis,* and he's the motherfucking patron saint of pain, believe you me. This guy knows more about torture than the fucking Tonton Macoute."

Digger Mussolino paused, fished in his shirt pocket for the last bent cigarette from his pack of Dunhills, pulled it out, and popped it between his teeth. He fired it up and took a long, exasperated drag, then settled back into the leather contours of the Lexus, its buckets as soft and supple as a handmaiden's womb. Digger had taken off his jacket, draping it carefully over the back of the passenger seat, and now he was sweating through his brand-new silk dress shirt. He was tired of waiting, tired of gazing through the windshield at the lazy street corner, and most of all, he was tired of making conversation with the kid. "Make no mistake," Digger added with a grumble, "this guy can do more with his thumb than one of your fucking AKs."

There was a pause as the kid thought it over. "All due respect, I ain't never seen a fucking thumb that can do the damage of one 47 on full auto."

"What the fuck do you know about it? All you young pricks with your fucking Berettas, shooting out the backs of cars, holding your guns sideways like some Pachuco punk from some rap song. You wouldn't know finesse if it crawled up your ass."

The kid mumbled: "All I'm saying is, there ain't no replacement for a good room-broom." He was sitting in back, chewing a wad of sugary-smelling bubblegum, clicking .357 magnum tracer slugs into an ammo magazine—*slide-click!—slide-click!—slide-click!* At first glance the kid looked as though he had only recently received his driver's license, his slender face sporting a peach-fuzz goatee, his lanky arms tanned from innumerable sandlot baseball games. But underneath the mesh dago-T, baggy shorts, razor haircut, and hightops beat the heart of an efficient mob assassin. They called him Tiny, but his real name was Anthony Dinello Sharpetti, and he had just celebrated his twenty-ninth birthday the previous weekend with a three-hundred-dollar whore and a Ziploc bag full of hydroponic weed that his crew had gotten for him. Now he was rested and ready for work, and the fact that he was working with the top guy in the family tonight just made him all the more talkative. "All due respect," he said again as an afterthought, "I ain't never heard of nobody gettin' washed by a motherfuckin' thumb."

Slide-click!

"How old are you?" Digger growled. "Fourteen? Fifteen?"

"Very funny."

"You don't know shit beyond those cannons you carry around in your lunchbox."

"That's what they pay me for," Tiny Sharpetti said softly, snapping the last three slugs in the clip—*slide-click!—slide-click!* He tapped the bottom of the magazine against the seat, making sure the rounds were seated properly, then shoved it up the butt of his Glock—*snick-clang!* "When's this mean muchacho showing up, anyway?"

Digger looked at his watch. "Any minute now, just cool your pits."

Digger glanced into his side mirror at the row of brick bungalows behind him, his gaze falling on the last one on the left. The psychic lady's bungalow was locked up, nobody home, and it had been that way ever since Digger and the kid had arrived about an hour ago, beginning their stakeout, and it was starting to piss Digger off. Where the hell was she? From all reports, Digger understood that the psychic lady worked out of her house, and rarely went out, and even when she did go out, she was back home within an hour or so. So where the fuck was this broad?

Digger wiped a bead of sweat from his brow and mumbled, "Any minute now . . ."

The Lexus was parked behind a Didy-Wash diaper service truck, pointing in the opposite direction, shaded by the long shadows of early evening. Even in the dusky, dying light, though, the air was heavy, the inside of the Lexus like a clay oven. Every few minutes Digger would start the car and run the AC for a while, but it didn't do much good. His silk shirt was sticking to the back of the seat now, and the kid's smell was starting to turn. Digger looked at his watch again. It was already a quarter past seven. Not only was the psychic late, but so was St. Louis, and Lou St. Louis was never late. Lou St. Louis was a machine. You could set your fucking watch by him. Digger just couldn't believe that the Doc would get lax in his old age.

"Who the hell is this?" Tiny was glancing over his shoulder, pointing his thumb at a figure coming their way through the heat rays.

Digger glanced in the side mirror and saw the figure coming. "That's him."

"That's him?!"

"Shut up."

"*That's* the guy?"

"Shut your mouth," Digger said softly, watching the little man in the JCPenney suit approaching the car.

"All due respect, Boss," the kid commented, looking over his shoulder, "but this guy don't look like he could put the hurt on my fat Aunt Rose."

"Shut the fuck up or *I'm* gonna be putting the hurt on *your* ass," Digger said. Then Digger opened his door and climbed out into the heat. "How ya doing, Doc?"

"Fine, thank you," Lou St. Louis said as he strode up to the Lexus. He couldn't have been more than five feet tall—if that—dressed in his smart little discount suit, black wing-tip shoes, and horn-rimmed glasses. In his left hand he gripped a scuffed, imitation leather briefcase. He looked like a toy, a toy man, his bald pate gleaming in the sun. Well groomed, but cheaply constructed. Hollow inside. When he extended his miniature hand for Digger to shake, Digger noticed the doctor's slender white fingers were powdered, soft to the touch. "How are you, Mr. Mussolino?"

"Same-old same-old, Lou . . . You know how it is."

"I do indeed," St. Louis said softly, then smiled, revealing his uneven front teeth, one of them capped in dirty gold, a sloppy job.

"The psychic hasn't shown up yet," Digger told him. "But we expect her any minute now."

"Very good."

Digger nodded toward Charlotte's bungalow. "The plan is, when she gets back, we'll go in through the front door, nice and quiet, make some excuse, pick her up, and then take her to the safe house. Then you can get to work. That sound right to you?"

The chiropractor smiled, the gold tooth catching a dapple of dying sunlight and glimmering dully. "Right as rain, sir. Right as rain."

8

Nightmare Blossoms

As the sun melted behind the skyline, Halsted Street became a carnival of neon delights. Boutiques vibrated with chartreuse light and shrill music, taverns spilled malty odors and noisy jukes out onto the cracked sidewalks, and the whole promenade oozed and churned beneath the golden mercury vapor lights. Charlotte barely noticed any of it. She was too busy ruminating on the passenger side of Junior's battered Chevy Geo, thinking about all the things that could go wrong.

Junior was next to her, white-knuckling the Geo north toward Fullerton, and he seemed more nervous than Charlotte. "There's an alley, right?" he said suddenly. "Behind your place?"

Charlotte nodded. "Yes, it's a mess now with the garbage men on strike."

"That's okay, we're gonna walk it."

"What do you mean?"

Junior glanced at her. "We're gonna slip in the back way, then get in and get out without making too much of a racket."

Charlotte nodded again, then gazed out at the passing storefronts and said softly, "How in God's name did I get myself into this?"

"Where's the alley entrance?" Junior asked.

Charlotte thought for a second. "It's off of Sheffield, just north of Fullerton, right before you get to Waitley."

"East side of the street?"

"Yes, it loops around, then it empties out onto Waitley."

Junior shot her another glance. "You're gonna be okay, Ace, don't worry."

"I can't imagine they would come after me, Junie."

Junior shrugged. "All I know is, these folks are very unsavory, and they know where you live."

"But if they were gonna mess with me, wouldn't they have done it already?"

"I don't know, kiddo. Better safe than sorry."

"But Junie, is the gun really necessary?"

"I hope not," he said, more to himself than anything else, and then he drove in silence for a while.

When they got to Fullerton, Junior turned left and went west a few stoplights to Sheffield.

By the time they found a parking place on Sheffield—an arduous task on the slowest of nights—the sunset had melted off the edge of the skyline and the day had turned into the magic hour, the moment just before dark, when the sky becomes a vast glacier of deepest blue, and the shadows deepen, and the landscape turns luminous. Junior parked on the west side of the street, facing south, and he left plenty of front-bumper space in case they were forced to make a hasty exit. Then he led Charlotte around back to the Geo's rear hatch. When he opened the nylon ruck-sack, the stainless steel Smith & Wesson gleamed in the vapor lights, which were winking on overhead.

"This isn't happening," Charlotte murmured, wringing her hands, staring down at the gun. She was terrified of handguns, probably because of the time a local homicide detective had asked her to handle one in a missing person case.

It had been an ugly, blocky, black gun—they called it a Gluck or a Glock, Charlotte couldn't remember for sure—which had been found in an abandoned building near the Robert Taylor Homes, the same building in which a young girl had last been seen. When Charlotte had picked the pistol up, wrapping her fingers around the ragged, duct-taped grip, she felt the sudden concussion blast to the back of her skull as though she'd been hit by a truck. She dropped the gun immediately. She knew what the feeling meant. She knew the owner of the gun had been killed, execution-style, right in that same abandoned building. And Charlotte knew it was the girl, and Charlotte knew it was gang-related and the police would never find the girl's body. But for Charlotte, it was merely another germ of misery, destined to take root in her psyche and repeatedly blossom in her nightmares from that day forward, for the rest of her life.

Needless to say, she wasn't too anxious to handle another gun.

Junior was glancing over his shoulder, making sure no one was watching. He had the gun in one hand and a little round cartridge of bullets in the other, and he was fiddling the bullets into the gun's cylinder. "It's just a lump of metal, honey, just a tool, don't let it shake you."

"Do we have to bring it, Junie?"

"Yes, darlin', we have to bring it." Junior was unzipping his light windbreaker now. He had a brown leather holster under the jacket, and he quickly slipped the weapon inside the holster. Then he put another one of those little bullet cartridges—Charlotte remembered someone calling them speed loaders—into his right pocket.

"Can I tell you something?" Charlotte said, watching him zip up.

"What is it, Ace?"

"I'm so scared right now, Junie, I could wet myself."

"Listen, if it's any consolation," Junior said, patting

her shoulder, "my bladder ain't feeling too wonderful either."

Then he gently ushered her toward the mouth of the alley.

"I am so fucking tired of staring at this fucking house," Tiny Sharpetti grumbled from the darkness of the backseat, the *snap-clang* of the Beretta's bolt ringing loudly, the sound of the kid's voice like a fucking parakeet squeaking in Digger Mussolino's ears. The car reeked of sugary bubblegum and bad armpits, and if something didn't happen soon, Digger was going to reach around and put a cap in the little snot's left eye.

"We'll give it a few more minutes," Digger murmured from behind the wheel, his gaze still glued to the side mirror. "If the bitch doesn't show, we'll call in."

"May I say something?" Lou St. Louis said from the passenger side. He was sitting like a perfect little gentleman, back erect, hands clasped in his lap, ratty little briefcase at his feet. He looked like a child at Sunday school class, a young boy waiting to see the principal. For the last two hours, he had spoken about a dozen words.

"What is it, Doc?"

"Well . . . I would never be presumptuous and tell you how to run your operation."

"It's okay, Lou—what is it?"

"Well, quite frankly, I've been wondering about the rear entrance."

Digger felt his stomach twist. "The rear entrance?"

"I'm just saying, it's conceivable the lady might slip in the back way, and nobody would—"

"Holy fucking shit," Digger murmured to himself, gazing into the mirror.

The bungalow sat in the moonlight a half a block away, nestled in a grove of maples at the end of the street. The front of the house—a tranquil still life of twin dormers, a varnished walnut door, and flower boxes brimming with petunias and impatiens—was still dark and shuttered, and it was obvious that nobody was home. At least nobody that wanted to be seen. Digger's scalp tingled suddenly, his teeth on edge as though someone were clawing fingernails across slate-rock in his brain. How the fuck could he have been so fucking stupid? Forgetting all about the goddamn back door!

Lou St. Louis was staring at the rearview. "I wonder if we might want to post a man—"

"Kid!" Digger twisted around and pointed a pudgy, manicured finger at the shooter. "Put a suppressor on that cannon, and get your ass back there!"

"Where?"

"The goddamn back of the house—what the fuck you think I'm talking about?" Then Digger grabbed the kid's arm for emphasis. "And, kid: Do not—I repeat, do *not*—hurt the psychic lady."

The kid nodded. "I got it, I got it."

Digger let go of the kid's arm. "Just make sure you don't get trigger happy."

The kid mumbled something under his breath and started screwing a silencer onto the Beretta's blunt-nosed barrel. A moment later he was climbing out of the car, then heading across the street.

9

The Taste of Pennies

As they crept across the back deck, approaching the rear door, Junior Parrick was starting to think that maybe this was a bad idea, maybe a very bad idea. The stench was unbelievable, a fog bank of stink from all the rotting garbage, so powerful the air seemed radioactive with it, and the wood was creaking beneath them, and Junior was wondering why he had never noticed how loudly a weathered wooden deck groans and creaks with the weight of people on it. Worse than that, Junior was tasting that stale, coppery taste in his mouth again, that old penny taste that he used to get in Vietnam. Either a chemical reaction from the nerves, or some kind of neurochemical signal that something nasty was about to happen. He wasn't sure. But he could feel the eyes of all the neighbors on the back of his neck—the inbred paranoia of a former sniper—and he could hear footsteps coming down the alley, crunching in the gravel.

Charlotte was pulling open the screen door, fiddling with her keys.

"Hurry!" Junior whispered urgently, wanting desperately to get out of sight.

Charlotte opened the door, and they both slipped inside the darkened house.

The door clicked shut behind them.

The first thought that occurred to Junior as he stood frozen in the dark, listening to the sound of a clock ticking somewhere out in another room, was the feeling that there was somebody else inside the house, waiting in the shadows, locked and loaded, waiting to ambush them. Or maybe there was a sniper somewhere who had them lined up in the crosshairs already. Junior's skin was prickling with nerves, and he considered pulling his gun out of its holster, but then he instantly thought better of it. That would only alarm Charlotte, and right now he needed her to stay calm and quiet.

Junior glanced around the shadowy kitchen, the odors of onions and nutmeg and Formula 409 all mingling to form a melange of images in Junior's mind, visions of his mother's kitchen on a cold, wintry night, a steaming bowl of bread pudding on the butcher block, his brother Dennis practicing slap shots against the pantry door. Junior had only been in Charlotte's house a couple of times since they had known each other, but each time he visited, he reeled at all the secret visions it evoked, secret images, secret love—

"No! Wait!" Junior suddenly lurched across the kitchen to the wall where Charlotte was about to turn on a light. Junior grabbed her wrist just in time and whispered, *"No lights."*

Then he gently urged her arm back down to her side.

"Sorry, sorry," Charlotte murmured softly. "I guess I'm not very good at this kind of stuff."

"Don't worry about it. I just don't think we should let anybody know we're home."

Charlotte nodded. "I understand."

"Let's just get the coin and get out, and remember not to turn on any lights."

"I got it, Junie—no lights."

"Where is it?"

"The coin? It's out in the dining room, in a jewelry box on the table."

"Okay, let's go get it." Junior nodded toward the archway.

They crept across the shadows of the kitchen and into the next room.

The dining room was just as Junior remembered it, cozy and warm, filled with antiques and books. But in the gathering darkness, it was taking on a slightly menacing quality. A long, razor-thin strip of vapor light was shining through the front window, slicing through dust motes and slashing the floor down the middle. The great hulking bookshelves along the back wall looked oddly sinister, and the wrought iron fixture above the dining table looked like a prop from a horror film, like a tangle of cobwebs and black candles. Junior watched Charlotte hurry across the dining room toward the big oak table.

"Make it quick, honey," Junior whispered. "Just grab the coin."

While Charlotte fished through the contents of a small wooden jewelry box, Junior turned and went over to the front of the living room, where three bay windows rose over an old Zenith console. Most of the wooden shutters were half-open—a few centimeters gapped between the louvers—and for some reason Junior felt compelled to take a little peak out at Waitley Street. He pressed his back against the wall next to the corner window and carefully lowered one of the wooden louvers until he had a clear view of the street.

He saw the burgundy Lexus a half a block away, the two shadowy figures huddling inside it.

"Okay . . . ," Junior uttered softly, barely audible above the ticking of the clock. He could see the figures glancing over their shoulders, gazing back directly at Charlotte's window. And all at once Junior's skin got very clammy, his scalp starting to crawl.

He could taste old pennies.

"Junior, I got it." Charlotte was behind him, holding

the coin between her thumb and index finger, holding it up as though it were a prize. The dim slice of streetlight caught the edge of it and it glinted dully. Charlotte frowned, cocking her head. "Is something wrong?"

"Don't move!" Junior hissed.

"What is it?"

"Just stay calm, Ace; stay put for a second; there's a car out there; I don't like the looks of it."

"A car? What car? What do you mean, Junie, a car?"

"Just don't move, stay in the shadows. If they don't see us, we should be okay."

Junior reached into his coat and pulled the gun from its holster. He didn't make a big deal out of it, just brought the gun out and let it drop to his side as though he were about to fix a broken toaster. Unfortunately Charlotte instantly made eye contact with the thing and started breathing a little faster. In fact, the very air in the room seemed to seize up for a moment, something psychic working between Junior and Charlotte. "Just don't move, Ace." Junior was trying to whisper as calmly as possible, trying not to make Charlotte too crazy.

The trouble was, Charlotte was standing directly in front of the bay windows.

"Junie—who is it? You're scaring me." She was still holding that goddamn coin up in the air like she was some kind of mannequin in a darkened store window.

Junior started to say something, then heard the sound, the faint sound coming from somewhere nearby. The reason he hadn't heard it when he first came in was the fact that it was a ticking noise, and it had blended in with the incessant ticking of the clock out in the dining room. But now Junior could hear it as plain as the beating of his own heart. A metallic clicking noise, very rhythmic, a click every couple of seconds. "What is that?" he asked.

"What?" Charlotte was still frozen in front of the window.

"That noise, that ticking noise."

"I don't—"

Charlotte fell abruptly silent, gazing down at the contraption on the wall near the TV.

Digger Mussolino had a weird feeling in his gut all of a sudden.

Twisting around, gazing back through the rear window, he couldn't take his eyes off the front of that frigging bungalow. The windows were still dark, and it still seemed as dead as a tomb in there—the kid was probably picking his nose in the backyard by now—but there was something about those shutters inside the front bay windows, something that Digger couldn't quite put his finger on.

From the moment he had arrived earlier that day, he had been staring at those shutters. His Aunt Helen had shutters like that back on Mulberry Street in New York, and Digger could remember being seven years old and running around the front walk, playing peeka-boo with his sister Rose, who was inside, snapping those shutters open and shut like a crazy person. And tonight, nearly forty years later, Digger was still half expecting one of those wooden shutters to snap open and reveal his sister Rose peeking out the slats.

But now the shutters were starting to bother Digger like never before, and he didn't know why.

"I'm probably just being paranoid," the voice said next to him.

Digger looked over and saw the chiropractor peering into the rearview.

"Yeah," Digger murmured. "Ain't we all."

Then Digger stared at the shutters some more and

pondered the shadows behind them and started thinking that maybe this whole surveillance idea was a big fat waste of time. Maybe the psychic was on a plane to Bermuda already, or maybe she had gone to the cops, or maybe she had just fucking *gone fishing*. But still, there was something about those front bay windows, and the shutters, and the feeling that was growing inside Digger.

He turned to Lou St. Louis and said, "Hey, Lou, you want to hand me that gun case on the seat behind you?"

The realization struck Charlotte right between the eyes, and for one horrible instant she was paralyzed right there on her hundred-year-old Amish rug, still holding the coin up in the air, still gaping at the small plastic device plugged into the wall next to the TV.

"What's the matter, Charlotte?" Junior was frozen in front of the corner window, his eyes full of panic.

"The lights—" Charlotte uttered, nodding toward the wall socket, unable to make her legs work or motivate her body to go rip the thing out of the wall.

"What about them?"

"They're on a—" Charlotte started to explain—

(—and in her mind she was preparing to warn Junior in as few words as possible about the little plastic gizmo that she had purchased a couple of years ago at True Value hardware after her garage had been broken into, a little plastic gadget that gave her peace of mind whenever she was away on a trip, the kind with the square housing and the dial in the center that allows a person to set a daily pattern of lights or appliances coming on and going off in order to keep up the appearance of somebody being home, *this same little plastic doohickey which Charlotte often completely forgot about and neglected to unplug even when she was home*—)

—but there was no time to even finish the sentence with the word *timer*—

—because the clicking noises had abruptly ceased—

—and there was a snap like a match striking flint—

—and the two large hundred-watt lamps flamed on like spotlights showcasing Charlotte's silhouette in the front windows.

10

Invasion

The next ten seconds or so—at least in Junior's mind—seemed to stretch unmercifully.

Several things were happening at once—sounds mostly—and because of the freaky way that time had ground to a halt Junior was cognizant of them all, even while lurching toward the lamps, quickly turning them off, then spinning toward Charlotte, grabbing her, and jerking her away from the front windows: There were the sounds of car doors bursting open out in the darkness, voices echoing across the dew-slick lawns; there were noises out back, the telltale creak of footsteps coming across the weathered deck; and layered over it all was a completely surreal, incongruous noise like the sizzle of high-voltage electricity running through high-tension wires. Back in the 'Nam, Junior would hear this crackling sound in his head every time a firefight was imminent, and right now it was screaming at him.

The bastards were staking the place out!

"Wait—!" Junior lunged at Charlotte and pressed his left hand over her mouth.

Then he yanked her across the room as gently as possible and pressed her against the back wall of the dining room, rattling porcelain figurines and books off a nearby bookshelf. "Don't move, Ace, don't move," Junior was uttering under his breath, his hand still over her mouth. Although only five or six seconds had transpired, he had already switched into some deeper mode, a sort of battle-smart muscle memory, because he was doing all the things a well-trained soldier must do in order to survive in the field. He was protecting his company's weakest link, he was gauging the killing zone, and he was taking instantaneous inventories of the escape routes all around him—the windows, the other rooms, the ceiling, the floor—the dead ends and the blind alleys.

Out in the kitchen: a sudden, harsh rattling noise like somebody futzing with the lock.

"Don't panic," Junior whispered to Charlotte, his left palm still cupping her mouth. "Just stay there, keep your back against the wall!"

With his right hand he thumbed back the hammer of the Smith & Wesson.

He aimed the gun at the archway leading into the kitchen, all the old lessons about handgun combat sparking and sputtering in his memory banks, the part about aiming low through the back-sight, compensating for the kick, relaxing on the squeeze, and breathing through the action. And even though only eight or nine seconds had passed since the lights had come on, Junior was already deeply in the game, making instant observations, coming to several conclusions. First, these figures closing in on the little bungalow were probably wise guys, because only wise guys would brazenly march up to the house and start fiddling with locks without a how-do-you-do. Junior knew enough mob lore to recognize the attitude. Second, the guys coming up the front walk were probably the bigger fish, since Junior had always heard that mob guys like to come at their quarry head-on. And third—and this was a big one—the guy at the rear was probably already inside the house, because Junior couldn't hear any more rattling noises out there.

Now there were footsteps coming across the kitchen's parquet floor.

Junior kept the gun aimed at that arched entrance, breathing through the panic.

A pimply-faced kid in a mesh dago-T appeared in the archway. "Who the fuck are you?" the kid said, aiming his semiauto rig sideways at Junior—real fancy like in the movies—real stupid, too. The kid was probably a low-level schlub from the family with an IQ somewhere south of room temperature. Which meant two things: He could be manipulated, and he could be dangerous.

"Screw you," Junior said as calmly as possible. "Who the hell are you?"

"I asked you first."

"I don't give a shit, this is my score, and I want you the hell outta here," Junior growled at him. The ruse was working, at least for the moment; in fact, every single second Junior kept on living and the kid kept on *not* seeing Charlotte in the shadows to Junior's left was a smashing success.

"You got three fucking seconds to tell me who you are, old man, before I cap your fucking ass!"

There was a glitch of silence then as taut as piano wire tuned to high C.

"Try the house next door, asshole," Junior said, his gun unwavering. "This score is mine, and you ain't takin it away from me."

The kid cocked his head, a dog hearing a high-pitched whistle, his little peach-fuzz goatee twitching. "You're telllin' me you're hittin' this place?"

"Brilliant deduction, Sherlock."

"You're a fucking B&E guy?"

"Give the youngster a stuffed teddy bear."

Again with the cocking of his head, the twitching of his little goatee.

Across the room came a muffled tapping noise,

knuckles against a window, and Junior knew exactly
what it was without even turning around, and the chills
started working their way down his spine. The wise
guys were out on the front porch, probably peering in
through the door's portal window, peering in through
ruffled curtains, trying to see what the hell was up
with this absurd little showdown. Junior started to say,
"Look, if you don't get the hell outta my face—"

Then Junior stopped abruptly because an opportunity had just presented itself.

It occurred over the space of a single instant, and
if Junior had blinked he would have missed it, but
sure enough, just for a split second, the kid in the
dago-T had glanced off toward the door, shrugging at
his bosses as though he didn't know how to play this
thing out, and in doing so had taken his eyes off Junior for one brief millisecond, and Junior realized he
had to act without hesitation.

He squeezed off a shot.

The Smith & Wesson barked in the silent dining
room, a flash of silver light, and the blast punched a
hole in Tiny Sharpetti's left thigh. The impact shoved
the kid off balance, jerking him to the left, so that
when he fired his own piece—a flat pop of suppressed
.357-caliber metal—the tracer shot up into the ceiling
like a Roman candle, chewing a ragged navel in the
plaster, and that's when Charlotte started screaming.
And then several things were happening all at once,
and it was hard for Junior to keep it all straight because his ears were ringing now, and he was moving,
moving toward Charlotte, reaching out for her with
his free hand, ignoring the high-pitched whistle in his
head and the sound of shrieking and the battering ram
slamming into the front door behind him.

He reached Charlotte just as the front door burst
open.

11

House of Cards

It was as though Charlotte were standing in the path of a freight train.

It wasn't exactly Junior's fault either; he was going so fast that when he tried to shove Charlotte deeper into the shadows of the hallway, Charlotte tensed at the wrong moment, her legs tangling, and she tripped backward, careening to the floor, her tailbone striking hardwood. A jolt of pain shot up her spine, and starbursts popped in her line of vision. Then Junior's feet got tangled in Charlotte's legs, and *he* went sprawling to the floor as well.

The coin went bouncing and spinning across the dining room.

It struck the far wall and came to rest near a potted ficus plant.

Charlotte yelped—a completely involuntary sound that tumbled out of her lungs—because the pain and the panic struck her all at once like a lightning bolt as she struggled to her knees. She could see across the living room—the front door gaping open, the lock broken like balsa wood, and the two hulking figures coming into her sweet, cozy, little bungalow with the swift, deadly certainty of poison clouding a clear pond. The kid out on the kitchen floor was curled into a fetal position now, holding his leg, howling like a gutshot dog. And worse, much worse, was the sight of that silver dollar lying near the dining room base-board, still gleaming in the dim light.

Charlotte started toward it.

"Charlotte!—Jesus Christ!—forget the coin!"

Junior's voice was bellowing somewhere behind her, but Charlotte could barely hear it now, her ears were ringing badly, and her spine was throbbing painfully as she tried to crawl across twelve feet of oak floor in her denim jumper and 9West boots. There was a big, ugly man in her living room now, coming toward her, raising a big, ugly-looking gun. And there was another one—a bit smaller, milder mannered—standing near the door, looking on like a referee. But Charlotte ignored them both and concentrated on getting that coin.

She reached the coin just as the next blast rang out behind her.

It felt as though the top of her head had just been peeled off like a pull tab, the sound was so immense, so abrupt, the dust raining down on her from a divot in the crown molding overhead. It took her a moment to realize that the blast had come from Junior's gun—just a warning shot to get everyone's attention—and the threat of it had driven the other two men behind the sofa out in the living room. And now the sound of the kid shrieking in the kitchen was blending with an angry voice coming from the living room.

"Stop your yappin', Sharpetti—it's just a slug, for Chrissake!"

From the kitchen: *"FUCK!—fuck-fuck-fuck—FUCK—FUCK!!"*

"Who's doing all the shooting anyway?"

More garbled shrieking, a torrent of profanity, but not much of an answer.

"Charlotte!" Junior's voice cut through the dark haze behind Charlotte, instantly reaching down inside her and touching something there, something primal,

something like the will to survive. She scooped up the coin and was crawling back toward the hallway when she heard the voice of the thug in the living room.

"Charlotte Vickers?"

"That's right," Charlotte was muttering, instinctively polite, scuttling across her floor like a madwoman, clutching the coin in her sweaty palm. She didn't even pause to glance over her shoulder at the intruder.

"There's no call for violence, ma'am. Miss Fortunato just wants to talk."

"Charlotte!" Junior was yelling at her again from the hallway. "Please!"

"I have to be going," Charlotte was murmuring now, crawling toward the shadows of the hallway. She almost made it, too, but when the sound of the kid screaming behind her rose to a wild howl, and then the sounds of thudding out in the kitchen signaled he was up on his feet, Charlotte made the mistake of glancing over her shoulder.

The lanky kid was standing on one leg in the archway, aiming his gun at Charlotte. "Bitch!"

Before the kid could fire, there was another thunderous blast from the hallway.

A momentary flash of strobe light, and the kid's skull snapped backward against the doorjamb, spewing red mist across the plaster wall. The kid folded like a house of cards to the floor. And at this same precise moment, Charlotte was yelping again—another one of those instinctive yelps that stole her breath away and nearly jerked her out of her skin—and again her body lurched.

The coin went flying.

"Oh no!—OH NO!"

Charlotte turned and crawled across an endless expanse of hardwood floor toward the coin, which was spinning now like a top toward the opposite base-board, and the fear and adrenaline surged through Charlotte's body—the absolute horror of seeing somebody killed in her own home like fast-growing cancer in her brain, driving her on, the noise in her head as bright and shiny as the blood splattered across the wall behind her—and she dove toward the coin, thinking if she could just save that coin, if she could just save the lives of those poor people in Colorado—

The coin skipped across a cold air vent.

Then it plummeted down inside the furnace.

12

Dirty Blue Flames

Junior lurched across the dining room toward the furnace vent, moving very quickly because he knew he only had one chance to get across the room, get to Charlotte, and get the hell out of there before the big guy out in the living room had a chance to do anything.

Junior was halfway across the room when the massive figure rose up behind the couch holding a 12-gauge coach gun, double trigger, loaded for grizzly.

Junior squeezed off a round, mid-stride, like he was spitting at the living room. The blast gobbled the wall out there, right behind the sofa, chewing through a framed embroidery that said *There's No Place Like Home,* shattering the glass, and knocking the frame off its hook. The bad guys ducked back behind the sofa. "This is ridiculous!" the big one bellowed. "We're all adults here, for Chrissake—all Miss Fortunato wants to do is talk!"

Junior reached the furnace vent and scooped Charlotte up, yanking her to her feet.

She was limp, almost in a daze, but Junior had no time to discuss her condition, or to placate her shock, or even to be gentle; he was a machine now, calibrated for one singular purpose: to get her the hell out of there. He jerked her toward the hallway, aiming his gun back at the living room couch just as the big guy's head was coming back up.

Junior fired twice—aiming for maximum noise and distraction, not really trying to hit anybody—and the first shot struck the side of the couch, tearing through fabric, gouts of stuffing exploding in the air. The second shot whistled past the bad guys and struck the wall, leaving a puckered hole that puffed plaster and dust.

"C'mon, honey!" Junior yanked Charlotte down the hall toward her bedroom, several things swirling through his mind now as he stumbled along. He was thinking that maybe they could get out one of the bedroom windows, or even use the phone in the bedroom to call the cops, and he was also thinking that he better get that speedloader out and get those last six rounds into the Smith & Wesson before the wise guys started bringing hellfire down on him. But all at once, these thoughts were shattered by a sudden surprise movement to his right.

Charlotte had pulled herself free and was staggering toward a door on the opposite side of the hall. "The coin, Junie! We can't leave it!"

Junior followed Charlotte through a doorway.

They descended a rickety wooden staircase.

Everything was happening too fast now, too fast, too fast to put on the brakes, because now Junior found himself descending into the cool darkness of Charlotte's basement, and the odors of cold rot and old brick were filling his nostrils, and the sounds of heavy footsteps were coming down the hallway above him. All at once, Junior rushed back up the steps and slammed the door shut, latching it with a chintzy little hook that probably wouldn't withstand a burst of harsh language.

A bare light bulb clicked on at the base of the stairs.

Junior rushed back down the steps and found Charlotte circling a filthy iron octopus slathered in cobwebs—an old rebuilt coal burner, probably transformed into a forced-air job sometime around the Jimmy Carter administration—and now Charlotte was reaching up and pounding on the ducts that led down into the beast from the first floor.

Junior gazed around the cellar, frantically looking for a way out. The basement was tiny and unfinished, with ancient cinder-block walls, a water-stained cement floor, and no apparent way out other than the stairs. "Jesus Christ, Charlotte, we're really screwed now."

"The coin, Junie, the coin is the only way," she was gibbering, pounding on the ducts, frantically searching for the fallen coin.

The sudden thud of a heavy boot against the door at the top of the stairs.

An angry, muffled voice: "I'm through playing around, folks, I mean it!"

Junior pulled the speedloader out, his hands trembling so badly it took him several seconds merely to get the tips into the cylinder. It wasn't because he was frightened for his own life, or because he had just killed a person (that kid was positively going to hurt Charlotte). It was the realization that was dawning on Junior, at this very moment, that he had started something with the mob, and these guys were heavily into vendetta, and they would bring their vengeance down on both Junior *and* Charlotte, and the last thing Junior wanted to do was put Charlotte in harm's way.

Another muffled thud from the top of the stairs, the hook rattling: "You're pissing me off now!"

Junior snapped the cylinder closed just as the sound of Charlotte's voice rang out.

"There it is!"

She was kneeling down in front of the monstrous boiler, pointing at the bulwark, pointing at something inside it. There were dirty blue flames pulsing inside a grated cover—the temperature had dropped enough this evening for the burners to cycle on—and now Charlotte was prying open the faceplate, and Junior couldn't believe what he was seeing.

"Charlotte, don't—!"

But it was too late; she had already pried open the ancient faceplate and thrust her hand into the flames.

13

The Chute

One thing saved her.

The chute.

She kept on thinking about it as she dipped her hand into the blanket of fire inside the furnace, the sudden gush of pain stealing her breath away. It poured up her arms and registered in her mind, and she saw nothing but Day-Glo pink for several seconds as she fished around for the prize. It felt as though her skin were peeling away, as though the tissue underneath were bathing in acid. But thank God she was able to get her fingers around that coin—which had fallen into the guts, lodging itself between two gas jets.

"Aaaaahhhhh—AHHH!!—darn it!" she hissed through clenched teeth as she plucked it out. She looked down at her arm and saw that the tiny hairs were gone. She closed her eyes, cradling her throbbing arm, holding that red-hot coin. She managed to put the coin in her pocket.

Above them, the door burst open.

Charlotte barely heard the creak of the steps, her ears were ringing too severely now.

Junior yanked her behind the furnace and started firing at the stairs—a string of five cherry bombs popping in the dim light, the sparks like strobe lights—and each blast sounded to Charlotte as though it were underwater. Then a pair of massive explosions—two shotgun blasts—striking the furnace, sending dust and

debris spurting across the basement. But Charlotte
was too busy to worry about it, she was too busy
searching the far corner of the basement where the
thing was buried in shadows, situated near the ceiling.

The chute.

It was one of those wonderful, funky old hinged
doors with the *Hubbard Fuel Oil* insignia stamped on
the steel; the same kind that her parents used to have
in their basement; the same kind that her dad used to
open up for the coal truck every month or so and let
that stream of smoky black rock rush into the cellar.
The coal chute. It was Charlotte's and Junior's ticket
out of this trap, and Charlotte saw it across the basement, less than fifteen feet away.

She grabbed Junior and ushered him toward the
chute.

What happened next occurred without words, because Junior glanced up and immediately saw what
Charlotte was pointing at, and he nodded quickly,
then turned and aimed his gun at the stairs. He had
one bullet left. His enemy was huddling at the top of
the stairs, reloading his shotgun, a couple of plastic
shell casings bouncing down through the open steps
and landing on the concrete below. "You folks are
makin' a big mistake," the voice said almost as an
afterthought.

Charlotte staggered over to the wall, stood on tiptoes, and wrestled the chute's bolt-lock open with her
good hand, then pushed the chute open.

The three-foot channel was covered in soot. It led
up to the alley where anther hatch was covered with
a flimsy painted panel. After a moment's pause, Charlotte planted one foot in a gap between two loose
bricks and lifted herself up. She negotiated the chute
in a matter of seconds—rubbing soot and filth across
the sides of her arms and legs, not to mention ninety
percent of her jumper—but when she pushed open the

outer hatch, the night air hit her face and it was delicious.

She climbed out, the weeds cool on her sore knees and her burns. She could hear the sirens in the near distance, police cars coming, the neighbors' windows filling with the silhouettes of onlookers.

More gunfire popped and boomed behind her, the sparks like flashbulbs in the basement.

Charlotte twisted back toward the opening, her heart racing, her lungs burning with panic. What if she had just heard the sound of Junior getting shot? What if they had shot him? Charlotte thought she had heard three shots—one from Junior's pistol, and two thunderous booms from the shotgun—but she couldn't be sure. What if—?

She didn't even get to finish thinking the question.

Junior's face materialized in the coal chute. "Let's get the hell out of here," he said, struggling out the hatch.

They climbed to their feet and hurried off toward the azalea bushes.

Within moments, they were gone.

The darkness swallowing them whole.

PART 11

THE SCARECROW

"Man is a fighting animal."
—SANTAYANA

PART II

THE SCARECROW

14

Real-Life Monsters

"You're worried about the kids again, aren't you?"

Sandy Stafford—née Lattamore—was sitting on a massive stump behind the modest two-story house that had come to be known as the neutral site. Paul was standing nearby, a long stick in his hand, staring off across the forest of birches and pines. The sun had slunk behind the trees, and the shadows had lengthened, and now the air was as crisp as a cold glass of cider. Paul glanced across the clearing and saw Timmy and Darryl playing quietly on a rusty swing set near the satellite dish. Actually, Timmy was the only one playing. Darryl was sitting stone still in his *Night of the Living Dead* T-shirt, staring at his parents, brooding like a miniature version of his father.

"No, actually, I'm worried about me," Paul said softly, his gaze fixed on the setting sun.

"What you mean is, you're worried about the trouble the kids are going to get *you* into," Sandy said bitterly, her breath visible in the chilled air.

It was a cutting remark, yet it was valid; Paul Lattamore had learned that the weakest links to protecting their anonymity in the witness protection program were the children. Especially in school. During free-for-alls on the playground or share-and-tell-sessions, the kids had to keep their stories straight, had to sign their phony signatures as though they had been doing it all their lives. For nine-year-old Darryl it was a

daunting task, but for six-year-old Timmy it was next
to impossible. Paul had tried turning the process into
a game, pretending the kids were spies, working
undercover, and he would reward them with little trin-
kets when they did well, punish them with "black
marks" when they slipped. It seemed to work at first,
but with each passing month, Sandy had become more
and more cynical about it. She felt Paul was projecting
his angst onto the kids, and she felt trapped by the
whole situation; and even though she still loved Paul,
she couldn't help but let some of that good old bile
come spewing out once in a while.

Paul couldn't blame her.

"It's something else," he said finally, speaking under
his breath so that Darryl wouldn't hear. The nine-
year-old reminded Paul so much of himself at that
age. Full of burning questions, smoldering hormones,
and a love of baseball, rock and roll, and comic books.
Darryl was a walking encyclopedia of both baseball
trivia and horror movies, and he reminded Paul of his
own childhood, and the days he used to put together
the old Aurora plastic models of the Wolfman, Fran-
kenstein's monster, and Dracula. Little did young Paul
Lattamore know, he and his family would one day be
hiding from real-life monsters.

"What does that mean—*something else*?" Sandy
was chewing her fingernail, watching her kids, and
across the clearing, little Darryl Lattamore was chewing his own fingernails, watching his parents.

"It's kind of hard to explain," Paul said, scraping
the stick against the ground, making cryptic symbols
in the fallen pine needles.

"Well, try."

"It's like these flashes I've been getting lately," he
said.

"Flashes?"

"Yeah, spells, I don't know what you would call them."

Sandy chewed her cuticle. "What kind of spells?"

"I guess you could call them flashes of paranoia," Paul said. "Except they're very intense, like little seizures, you know what I mean?"

"No, Paul, I don't have any idea what you mean."

Paul licked his lips and tried to figure out how to explain it, but it was futile. He couldn't put it into words. Besides, even if he *could* articulate it, it would probably only serve to make Sandy more anxious than she already was. "It's probably nothing," he finally said, tossing the stick into the woods. "I'm sure it's nothing, I'm sure I'm just imagining it."

Sandy shrugged. "If you say so."

Paul turned toward the kids and called out. "C'mon, men! Time for supper!"

The boys climbed down from the jungle gym and trotted across the clearing toward their parents. Timmy jumped up into Paul's arms, and Darryl walked alongside his mother, and the four of them strode back inside the neutral sight.

But even after they were safely inside, doors locked, good smells engulfing them from Sandy's Swiss steak dinner, Paul Lattamore could not shake the feeling that another spell was on the way.

Another electric jolt in his brain, as though somebody were trying to reach him from a long distance.

15

Broken Pastels

The Geo was screaming down Fullerton Avenue toward the I-90 entrance, the dark granite warehouses streaming by them on either side, the flashbulb blur of dirty lights flickering against the windows.

Thank God there was a small first-aid kit in Junior's glove box. Charlotte had pried it open as soon as she was inside the car, and had found enough gauze and antibiotic ointment to wrap her burned right hand. From the looks of her blistered palm and swollen fingers, it seemed as though she had sustained serious second-degree burns. Nothing too deep, but nasty enough to provide a constant drone of pain. Now she sat mute on the passenger side, her hand throbbing in her lap, her brain buzzing like a faulty electrical connection. Every few moments she would nervously glance out at the side mirror, expecting to see some big black sedan looming behind them, but so far none had appeared. Still, her heart was thrumming so loudly it felt as though it were about to split apart at the seams, and every distant backfire or screeching tire made her jump.

They drove in agonizing silence for several more minutes, as if the mere act of talking would steal their concentration or jinx them somehow.

By the time they reached the freeway ramp and slipped into the flow of eastbound traffic, Charlotte was breathing well enough to speak: "I feel so terrible, Junie, dragging you into this. I'm so sorry."

"Nobody twisted my arm, Ace."

After a long pause, Charlotte said, "That boy you shot . . . he couldn't have been more than twenty years old."

"That 'boy' was a stone killer, Charlotte, don't kid yourself."

"He was just a teenager."

Junior shot her a glance. "A teenager who was about to blow the back of your skull off."

Charlotte shuddered and looked back out the window. Her brain was sore from all the cacophonous emotions and noise and pain that had been bombarding it over the last few hours. The image of that kid in her living room kept replaying in her mind, the muzzle flash, the puppet snap of his head, and the red mist against the crown molding. Charlotte felt as though she had shaken a wasp nest, and now all the wasps were getting ornery and noisy. People were going to get stung, and it was all Charlotte's fault. But there was a deeper feeling turning inside Charlotte now, and it was magnetic, inexorable, drawing her westward toward Colorado, toward the only mode of redemption: to save the Lattamore family. It was the only way to make things right, the only way for Charlotte to live with herself. All she had to do now was pinpoint the exact location . . .

She was reaching into her pocket for the coin when she caught a glimpse of her reflection in the side mirror.

At first it seemed as though she were looking at another person. Her round face was moist with sweat and grime, her dark curls tossing in the wind, her eyes glassy with pain. Her jumper was filthy, covered in soot and pocked with tiny rips along one shoulder strap from having crawled out of the cellar. To make matters worse, her lower back was throbbing painfully now, as well as her hand, and she felt a twinge in her ribs every time she took a breath. She wondered if Junior had injured her when he tackled her to the ground. She wiped a strand of hair from her eyes and longed for her overnight bag. How in God's name was she supposed to track down the Lattamore family without a change of clothes? Without toiletries? Without any supplies whatsoever?

Charlotte shuddered suddenly, a fluttering in her ear making her shiver.

She glanced over at Junior and saw his chiseled face reflecting the orange glow of the dashboard instruments, his jaw set, his brow furrowed gravely.

He looked as though he were concentrating on solving some complex calculus equation.

Charlotte suddenly felt a jolt of panic run through her. If anything happened to Junior, she would never forgive herself. She started thinking that maybe they were on a suicide mission, and maybe they should go to the feds after all. "Junie, look," she said softly over the engine and wind. "Maybe you're right about going to the FBI."

"Whattya mean?"

"Maybe we should find the nearest phone, call the FBI, and tell them everything."

He looked at her. "You really mean that?"

"No," she said.

Junior managed a tepid smile. "That's what I thought."

"On the other hand, I don't want to just blithely lead these people to Lattamore."

"Meaning what?"

"Meaning . . . they could be following us right now."

"I doubt it."

"How can we be sure?"

"We made a big racket back there, Ace," Junior

said, his eyes shifting across the dark expanse of highway before them, his gaze darting from car to car. "I don't think they were quick enough on the draw to follow us."

"But how do we know for sure?"

Junior shrugged. "*You're* the psychic. See if you pick up any signals back there."

Charlotte glanced out at the side mirror, the blur of headlights streaming behind them. Her mind was a whirlwind. Fragments of feelings and sensations, colors and shapes and sounds, percolating noisily. It felt as though her mind were a faulty videotape recorder, replaying glimpses of the evening, backward and forward over sputtering magnetic heads. It was threatening to crack her skull open. She had to slow down, turn the VCR off for a few moments.

"I can't tell, honey," she uttered finally, blowing on her injured hand.

"Don't worry about it," he said. "Soon as I get a chance, I'm going to ditch this car."

Charlotte thought about it for a moment, then started to say, "You think that's the best—"

Then she stopped.

A spot on the cloth seat beneath Junior had caught her eye. She had noticed it earlier, but she had thought it was merely a worn spot where the fabric had gotten shiny. Or maybe a coffee stain. In the dark interior it was hard to tell. But now she realized it had grown over the last few minutes, and it was as black as tar.

"Junie— That's not—" She reached over and touched the dark spot with her mitten of gauze.

It was wet to the touch, and it soaked into the gauze around her fingers.

"Whatsamatter? What's wrong?" Junior was glancing down at his seat, his eyes widening. In the darkness his pupils shimmered. "What the hell *is* that?"

Charlotte took a closer look at her fingertips. The tiny spots had the consistency of thirty-weight motor oil.

"What is that?" Junior asked, his voice dropping an octave.

"Omigod—Junie." Charlotte's fingers hung in the air before her lips. "It's blood."

"Bullshit! BULL-FUCKING-SHIT! How could this happen? How? HOW?!"

Natalie Fortunato had the cordless phone receiver pressed to her ear as she sat forward on the edge of a Tiffany chair in her bedroom, breathing hard, glowering at her reflection in the oval mirror of her makeup bureau. Her face was covered with an avocado green gunk—an astringent mask that she applied every night before bed—and her eyes blazed red like lit fuses as she waited for an answer. Her right hand had pieces of cotton sandwiched between the fingers where she had been removing fingernail polish, and now a cigarette smoldered between the cotton balls. She could hear the telltale rush of wind on the other end of the line, the slightly dead, tinny sound of a man's voice calling from a moving car.

"I'm real sorry, Miss Fortunato, but the thing of it is, nobody expected the psychic to have this mutt with her." The voice on the other end of the line was Digger Mussolino. He was speaking loud enough to be heard over the engine noise, his tone an odd mixture of annoyance, anger, and embarrassment, as though he had just banged his thumb with a hammer.

"What mutt?!" Natalie demanded.

"Some mutt with a .357—probably some boyfriend or neighbor or something—we're not sure."

Natalie growled, "For Chrissake."

"The prick popped one of our guys, too, one of the kids from Tony's crew—"

"Shut up, just shut up for a second!"

"We got outta there before the Boy Scouts arrived, but we lost the—"

"I said shut up!" Natalie angrily snubbed the cigarette out in a marble Venus-on-the-halfshell. "I need to think for a second."

There was a moment of staticky silence on the other end as Digger waited for Natalie to think.

Natalie glanced across the bedroom, across the plush berber carpet and the fine French Provincial furniture, across the chintz and ruffles and pleats. It was her inner sanctum, this soft warren of pink and baby blue and peach, a place to unwind at the end of the day. But now it bristled with hateful feelings and venomous thoughts. Natalie wanted to strangle that bitch of a psychic for holding back. Natalie wanted to dig her deluxe Lee press-on nails right into that slut's eyes until her eyeballs popped like poached eggs. The bitch was probably heading west right at this very moment, heading west toward that rat-prick accountant's new home in Colorado in order to warn him. The rage pulsed inside Natalie's scrawny little form like white-hot embers in the pit of her belly, and she felt like screaming, and she felt like throwing things, but she didn't. She didn't let her emotions get the best of her this time.

Instead, she focused.

"Okay, Digger, pay attention," she finally said into the phone.

"Go ahead."

"I want the five families behind this thing. I want every last bit of muscle we got from here to the West Coast on this case—you understand what I'm saying?"

"Yeah, I guess," came the flat reply.

"Listen to me, Digger, I'm talking about every cop and state trooper we got in our pocket." The cold rage was stitching down Natalie's spine, making her fingers tingle, making her sinuses burn as though she'd just sniffed a vial of smelling salts. "I want them all on the lookout. I'm talking about every inch of major interstate between here and Colorado."

"That's gonna be kinda difficult—"

"I don't want to hear about it, Digger. I want people at O'Hare, and I want people at Stapleton in Denver, and I want people at every other airport you can think of in Colorado. I want people at the train depots and the bus depots, too. You hear me?"

A spurt of static, then: "Yes, ma'am."

"We're gonna find that psychic, Digger, and she's gonna lead us straight to that fucking rat."

After another moment, Digger's voice returned. "They got a jump on us, Miss Fortunato—"

"GODDAMNIT!" Natalie lashed out at the tabletop, flinging dozens of tiny glass cologne bottles across the room. Pastel-colored glass shattered against the pastel-colored wall, spraying hundred-dollar ounces across the floral print wallpaper. "I told you!—I don't want any more fucking excuses!"

"I'm sorry, Miss Fortunato, you're right—we'll find them—I'll get right on it."

Natalie got herself under control. "And one more thing," she said then.

"Go ahead, Miss Fortunato."

"I want you to get the fat man."

"You're kiddin'? Really? I mean . . . you think he's necessary for this thing?"

Natalie clenched her teeth, felt her stomach tightening like a steel band. "Digger, don't argue with me. I want you to wake him up, get his lard ass outta bed, and tell him this is for John."

"Right, we'll get the fat man, don't you worry."

Natalie hung up the phone, then started pacing across the bedroom.

Right through the broken glass.

16

A Vast Ocean of Radiance

Interstate 80 was Chicagoland's carotid artery, carrying rich arterial blood from the industrial cities of the east into the capillaries of western suburbs. At night, the artery pulsed and surged with constant traffic, the lights of big rigs hauling ass for the Mississippi, and the endless drone of commuters in their little metal cells. Beyond Chicago, I-80 snaked and coiled all the way across the country's spine, not stopping until it reached the Pacific Ocean just north of San Francisco. It was America's true circulatory system. But like any bloodstream, there were certain veins that could use a little angioplasty.

One of the most diseased of these veins was just south of Joliet, Illinois, where exit number 124 wound down into a valley of spindly trees, festering sewage treatment plants, and rows of boarded storefronts. A quarter mile beyond these storefronts, the horizon exploded with fluorescent light, as white as a near-death experience, teeming with bugs and carbon monoxide. The light was so bright, in fact, that it made the surrounding landscape look like nuclear daytime, like a flashbulb frozen in mid-explosion. It was here, in this vast ocean of radiance, that Junior Parrick finally worked up enough nerve to pull his torn shirttails out of his pants and look at the wound.

"It's the damnedest thing," he murmured, looking down at his pasty white belly. He was sitting behind the wheel of the Geo, which was parked and idling behind a row of Dumpsters on the edge of the Conoco Truck Stop Complex. He ran a fingertip along the bloody patch, then mumbled, "Can't feel a stitch of pain down there, just feels numb."

"All that blood though," Charlotte uttered, leaning over for a closer look. She had a pained expression on her face, and she was biting her lower lip, and it looked as though she didn't know what to do with her hands. "It doesn't look like a bullet wound, not exactly."

"I think it's a piece of your furnace," Junior said, rubbing his fingers along the sticky puckered area on his side. It looked as though somebody had drawn a jagged black line across his love handle in ballpoint pen, the blood already crusting around it, the serum glistening in the ambient light. He pressed his fingertip to the wound and felt the hard object embedded in his flesh. Probably a piece of shrapnel, probably from one of the furnace ducts that had gotten in the way of the 12-gauge. Junior wasn't surprised that he had missed it. Even now, he had so much adrenaline sluicing through him, he could barely feel the wound. Nevertheless, it was beginning to sting, and just beneath it, a deeper heat was building.

"A piece of my what?" Charlotte was staring at the wound, looking as though she might be sick again.

"Your furnace—a piece of metal from one of the ducts, probably nipped me as I was heading for the chute."

"Jesus, Junie, you've lost a lot of blood."

"Looks worse than it is, believe me. Why don't you hand me that first aid kit?"

"But, honey, we gotta get you to a doctor, get it cleaned up, get you a tetanus shot maybe."

"I don't think that's a good idea right now."

Charlotte looked up at him. "Don't argue with me,

Junie. Besides, I should probably have my hand looked at as well."

Junior took a deep breath. The stinging sensation was starting to make him dizzy. "These mob guys are smart, Charlotte. If they think we're hurting, they'll be keeping tabs on every emergency room and clinic from here to Denver."

After a moment, Charlotte said, "You think they know we're injured?"

Junior shrugged, told her he had no idea.

Charlotte reached down, scooped up the first aid kit, and started rifling through the remaining vials of antiseptic, rolls of gauze, and bandages. "How in God's name are we gonna make it to Colorado, Junie? We got no clothes, no supplies, and I don't know about you, but the only money I've got on me is that damn coin, and I need *that* to find the witness."

"I've got money, plastic, you name it," Junior assured her. "We'll make it."

Charlotte had found a pack of sterile Handi Wipes, and now she was tearing into it with her teeth. She unfolded one and started dabbing the edges of Junior's wound.

Junior watched. "The good news is, they didn't see our car, so we don't have to worry about somebody spotting us."

The Handi Wipe quickly became sodden with blood, and was starting to disintegrate. "I'm thinking about going to the nearest airport," Charlotte announced then. "As soon as I pinpoint the city, I can fly down there and—"

"Sorry, darlin', but planes and trains are definitely out of the question."

After thinking it over, Charlotte said, "Because they'll be watching for us at the airports and depots?"

"Yeah."

"But it seems like we're more vulnerable on the highway."

"Maybe, maybe not," Junior said, and grimaced at a twinge of pain.

"Sorry, Junie, sorry—" Charlotte was obviously trying to be gentle, trying not to jostle the wound.

Junior watched her for a moment and felt a sudden, unexpected tremor of emotion deep in his gut. Funny . . . how quickly he followed her right into this nightmare. Hell, he was no hero. Truth was, he had plunged into this mess because of one reason and one reason only—his unrequited obsession for Charlotte Vickers. He would do anything for her; he would fight the mob; he would take a piece of shrapnel in his side. Hell, he would even get in a gunfight with a crazed young man.

All for Charlotte.

"We gotta get you inside, Junie. Get you cleaned up, get the fragment out of you."

Junior glanced over his shoulder at the truck stop.

The Conoco complex was a favorite haunt among southbound long-haulers passing through Chicago. A couple of acres of weathered cement and low-slung buildings, the truck stop was laid out in an inverted V, the diesel pumps lined up down one leg, the gas pumps down another. At the top of the inverted V was the combination office/mini-mart/restaurant. The place seemed busy for a weeknight, crawling with truckers and travelers stocking up amid the lurid displays and harsh fluorescent overheads. Behind the restaurant glowed the lights of a car wash, and behind the car wash, a grove of emaciated oaks stretched back into the darkness beyond the property line.

In the shadows of the trees a flickering neon sign said *Stardust Motel—Color TV—Cottages—Vacancy.*

"Yeah, maybe you're right," Junior said at last. "Maybe we ought to lay low for a few minutes." He nodded toward the woods. "Looks like there's a place back there we can hang out with the roaches for a while."

Charlotte agreed with him.

And so they went about the business of hiding the car and checking in.

Rondo Hatton was dreaming he was thin. He did that a lot. In this one, he was the ancient Greek god Apollo, kingpin of the sky, guru of inspiration and art and prophecy. He was cut. He was buff. He was Major Beefcake, his oiled biceps reflecting the sun, his rippling six-pack tummy glistening. All the lesser goddesses were gathered at his feet—Hera, Aphrodite, Athena— their arms wrapped around his muscular legs. Dressed in skimpy togas, their enormous breasts heaving, their huge blond bouffants shimmering in the sun, they looked suspiciously like the gold diggers from the old Dean Martin television show. (. . . Hey, it was Rondo's dream, so give him a little leeway for artistic license.) And there was a thunderous pounding now, reverberating across the sky, shaking the hills, rattling the earth down to its core. And Apollo (Rondo) was becoming very distracted by this pounding, and he finally raised his powerful fists to the heavens and—

—he woke up with a start in the back room of his bungalow on Damon Avenue.

He was slumped in a BarcaLounger in front of a television set tuned to snow, and it was some godawful hour in the morning, and he was fat again. He was a fat, sweaty, balding private detective with fallen arches, a prostate the size of a grapefruit, and monthly alimony payments to an evil woman down in Peoria. But Rondo Hatton was still one of the best snoops in the business. And he still had his dignity—despite the fact that most of his peers referred to him as "the fat man." Therefore, he saw no reason why he should be awakened in the middle of the night by some idiot knocking on his door.

And yet.

The tommy-gun rapping continued.

Rondo struggled out of the easy chair—no small feat—and stood there in his boxer shorts for a moment, scratching his rotund belly, then rearranging his testicles, wondering who the hell might be knocking on his door at this hour. He waddled across the room—there was no other way to describe his walk—trying to suck in his gut along the way. Which was impossible. He was all gut. In fact there wasn't an inch on his body that wasn't round and flabby. Even his ears were fat. He looked like a conglomeration of overstuffed sausage casings. To make matters worse, his missile-shaped head was almost completely bald except for a delicate little widow's peak of black hair above his brow, which made him look even more comical. Like a porno actor playing Humpty Dumpty.

He answered the front door in a huff.

"The hell's going on?!" he said to the beefy figure silhouetted by the porch light.

"Got a job needs immediate attention," the figure said.

"Do I know you?" Rondo asked, squinting to see the beefy man's face in the shadows.

"Mussolino," the man said.

Rondo frowned. "Mussolino?"

"Digger Mussolino. Friend of John Fabionne's. Working for Natalie Fortunato."

It didn't take long for the magic word to make its way down Rondo's auditory canal, across his neural pathways, and into his cerebral cortex. It was like a splash of cold water on his face.

Fabionne.

"Yes, of course," Rondo blurted. "Just give me a minute to get dressed."

17

Chickenskin

The moment Charlotte stepped through the door of the musty little cottage, she felt the chill bumps working their way down the backs of her thighs, along the backs of her arms. *Chickenskin.* That's what her mom used to call it.

This was not a tranquil place. This was not a place of vacations and honeymoons and happy travels. This was a moody, agitated place. A way station on the road to purgatory. And the feeling was everywhere. It leapt out at Charlotte from the moldy braided rugs, it called to her from the cheap desk and chairs, from the swayback queen-sized bed with its tattered, pilled bedspread and twin lampshades the color of urine. Tormented spirits clung to the drapes here, the residue of much anguish, and whenever Charlotte walked into a room such as this, her mind would almost pucker, as though sampling the taste of strong vinegar.

But tonight she was far too preoccupied to even worry about it.

"Over here, Junie," she said, ushering the stocky man across the room to the john.

The bathroom was a moldering, closet-sized cubicle that smelled of dried piss and Lysol. The vinyl flooring crackled as they entered, and when Charlotte flipped on the light switch, an overhead donut of fluorescent tubing flickered and ticked, the bugs imprisoned in its housing swarming noisily. Junior took a seat on the commode as Charlotte glanced around the bathroom for any sign of the linens. She found two threadbare little towels embroidered with the Stardust logo hanging on a rack near the tub.

Charlotte grabbed a towel and went over to the sink, turning on the hot water.

"Off with the shirt," she instructed, soaping the towel as Junior set the first aid kit on the edge of the sink, unbuttoned his chambray shirt, and peeled it off. Charlotte had never seen the man shirtless before. In the year since they had met, they had frequented countless coffee shops, restaurants, and movie theaters, but they had yet to go to a beach or a pool or any other setting where Junior would disrobe. Now, in the cold light of the tiny bathroom, Charlotte was slightly taken aback at the sheer girth of the man. He looked like a linebacker who had gone to seed, his shoulders broad and thick, his neck corded with old muscle. He had a farmer's tan—a distinct V at the neck, and stripes at the short-sleeve point—and his chest hair was surprisingly prominent against the pale parts, like thick, curly steel wool—starting to gray slightly—cascading down his sternum and around his magnificent belly.

Charlotte felt an odd fluttering in her tummy as she leaned over and started cleaning the wound.

"Give it to me straight, Doc, I can take it," Junior muttered sheepishly.

"You're gonna live," she said, wiping away the last of the dried blood, making sure the wound site was clean.

Taking a deep breath, Charlotte turned back to the first aid kit and found the tweezers. They were pretty small, and were fairly difficult to maneuver with the gauze wrapped around her right hand and the dull pain still making her fingers throb, but she managed to grip them tightly, reach over to the wound, and carefully probe the jagged pucker in Junior's side.

Junior barely flinched.

"Ouch!" Charlotte yelped instinctively as she extracted the jagged fragment.

It came out easily, much more easily than she had expected, like a rotting tooth slipping out of a dead gum, and she glanced down at the fragment in awe. It was the size of a large paper clip, shiny with blood and serum, and when Charlotte looked back up at the wound she saw a fresh bloody tear falling from the site. She tossed the fragment in the sink, grabbed the rag, and held it on the wound.

Junior was grinning. "You said *ouch*."

"What?"

"When you pulled the thing out, you said *Ouch!* Don't gimme that routine about this 'hurting you more than me.' "

She thought about it for a moment. "It *did* hurt me, Junie—believe me, it *did*."

Charlotte finished cleaning the wound, applying some more antibiotic and a fresh dressing. When she was done, she picked the fragment out of the sink and tossed it in the wastebasket.

Junior was watching her. "How's the hand?"

Charlotte flexed her right hand. Her fingers felt stiff, as though they were covered in fast-drying glue. The intense pain had dulled to a low simmer but the ache was still there, throbbing faintly. "It's okay, actually," Charlotte reported. "Considering."

A sudden thought crossed her mind like a gust of ill wind. What if her hand had been injured permanently? What if she had damaged her instrument beyond repair? Her hand was her pipeline to psychic insight, her pipeline to the other realm—her gift, her curse. She knew enough about burns to know they often caused permanent nerve damage, and now she was starting to panic, her heart starting to race. What if her fingers were completely numb to the sensations of the coin?

"What's wrong, Ace?" Junior must have noticed her terrified expression.

"Need to check something," Charlotte murmured, tearing at the gauze, her fingers tingling hotly, itching. She got the gauze off and saw her swollen flesh, a circle of blisters on her palm like a faint tattoo where the coin had burned its impression into the skin. Charlotte reached into the pocket of her jumper and felt the cool, hard coin.

(—static—)

She brought the coin out and cupped it in her burned palm, fondling it with her swollen fingers, opening the channel in her mind that received the feelings. She ignored the pain—the hot sutures along the surface of her index finger—and she concentrated on receiving. The signals were crackling and popping behind her eyes, the pressure on the bridge of her nose coming in arrhythmic bursts—

(—searching a dark path—static—searching, feeling alone, afraid, afraid for Timmy and Darryl—more static—the cold in my joints like ice shavings—)

Charlotte slammed her eyes shut, squeezing the coin in her sore hand.

"Charlotte—what is it?" Junior had risen to his feet and was standing next to her now.

Charlotte gazed down at the coin. "It's my hand. The burn messed me up something fierce."

"What do you mean? Your sensitivity?"

"Yeah, it's like a short wave in a storm or something—it's hard to explain."

"It'll be fine, Ace, it'll heal."

"We don't have time for that, Junie." She looked up at him and tried not to let her nerves get the better of her, tried not to cry. But her eyes were stinging now, her chest seizing up with panic. She felt like a little girl who had run away from home and gotten lost, and now all she wanted to do was wail for her mother to come get her.

"Listen to me, Ace, you gotta try and stay calm, take one thing at a time." Junior put a big beefy hand on her shoulder and gently squeezed. "Lemme see the hand."

Charlotte put the coin back in her pocket and showed him the sore hand, palm open.

Junior carefully took her hand and tenderly ran his fingertips along the edge of her thumb. "You feel that?" he asked softly—

(—adore her—)

Charlotte blinked.

(—absolutely adore her touch—)

She blinked again, inhaling suddenly, the chicken-skin crawling down her back again. Something had arced out of Junior's touch like static electricity, and it had entered Charlotte, instantly conjuring a feeling, a feeling so strong and clear it had nearly stolen her breath away, and she had immediately closed her mind down like a steel shade snapping shut. She gazed down at her hand, and she saw Junior's big fingers brushing her wound, and she realized what was happening.

"What's the matter, Ace?" Junior was giving her a sidelong glance.

"It's nothing, Junie, it's just—"

She opened her mind again.

And the feelings flowed into her—

(—never before, never felt this way, and I don't even know how to tell her, I would do anything for her, I would give up the rest of my life to hold her in my arms, so beautiful, so goddamn frigging beautiful, God help me, I love her, I really do, I love her so frigging much—)

—then Charlotte jerked away suddenly, pulling her hand free.

"What is this?" He was staring at her, oblivious to what had just happened. "Charlotte?"

She stood there for a moment, speechless, stomach tightening with emotion.

She never thought it even possible to encounter such feelings, especially not directed toward her, but here they were, coming from Junie, of all people, her buddy, her platonic pal—*directed toward Charlotte!* She was paralyzed with shock. It was as though the entire world had suddenly passed through a crazy kaleidoscope that Charlotte didn't understand, a million new colors that were making her dizzy, colors that she could only stare at in mute wonder. She realized her eyes were welling up now, so much so that she could barely see, and then the tears broke and tracked down her cheeks, and she felt her shoulders trembling, and she realized she was crying. She was crying because up until now she had resolved to be an old maid the rest of her life, and continue dredging through other people's feelings, and never face her own pain, and never-ever-ever taste the kind of love that was currently radiating off Junior's hands. But here it was, flowing into her like a wonderful transfusion that she'd been waiting for her entire life . . .

"I didn't know, Junie," Charlotte suddenly blurted through her tears.

Junior looked mortified. "Ace—what is it? Didn't know what?"

"I didn't know," she whispered again, her voice barely a whisper.

Then she leapt into his arms.

It was a newsreel kind of hug, the kind of embrace that evoked memories of V.E. Day and old Pathe movie trailers and Walter Winchell's ebullient voice describing "a homecoming fit for a king," and all at once Junior wrapped his big ham-hock arms around her and they were clinging to each other with a weird kind of desperation, and Charlotte was breathless, trying to say something, trying to explain, but she couldn't get any words out, because the love surge was swirling around her like a magnetic field, and it wouldn't have mattered anyway, because now Junior was searching for her lips.

Explanations were no longer required.

When Junior Parrick was eight years old, his older brother Dennis took him to the Ohio State Fair. The fairgrounds were fifty miles or so from their home, and it was a beautiful summer afternoon, and the long journey was glorious. Riding on the back of his brother's Yamaha, the wind in his hair, Junior found himself slipping into a sort of blissful fugue state. He wanted so very badly to be cool and poised like his brother, and now he was Dennis's buddy for the day, and he was going to the big fair! When they finally arrived at the fairgrounds, the sensory overload hit Junior like a tsunami. The girls in halter tops, the steam from the corn dog venders, the yammer of the freak show barker, the thrill rides, the smell of cow shit and tap beer, the taste of cotton candy and cinnamon apples and lemonade shakeups—it was beyond overwhelming—it was Valhalla for an eight-year-old boy who wanted to be grown up. Little Junior lost himself in a fog of pleasure that day. He had never felt so alive—never so *right* in his little eight-year-old skin—and would never feel quite that wonderful again.

Until tonight.

Tonight Junior was lost again, but this time the fairgrounds were replaced by a tangle of blankets in a queen-sized bed in a cottage just east of Minooka,

Illinois, and the textures and smells were emanating from a woman named Charlotte.

Junior was engulfed in her breasts, in the nape of her impossibly gorgeous neck, in the curve of her chin and the moist glow of her lips. Junior was in that fugue state again, oblivious to the room around him, or the trail of discarded clothing strewn across the floor, or the moths fluttering around the faded lampshade next to them. He had lost track of everything but her. She was a dream in his arms, naked and soft as a prayer, undulating under him as he thrust into her. Every intimacy, every sensation, every moment was being burned into Junior's midbrain for later retrieval—the generous thatch of dark pubic hair under her tummy, the faint curry smell of her armpits, her heavy breasts, marbled with delicate veins, splaying back and forth across her sternum, and the way her back arched, lips curling away from her teeth, Medusa mane of hair tossing against the sheets. But mostly Junior was fixated on her dear, sweet, injured hand— Junior was constantly aware of its position, of its touch, brushing across the back of his neck or around his nipple or under his cock, fondling him so delicately it felt like a whisper. It seemed to be drawing something out of him, some deep and secret well of desire.

Eventually—over a period of time that seemed both instantaneous and eternal—the wave of passion crested, and they both fell gently back to earth, sweaty bodies disengaging.

"When you touched my hand, I felt it," she confessed a few minutes later, catching her breath, staring up at the ceiling.

"Felt what?" He couldn't take his eyes off her.

"Your feelings, the way you felt about me."

"I *knew* it," he said, then leaned over and kissed her earlobe. "I could see something in your eyes, in the way you drew back."

She smiled. "Gotta admit, Junie, it took me by surprise."

"I didn't know how to tell you . . . I was scared shitless."

"Scared of what?"

There was a pause as Junior thought it over. "Guess it was all the standard stuff—fear of rejection, fear of making an idiot out of myself."

This time it was Charlotte who did the kissing. She leaned over and planted one on Junior's nose. "God, Junie, if you only knew."

"Knew what?"

She looked at him and said, "How scared *I* was."

Junior grinned. "I guess the days of us respecting each other's space are long gone."

They both looked at each other for a moment, then they broke into sudden and spontaneous laughter. The laughter came from a dark place, a place that had suddenly been exposed to the light, and now they were chortling over the absurdity of it all. Charlotte giggled uncontrollably for several moments, and Junior couldn't help noticing how beautiful she looked in the yellow light.

Then, a moment later, Charlotte quieted down, abruptly turning away.

"You okay, Ace?" Junior was wiping the tears from his eyes, watching her.

She sat up on the edge of the bed, her lovely, pale back facing Junior.

"Charlotte?"

She didn't answer. Instead she swallowed hard, like she had something stuck in her throat, then cocked her head at an odd angle. "It's nothing," she murmured finally.

"You sure?"

"Yeah, Junie, it's nothing, really."

"Look, Charlotte, if you're feeling weird about this . . . about us . . ."

"No, Junie, that's not it at all. It's just a migraine. They come on suddenly sometimes."

"I saw some aspirin in the first aid kit," Junior said.

She waved him off, her back still turned. "It'll pass, honey—really—it's nothing."

But the more Junior stared at her, the more he suspected it was anything but "nothing."

18

Before Dawn

Gleaming in the silver artificial light, cinders crackling beneath their feet, three figures were striding across a deserted Chevy lot in Ottawa, Illinois. Grim, stony faced, joined in silent lockstep, they walked briskly, with a purpose, their shadows stretching across luminous pavement. A big man, a small man, a portly man. Each dressed in dark attire. They looked like undertakers. The only sounds were the distant highway to the north, the lonely moaning of a barge on the Illinois River to the south, and the incessant ticking of moths around the brilliant Lucolux sodium lights overhead.

And their footsteps.

They were approaching a blue-green metallic Chevy Express van with full conversion kit on top. They paused a few feet away from the vehicle.

"Will this do?" the big one asked. It didn't sound like a question as much as an order.

"Suits my purpose nicely," the small one said.

"Is there enough room to stand up in back?" the fat one asked, motioning with pudgy fingers at the cap.

"Depends on who's doing the standing," the big one said. "Wilt Chamberlain, no. Any one of us, you bet. Got a six-foot-something clearance."

The fat one nodded. "Good."

The van's windows were all shaded, black as purest obsidian, and the detailing was magnificent. Ribbons of bright scarlet swirled back-to-front like on a birth-day present. They went around to the rear.

The big man opened the cargo doors. "Should be stocked with everything you said you need," he said, glancing inside at the fully furnished custom interior. Almost four hundred square feet of carpeted space. Four contour buckets in front. Enough space in back to dance the two-step. There were metal objects folded neatly against the wall. Road cases stacked against one of the braces. And a small cooler.

The fat man pulled a tiny spiral notebook from his jacket and said: "Police scanner?"

The big man nodded. "You bet."

"CB radio?"

"Check."

"Cellular phone?"

"Yep."

"Fax?"

"Yep."

"Thomas Guide maps?"

"Yep."

"And you got the mobile data transformers I requested?"

"Yep, we got four of 'em."

"Good . . . and the petty cash?"

"Yep."

"And the bagels?"

". . . What?"

Rondo Hatton looked up at Digger. "Bagels . . . Are there bagels in there . . . with cream cheese and lox?"

Digger sighed. "Yeah, yeah, sure, there's bagels."

"And vodka and Bloody Mary mix?"

"Yeah."

"And smoked salmon?"

"Yeah, I think there's salmon in there, too."

"And Frappucino?"

"What?"

"It's a delightful beverage in a bottle," Rondo explained. "Starbucks puts it out."

"FerChrissake, yeah, there's Frappa-rappa-whatever."

"You oughtta try it, it's incredible."

Digger glowered at the fat man. "Look, just find this bitch for us, and you can stuff your face with whatever bullshit you want."

"Fair enough," Rondo said. Then he motioned at the cab. "Why don't you drive . . ."

Digger and St. Louis were already marching toward the front of the vehicle. The keys were in the ignition waiting for them, courtesy of the local outfit, which owned the dealership.

The van roared to life, four hundred horses chomping at the bit.

". . . and I'll ride in back with the food," Rondo said softly, more to himself than anybody else.

Then he climbed in and slammed the cargo doors.

And the van shot toward the exit.

It wasn't anything psychic. It was just a feeling. And sometimes a feeling is just a feeling. But right now, Charlotte felt an overwhelming urge to get back on the road. Before dawn broke, and the morning light made their faces more visible inside the little Geo.

"C'mon, honey, let's motivate," Charlotte was saying, nervously stuffing her purse with packets of instant coffee, Handi Wipes, teabags, and plastic-wrapped utensils that she had found in the basket of complimentary goodies next to the bathroom sink. She had just taken a quick, cold shower and cleaned and dressed her hand. There was no time to bathe in any afterglow. She was antsy to get going.

Junior was across the room, tying his shoes. "Nag,

nag, nag," he said, trying to lighten the mood. "Always nagging."

Charlotte managed a halfhearted grin in spite of her nerves. "I warned you about getting mixed up with a pushy broad like me."

"Always in a hurry, it's bad for your heart."

"Yeah, you're right. These impromptu cross-country suicide missions are murder on your blood pressure."

"Not to mention your sleep."

"Okay, okay, I get the message," Charlotte said. "Now, c'mon, you can torture me in the car."

Junior looked at her. "Is that a promise?"

"Very funny. Now, let's go."

Junior finished tying his shoes, then grabbed his watch and loose change from the bedside table. In the doorway, Charlotte was fidgeting, watching him. In the harsh yellow glare of the bedside lamp, Junior moved with the casual grace of an old jock. All shoulders and swagger. His hair still wet from the shower, combed back slick against his scalp, he looked older than usual. Older and wearier. But gentler, too. Gentler and sexier. Charlotte couldn't believe the wellspring of passion this stocky, tough-as-nails man had touched off in her. Was it love? God help her, yes. Yes, she was in love with him. She probably had been for months, but just hadn't been ready to admit it.

Now look at her.

Funny . . . what an impromptu cross-country suicide mission will do for a girl.

"Let's go, Ace," Junior said softly, joining her in the doorway.

He gently put his hand on the small of her back and escorted her through the door.

Paul Lattamore sat up with a jerk, his pulse racing, his legs tangled in blankets.

For a moment he didn't know where he was. His

mind was racing, the room engulfed in absolute darkness, the echoes bouncing off the walls. What were they? Voices? Sirens? He couldn't tell if the noises were coming from somewhere inside the house, outside the house, or from within his *own skull*. Eyes adjusting to the darkness, he swallowed the acid-sharp panic and realized the sounds were in his head. *Afterechoes.* Ghostly reverberations from the half-whispered warnings that had been plaguing him for the last twenty-four hours. Was he finally heading for the booby hatch? Hearing voices, feeling phantom pains and twinges in his head? Was he cracking under the strain? He took deep breaths and looked over at Sandy.

She was still asleep—albeit restless sleep—her face buried in the crook of her arm, her eyes worming under her lids, tracking ghosts. She, too, seemed to be weathering some stormy nightmare. Paul felt a sudden and unexpected bolt of emotion shoot up his gorge, tightening his stomach muscles. He felt like such a coward. A self-absorbed, narcissistic coward. He had let the boogeyman into their home.

He looked at the clock: 4:17 A.M.

He gently leaned over the edge of the bed—careful not to jostle Sandy—then reached down to the floor. There was a slight bulge under the edge of the braided rug, and Paul dug out the small metal object lodged there. The Taurus felt puny in his hand, like a little nickel-plated toy. He sat back against the headboard, holding the revolver up in the pale moonlight. He regarded it for a moment, the dull gleam of its snubnosed barrel, the empty black socket at the end. So small. So impotent. Paul felt a strange buzzing sensation at the base of his neck, as though his nervous system were a lit fuse, and the bomb was about to go off.

He aimed the gun at the far wall, drawing a bead on the doorknob.

All at once he realized what he had to do.

The only way out.

19

Poker

The Egg McMuffin sat in Charlotte's stomach like a stone. A few miles back, they had stopped for some drive-in breakfast—during which time Junior had put in a quick call to a neighbor to go check on his dog—and now the fast food was about to wreak havoc in Charlotte's colon. Her nerves were like frayed wires. Her head was spinning. So many things they needed to do. They needed to get supplies. Some more cream for Charlotte's burns. Maybe some aspirin, some caffeine pills, antacid tablets. Maybe some bottled water, a map, a notebook for Charlotte to keep track of her impressions. If she was going to find the Lattamore family, she was going to have to focus like never before. But overriding all these needs was the primary need to keep moving.

In a westerly direction.

They had just passed a little wide spot in the road called Seymourville, about fifty miles or so west of Rock Island. Emerging out of the pre-dawn light like some rural Brigadoon, it was one of those blink-and-you'll-miss-it burgs along the highway with the single exit, a couple of dusty little gas stations, a dirt road trailer park, and a few acres of storefronts. For a moment, Charlotte had felt compelled to turn around and go back to Seymourville, hide out with Junior, stay there forever, and pretend that none of this ever happened. But the notion—just like the town—had passed in a flash, and now there was only the vast ocean of corn on either side of the car, as far as the eye could see.

"Kinda vulnerable out here," Charlotte said loud enough to be heard over the whine of the engine. "Don't you think we oughtta get off the main drag?"

Junior shot her a look. "You mean Highway 80 West?"

Charlotte nodded.

Junior shrugged. "I don't know. Right now I'm thinking it's a poker game, and we're the marks."

"What do you mean?"

"In poker, it's all about the face. Old vets are always studying each other's faces. We gotta put on a good poker face."

"I'm still not following, Junie."

"It's like . . . when you're playing poker with somebody, you're looking at their face . . . Do they have a good hand? Are they trying to 'look' like they don't have shit when they actually got a big slab of juicy meat?" He paused, wiping his mouth, thinking. For a moment, Charlotte thought she saw his hand shaking, but maybe she was imagining it. "Right now, we got all the cards," he went on. "We got you, we got the coin, we're a threat to the whole bunch of wise guys out there trying to get to Lattamore."

Charlotte thought about it for a moment. "So how do we fool them?"

"By doing the unexpected," Junior replied.

"Huh?"

"By staying on the main drag, staying in plain sight, playing it cool . . . until we get a chance to get rid of this tin can we're in."

Charlotte gazed out at the cornfields flowing past the car like a blanket billowing in the wind. "But why get rid of this car? How could they possibly find out what kind of car we're driving?"

"Make no mistake, Ace, they'll find us if we stay in this car."

"But how?"

"They'll figure it out. Process of elimination. I don't know."

There was a noisy pause as Charlotte ruminated on their pursuers.

Again that dreadful thought crossed her mind: What if these wise guys were already back there somewhere locked onto their tail? What if Charlotte was being used like a homing pigeon, leading the jackals right to Lattamore's door? A cold flutter passed through her stomach, raising gooseflesh on her arms. She turned and glanced through the back window.

The sun was still low in the sky, the long shadows slanting across the highway from telephone poles and overpasses. It was still fairly early, and traffic was sparse. Only a couple of all-night semi-trucks were loping along in either direction. Charlotte could see the heat waves shimmering off the grill of a Kenworth about a quarter mile behind them.

She turned back to the front.

"You okay, Ace?" Junior asked.

"Fine, Junie, it's just . . . I need to get a better fix on Lattamore."

She started fondling the coin some more.

And it was quite a few minutes—and many miles— before something started sizzling through the static.

"Fax coming in!" Digger announced from behind the van's steering wheel. He was cruising west along I-80 just outside of Iowa City, the sunlight strobing through the big windshield. He had his coat off, his shirtsleeves rolled up, and a Dunhill jutting out the side of his mouth. He was itching to get this thing done.

Lou St. Louis sat in the bucket beside him. Staring

straight ahead, hands folded neatly in his lap, the little guy had said maybe two words since they had left the Chevy lot back in Ottawa. Gave Digger the creeps.

"Did you hear what I said, Hatton?" Digger called toward the back.

The obese detective was sitting on a road case in back, munching a Bremner wafer iced with soft cheese, his jacket off, his belly straining the girth of his oxford shirt. He gobbled the rest of the cracker, licked his fingers, and said, "That'll be Toni, my operative down state. Probably got the boyfriend's license number, make of his car."

"You're shitting me," Digger said, truly impressed by the fat man's efficiency. "You got all that already?"

Rondo waddled up to the front of the van—holding the side braces for support—and hovered over the portable fax machine, which was plugged into the cellular. A page of thermo paper was curling out of the machine. "Wait till you see my bill," Rondo murmured, brushing crumbs off his shirt.

He tore the page off the fax's serrated edge. "Name's Parrick," the fat man announced. "Robert James. Goes by 'Junior.' Drives a green Geo Metro. License number HYX 118."

"Nicely done," the chiropractor commented softly from the passenger seat.

Digger threw Rondo a glance. "How the hell'd you get that so fast?"

"Nothing to it," the detective said. "Had my operative back in Chicago break into the psychic's place. Dug up a phone bill. Got the boyfriend's name." The detective paused, pulled a Twix bar from his pocket, opened it, and gobbled half of it in a single bite. "Had another operative down in Springfield—young gal, great ass—go over to the secretary of state's office. Flash her ass a little. Fill out a freedom of information form, give the clerk a C-note. Got the make and model in ten minutes."

Digger shook his head. "Un-fucking-believable."

"All it takes is a little money and a lot of experience," the fat man said.

"What's the next step?"

"Give me the phone," Rondo said, polishing off the last of the Twix bar.

Digger handed the detective the cellular receiver.

After dialing a long strand of numbers, the fat man said into the phone: "Larry, it's Hatton . . . we got a make and model, license number, the whole shot." The fat man read off the information into the phone, then looked at his watch. "They can't be too far ahead of us . . . I'd bet they're still in Iowa . . . so let's put an operative outside Iowa City, Des Moines, and Omaha . . . That's right, maybe a toll booth or overpass." There was another pause, and Rondo listened for a moment. "I don't care how much it's gonna cost, Larry . . . I want them eyeballing every car that comes past their checkpoint . . . and make sure they all have MDT units . . . okay? Call me back when you got something."

The fat man hung up the phone, then started opening another Twix bar.

Digger couldn't stop shaking his head.

Un-fucking-believable.

Sensations were popping and crackling off the edges of the coin.

Charlotte closed her eyes and saw threads of light stitching across the backs of her eyelids, spots of luminous fire. The ice cream ache was back with a vengeance, throbbing above the bridge of her nose, and someone else's thoughts and sensations were arcing across her mind, smelling of wet pine needles and car exhaust. If asked to describe it, Charlotte might have said it was like experiencing an electric shock through a membrane of water, the sensations flowing into her in jerky currents, the muffled, indistinct images rippling in and out of focus . . .

She squeezed the silver dollar tighter with her sore fingers and felt another wave breaking—

(—*moving, moving fast, past trees, down a dusty side road outside of town, the Suburban kicking up gravel, all the while wondering if I'm doing the right thing*—)

—and Charlotte held her breath, gripping the coin, the feelings flowing into her, knowing, somehow knowing that this was a key to Lattamore's location—

(—*jitters, that's all it is, just the jitters, but I can't let the boys see their daddy like this, all jacked up, hearing things, feeling odd feelings like somebody's trying to get into my head, and then . . . Wait a minute, wait a minute, there's the bar, the sign above the thick oak door reading* PACKARD'S . . .

. . . *and underneath it, the white plastic banner proudly proclaiming:* Best Barbecue in the Rockies!)

Charlotte didn't move, didn't breathe.

She was inside Paul Lattamore's head now, and she was seeing and hearing the world through his eyes and ears . . .

. . . and she realized something important was about to happen to him . . .

. . . and it was about to happen at a little tavern in the Rockies called Packard's . . .

20

Home Security

"Why we stoppin' here, Dad?"

Little Darryl Lattamore was slumped in the back-seat of the Suburban, buckled next to his little brother, watching his dad pull up in front of some bar called Packard's. Darryl had never been inside a tavern before, and he secretly longed to be in there with the grown-ups and drink beer and smoke cigarettes and tell dirty stories. Grown-ups got to do so many cool things like watch R-rated horror movies and stay up late and read Stephen King books and drive at night up in the mountains where the road got twisty and dark and spooky. But on the other hand, grown-ups sometimes kept secrets from kids and acted weird, just like his dad was doing at this very moment.

"This'll just take a second, men," Paul Lattamore said, glancing over his shoulder at the backseat. Darryl could see something shimmery in his dad's eyes, but he couldn't quite identify what it was. Then Darryl noticed the man's hands were trembling.

"But Mom said she needed the milk and eggs to make dinner," Darryl protested feebly. Deep down inside, he knew what was going on.

"I'll be back in a flash," Paul said. "Gotta see a man about something. You watch your brother for me."

Then Paul climbed out of the rover and slammed his door, the sound of it making Darryl jump.

"Daddy gone, that place!" Timmy chirped, pointing at the dark windows of Packard's tavern.

"Chill out, Timmy," Darryl said. "He's gonna be right back."

Then Darryl slumped even farther into his seat, watching Paul vanish inside Packard's front entrance.

Darryl had a bad feeling about this unscheduled stop on the way home from the grocery store. In fact, he didn't like the way his dad had been acting for the last couple of days. The man hadn't been this jumpy since the day the Lattamores moved into the Program. To this day, Darryl still didn't understand a whole heck of a lot about the Program. He had overheard a few nervous whispers, had sat through oversimplified explanations from nice men with plastic ID cards on their suits; but he had just assumed it was a top secret program to hide really bad kids from the police. And now, after twelve long months, Darryl was starting to think that maybe the truth was going to come out at last. Maybe this was the beginning of the end, the end of Darryl Lattamore's exile.

All because of a few baseball cards.

The sad truth was, Darryl had never meant to hurt anybody. He had never meant to throw his family into this kind of chaos. But like all addicts, Darryl had been unable to stop himself. He would go down to the Penny Whistle or Larry's Collectibles, and he would wait until three o'clock rolled around. At that point, school would let out, and the store would get very busy, and Darryl would stand at the counter and point to a '67 Mickey Mantle or a '72 Hank Aaron, and when the clerk would bring one out, Darryl would stare at it, feigning indecision, stalling. When the clerk finally got distracted by the other kids, Darryl would pull the dummy card out of his pocket and make the switch. It was foolproof. Over the course of three years, Darryl had stolen nearly fifty vintage cards in this fashion from various hobby shops around the Cicero area.

But now it was all coming back to haunt him. His family had sacrificed their own happiness—even though they refused to admit it or discuss it with him—in order to protect him from the angry hobby shop owners and bad cops, and now it was about to blow up in Darryl's face.

He had to do something about it.

"I'll be right back, Timmy," Darryl said, unbuckling his belt and easing the door open.

Timmy started whining.

Darryl slipped out of the Suburban and crossed the gravel threshold to the bar's entrance. He paused for a moment in front of the oak door, thinking that if he went in the front way he would instantly be busted and kicked out for being a minor. Instead, he turned and crept around the side of the building to the back.

The rear of the tavern was a battlefield of petrified deadfalls and rotting pinecones, the morning sun filtering down through the birches, the air stinking of sweet-rot and alkali. A mound of firewood cords was piled against the clapboard back wall, and a row of metal garbage Dumpsters jutted out across the clearing. The sound of a nearby stream mingled with the kitchen noises and voices drifting out the back door. Darryl paused just outside the door for a moment, girding himself, trying to work up enough nerve to slip inside.

"Get rid of that slop!" A voice barked from the kitchen. The voice sounded mean, and Darryl figured it was the boss of the place.

"What about the burners?" asked another voice.

"Just leave 'em on," the angry voice said. "Take your break out front today."

Then there was a shuffling noise, like boxes shifting and footsteps approaching. Darryl spun away from the door and crept around behind the woodpile, crouching down on the moist earth and waiting. His heart was thumping quickly, his pulse throbbing in his ears. He knew he was in deep shit if his dad caught him, but he also had the feeling something terrible was happening and he wanted to make sure his dad wasn't in danger. Next to Darryl a rusty axe head sat embedded in a stump. And all of a sudden everything was taking on a weird, grotesque quality, like that of a fairy tale, like the woods in a Berni Wrightson comic such as *Creepy* or *Vault of Horror*. Berni Wrightson was Darryl's favorite comic book artist, and it was probably because Wrightson characterized everyday objects with such horrific, lurid zeal. A simple rusty axe blade embedded in a stump would become a blood-dripping murder weapon—

"Back here, Stafford, this is just fine and dandy."

The angry voice had returned, a pair of figures filling the rear door. Darryl froze. His mouth went dry as he watched the meeting unfold.

"You're sure this is okay?" Paul Lattamore was fidgeting, glancing over his shoulder at the woods, eyes darting nervously. Darryl had never seen his father this nervous, and it was not a good thing.

"I told you it was okay. Jesus, when I say something's okay, it's okay," the other guy was mumbling. He was a lot taller than Darryl's dad, older, with a greasy vest and a cowboy hat and a leathery face like the Marlboro man. He was holding a green canvas duffel bag.

"I don't have much time," Lattamore said. "Guy at the Trading Post said you were the man to see."

"That's right, Stafford, I'm the guy." Marlboro Man lifted the duffel up, then set it down on a battered garbage can. The can squeaked with the weight of the bag. "I understand you're in the market for a little home security, something heavier than you currently got."

"You could say that, yes."

"Are you a law enforcement officer? ATF? Federal Bureau?"

Lattamore stared at him a moment, then shook his head. "No, absolutely not."

Marlboro Man smiled. "Just a formality, son, don't worry. I pegged you as a civilian the minute you walked in. Besides, Joe Banes wouldn't send me no cop." He was unzipping the duffel as he spoke. He pulled out an ugly-looking gun with a long, fat barrel and a shoulder attachment. "This here's a gorgeous piece of iron."

"What in God's name—?" Lattamore was staring at the thing as though it might bite. Behind the woodpile, little Darryl felt goose bumps on his arms.

"Sterling L-2 submachine with a suppressor attachment—go ahead." Marlboro Man stuck the weapon in Lattamore's face. "Ain't gonna bite. Unless you're on the business end."

Lattamore took the gun and held it awkwardly. "It's pretty huge."

"Weighs about eight pounds, chambered for nine-millimeter."

"Hmmm—"

"I'm telling ya, if that boy been firing one of these up ta Ruby Ridge, there woulda been at least two dozen less FBI faggots crawling this earth. Baby cycles at five hundred and fifty rounds a minute."

"I don't think so." Lattamore handed the Sterling back to Marlboro Man. "I'm looking for something a little less . . . cumbersome."

Marlboro Man put the machine gun back in the duffel, fished around, then pulled out a couple of hard plastic cases. He put the cases on the garbage can, then opened them, revealing their contents like a jew-

eler showing his wares. "First, you got your basic
Mini-Uzi with the folding metal stock, shoots at a rate
of nine hundred and fifty rounds a minute, best thing
the Jews ever invented." He pointed at the other one.
"And over here you got your miniature Heckler &
Koch MP5—slightly slower, not as many bells and
whistles, but just as nasty—which could solve the nigger problem down in Denver faster than you could
say O.J.-fuckin'-Simpson."

Lattamore seemed to be ignoring Marlboro Man,
staring at the weapons, rubbing his mouth with a
trembling hand. He took the Uzi out of its blister case
and aimed it at the air.

From the woodpile Darryl watched, transfixed by
the sight of his dad testing guns. This was bad; this
was very bad. All the secrecy, all the fake names and
documents—all the spy games that he and Timmy had
been playing—they had not been enough. The family
was in more danger than Darryl had ever imagined,
and it was all his fault. But the worst part, the part
that was making Darryl sick to his stomach right now,
was the way his father was behaving, the way his eyes
were all glazed and watery, and mostly the way he
was handling the Uzi.

Gripping it so tightly his knuckles were white.

21

Fireballs

It starts in the air, like a faint, low buzzing noise. Like a big fucking yellow jacket. Then it rises. And rises. And soon the whole goddamn rice paddy is shaking, the whole goddamn La Tho River valley. Junior looks up at the sky and sees the source coming from behind him: two big honking F-100s flying in low—attack formation.

Junior is trying to crawl away when the air around him suddenly implodes.

The jets roar overhead, and the sky cracks open, a sonic boom that peels off the top of Junior's skull. Junior ducks down into mire. The F-100s curl apart, then ejaculate all over the jungle. Tendrils of white vapor spiral down across the foliage three hundred yards away, and then the telltale WHUMP! *as the napalm erupts into a wall of fire.*

Night turns to day.

Junior shields his face from the heat. He can see Spider Baumgarten—his fellow sniper—twenty feet to his left, in the shadows and foliage, flinching at the sonic boom. The heat is so intense it feels as though Junior's eyebrows are singeing. He can smell the odors of cooked weeds and scorched paddies. It smells like a kitchen fire. Like burning grease. Junior can barely draw a breath.

But something worse is happening, something far worse.

Three hundred yards away, there is movement.

Junior tries to see through the haze, but it's no use. He puts his scope to his eye. In the green blur he sees the most amazing sight he's ever seen: brilliant fireballs pouring down a tree, then flowing across the jungle floor. High-pitched noise coming off them. Like broken wind chimes, sped up, reversed, a crazy sound. The fireballs look almost liquid as they roll across the ground.

Junior swallows hard.

The fireballs are not fireballs.

The fireballs are children.

The fireballs are burning children.

"Take 'em down! Put 'em outta their motherfucking misery!" Spider's voice is a paroxysm of madness in Junior's ear.

Junior puts his eye to the scope and starts firing, and he fires and fires and fires—

—until he's out of shells, and his throat is raw from screaming, and his eyes are burnt to crisps from the smoke and tears.

And he keeps firing, long past the point his sanity has snapped like a rubber band, trying to stop the sound of tiny screams like broken wind chimes.

But they never stop.

Not ever.

Not even in his dreams.

Junior shuddered, muttering to himself, "Stop already, stop thinking about that shit."

Shaking off the memories, wiping his mouth with the back of his hand, he kept staring at the dusty phone booth, trying to think, waiting for Charlotte to finish making her calls. A hot, southerly wind was flapping Junior's jeans and chambray shirt, the textures of Vietnam still clinging to his memories. A hundred yards away, the overpass rose up in the sky, the concrete viaduct baking in the sun. Every few moments a semi would scream by, raising Junior's blood pressure. He felt exposed out here at this lonely interchange—again his sniper's instinct kicking in—and he wanted to get going as soon as possible. But Charlotte had been adamant about stopping.

Inside the glass booth, Junior could see Charlotte's voluptuous form hunched over the phone, still dressed in her soiled jumper and sandals, still favoring her bandaged hand. She'd shut herself inside the dusty little booth with Junior's long distance calling card over ten minutes ago, madly punching in numbers for long distance operators and chambers of commerce, and now, from the anguished look on her face, it was clear she was getting nowhere. But she was driven now, driven like never before. She had experienced some sort of epiphany a few miles back, holding that coin, jerking against the seat in psychic seizures for minutes on end. It was downright scary. She had catapulted herself into Lattamore's head, breathing his breath, smelling his smells, tasting his tastes, and she'd gotten names and places and addresses. But now she was having a hell of a time making sense of it all.

Junior turned away from the booth, glancing across the scarred cement lot.

They were huddled on the edge of an abandoned gas station. The station's pumps were removed, its office windows blackened and taped, its sign ravaged with holes. It was a typical roadside ruin, a million others just like it across the farm belt. Whiskers of weeds grew along cracks in the lot, and the wind made whipcord noises through the sign. The Geo was parked nearby, its engine ticking softly.

The sound of the phone booth rattling open nearly made Junior jump.

"So damn close, Junie—but still coming up empty." Her voice was hoarse, cracking with tension as she emerged from the booth. Junior spun toward her. She was standing there in the wind and the sun, squinting off toward the western horizon, her bandaged hand shielding her eyes from the glare.

"What was the name of the tavern again?" Junior asked.

"Packard's."

"Packard's, yeah—you tried Aspen?"

"I tried Aspen, Estes Park, Boulder . . . I tried Denver, Fort Collins . . . Junie, I tried every town I could think of in the Rocky Mountain area. They all have dozens of Staffords listed."

"But nobody's got a bar called Packard's?"

"No Packard's." She kept squinting at the horizon, and Junior could tell she was buzzing with nervous energy. Her hair was flying every which way in the wind, and her jaw was clenched and grinding. She had heard the names in her most recent vision. Evidently, "Stafford" was what Lattamore was calling himself now. But the real magic word was "Packard's."

Junior found himself desperately searching for the right words of encouragement, realizing that he cared far more about protecting Charlotte than he did about saving another pathetic accountant who had ratted out a mob boss. Unfortunately, both Junior *and* Charlotte were now inextricably linked to this melodrama. Junior had killed one of the mob's own, and Charlotte had stolen their magic coin, and the mob didn't take kindly to people who did either of those things. Junior could feel the bandage around his belly stinging suddenly; the dressing probably needed changing.

"Maybe you got the wrong name," Junior said at last, ignoring the heat in his belly.

"No, Junie . . . damn it, no. I felt it very clearly— Packard's Bar and Grill."

Junior thought for a moment. "What did you say about the Rockies?"

"The sign on the bar, it said *Best Barbecue in the Rockies*."

Junior grimaced at the twinge in his side, the cut stinging fiercely, itching. "I wonder if you called the park, you know, the headquarters."

"What park?"

"The Rocky Mountain State Park."

Charlotte chewed on her fingernail for a moment. "I think it's a national park."

"Why don't you try Information in Denver, ask for the main number for the park headquarters."

Charlotte ducked back into the booth and started dialing—leaving the door open so Junior could listen. Junior leaned against the door frame, feeling as though he had just eaten a plate full of jalapeño peppers, and now the things were burning a hole through his stomach lining—

"Is this the park headquarters?" Charlotte's voice was taut with nerves. "Yes, I'm trying to locate a tavern in your area, name of Packard's . . ." Junior listened as Charlotte spelled the name, then waited for the head ranger to ask the other rangers if anybody knew of such a place. "Yes, I'm still here," Charlotte said after waiting endless moments.

Her eyes widened suddenly, and she started snapping her fingers at Junior, making writing motions. "One moment please," Charlotte said into the phone. "Let me get something to write with."

Junior handed her a ballpoint from his shirt pocket, along with a torn piece of a receipt.

"Okay, go ahead," Charlotte said and started writing. "Okay, I got it—Highway 40 from the south, 34 from the north—okay, got it—thank you, thank you very much."

She hung up, then dialed another number. She got the Information operator on the line and asked for a place called Grand Lake, then asked if there was a residential listing for a Stafford. Charlotte stood there for a moment, listening, then hung up.

When she emerged from the phone booth, her eyes seemed fixed on some distant point.

"Well?" Junior was looking at her.

"There's a place called Grand Lake," Charlotte said softly, staring off into the distance, her voice barely audible above the wind and highway noises. "It's just south of the Rocky Mountain National Park." Then she looked at Junior, her eyes watery with emotion, her voice shaky. "They got a place called Packard's Bar and Grill there."

Junior felt his gut tighten. "You tried Directory Assistance?"

"There was no Stafford listed, but I have a strong feeling this is the one." She started toward the car. "C'mon, Junie, let's roll."

Junior paused for a moment . . . then he followed her.

He wasn't about to start second-guessing Charlotte's feelings.

22

The Shooting Lesson

Less than sixty miles west of the phone booth in which Charlotte first heard about Grand Lake, a butterscotch yellow Lincoln Town Car was sitting under a scabrous viaduct. The car was idling softly on the shoulder. It was pointing westward, and its emergency flashers were on. There was an orange safety cone about ten feet off its rear bumper. And there were tools scattered near the rear tire. But it was all for show. All designed to avoid suspicious passers-by. There was no flat tire, no engine difficulty, no mechanical reason for it to be pulled over. In fact, it was as though the thing were coiled like a snake, ready to pounce.

Inside sat Conrad Horgan, a cellular phone pressed to his ear. He was chewing his stale Juicyfruit so quickly and furiously it sounded as though a clock were ticking in his mouth. A wiry man of indeterminate age, dressed in a purple silk baseball jacket, his India-ink hair greased back with pomade, Conrad D. Horgan was a jack of all trades, and the master of many. He could tear apart and put back together any late-model American engine you'd want to give him. He could crack most consumer-grade strongboxes and safes. And he could hack into the most secure corporate computer network in the world. He could also follow somebody and remain unnoticed for hundreds of miles.

Which was precisely why, at the present moment,

he was working as a subcontractor for the Hatton Investigative Group.

"Keep your eyes peeled, Connie," the voice crackled through the receiver. It was Rondo Hatton on the other end. The detective was calling from a van a few hundred miles away.

"Gotcha covered, Chief," Horgan said. Horgan liked the fat man. The two of them went gambling down at the Empress Casino whenever Horgan was in Chicago. "Believe me," Horgan added. "They come by here, I'll pick 'em up."

"How long you been in position?"

Horgan glanced at his watch. "Christ, I don't know. Since about eight o'clock this morning."

"Good," the voice said. "Keep eyeballing the road; they gotta be passing by there soon."

"You got it, Chief," Horgan said.

And then there was a click, and Rondo was gone.

And Horgan went back to watching the road and chewing his gum.

"They're getting closer, Junie, I can feel it."

"I believe you, Ace," Junior said, pulling the Geo down an exit ramp, the car's springs complaining loudly over the potholes. They had just made a quick pit stop at a Marathon Mini-mart, emptying their bladders and filling the gas tank up. They also got some crappy coffee, a couple of turkey sandwiches from a vending machine, and a fresh bottle of Tylenol caplets. Back in the car, they had gobbled the sandwiches like hungry stray dogs—amazed at how low sleep and high stress can give a person an appetite—then had sloshed the pills down with the coffee. Even stranger was how Junior's sweet tooth had kicked in with a vengeance. He would have given his left testicle for a goddamn Twinkie, a Snickers bar, even a fucking Gummy Bear.

That was Junior's cross to bear. When he got nervous, he started eating junk.

They reached the bottom of the ramp, turned south, then headed down a narrow dirt access road. Junior could feel Charlotte's panic like a sharp odor in the car. "There's something I want to do before we continue," he told her, glancing nervously into his rearview.

The afternoon sun was glinting off the Geo's rear window, a thunderhead of dust billowing off the back tires. Junior felt exposed, the skin prickling along the back of his neck, the heat building in his stomach. They were very vulnerable out here in the open like this, but Junior was trying not to think about that right now.

He had to be sure of one thing before they got back on the interstate.

A minute later they pulled up in front of an immense sugar maple, and Junior parked the car.

"Follow me," he said, getting out of the car and leading Charlotte around to the back. He opened the hatch and dug under the tire for his .22. He found the little greasy drill case wedged between the tire jack and the spare, and he pulled it out carefully. "Before we go any further," he explained, "I'm gonna give you a little shooting lesson."

Charlotte glanced over her shoulder, fists clenched at her side. "Damn it, Junie, we don't have time for this."

"We gotta make time."

"But you *know* how I feel about—"

"Won't take no for an answer, Ace." He took her hand and ushered her over to the tree.

The maple tree was a colossus, a couple of centuries old, so huge it looked as though its roots were intertwined with the next county. It stood sentry along the edge of the dirt road, shading at least a half an acre

of early corn. Fifty yards away, a double post fence
snaked down a gentle decline toward a distant compound of farmhouses. The air beneath the tree smelled
of cottonwood and manure, and it was as still as a
church. Junior found a tin can buried in weeds, and
he carried it over to a stump that sat near the fence.

Then he came back, opened the case, and handed
the Ruger to Charlotte.

"Junior, *please*—" Charlotte was holding the gun as
though it were covered with shit.

"Just a quick lesson," Junior said, moving around
behind her. "Just so you can handle the weapon if
you have to."

"They're getting closer every second—"

"We'll be outta here in a second. Just let me show
you how to defend yourself."

Then he taught her how to hold the weapon, how
to load the rounds into the magazine, how to load the
magazine into the stock, and how to inject a bullet
into the chamber by snapping back the slide mechanism. The Ruger was not the smallest handgun in the
world, but it was lightweight and easy to fire and
seemed just right for Charlotte. Finally, Junior showed
her how to flip the safety off and aim. "Go ahead,
sweetie," he said finally. "Kill that tin can for me."

She aimed and fired.

The bullet went high into the corn, the blast a flat,
hard pop like a firecracker.

Charlotte gasped at the sound of it, then she
blinked, and Junior felt a stitch of chills working their
way down his back. It wasn't exactly the sound of a
gun going off that was so creepy—Junior had spent
the bulk of his early adult life hanging out at gun
ranges—instead, it was something behind Charlotte's
eyes that took Junior by surprise, something unexpected. If asked to explain it, Junior would have been

hard-pressed to put it into words. It was so subtle, so abrupt, that he thought he might have imagined it.

But goddamn . . . it was there, just for an instant, in Charlotte's expression.

Junior had seen that expression once before, back in the mid-seventies, during the lost days after his discharge. On an impulse he had decided to ride his motorcycle across Europe in a misguided attempt to recapture some romantic Whitmanesque image of himself as poet-wanderer. But all he found were countless crowded hippie hostels full of equally lost souls searching for equally naive visions of themselves. One of the worst places was in Spain near the Ebro River, not far from Barcelona. It was there, in a squalid *pensión*, that Junior saw a young Andalusian girl get the same expression on her face that Charlotte Vickers had just gotten on hers—a mixture of complete surrender and horrible awe.

The Spanish girl had gotten it immediately after she had tried her first syringe of heroin.

"Do it again, Ace," Junior said. "Try to relax through the shot."

"It jumps," Charlotte said, aiming the gun. She was grinding her teeth now.

"I know, just relax and don't compensate for it."

Charlotte fired again, and again, and once again, missing the can each time, the shots ringing out across the deserted corn fields. Her face was hardening with each blast, like a marble sculpture taking on a new shape. On the fourth try, she clipped the can, tossing it thirty feet across the dirt.

Across the clearing, a flock of black crows suddenly burst out of the corn stalks.

Junior glanced across the clearing and noticed an object near the base of a telephone pole, an object that he hadn't noticed when they first arrived.

He walked over to it.

It was at least five feet high, maybe six, tied to the pole. Somebody had spent quite a bit of time and effort constructing it. The arms and legs and torso were perfectly formed, stuffed with taxidermical care. The hands were splayed pieces of straw. The head looked to be made of an old deflated basketball, torn in half, facial features molded and painted, crowned with a straw hat.

There was even a pair of old wing tips on its feet.

"What is it, honey?" Charlotte had walked over and joined Junior, and now they both stood there, staring up at the scarecrow.

"I have an idea," Junior said finally. "I think it's the only way we're gonna get you to Colorado in one piece." Then he looked at Charlotte. "But you're not gonna like it."

23

Nice Girls Don't Explode

The chiropractor was driving, the van roaring across the Platte River.

Digger Mussolino was in back with the fat man. Digger was getting frustrated—not a word from any of the operatives—and when Digger got frustrated, he got restless. So now he was in back, digging out the anvil cases, opening them one by one, a Dunhill dangling from his mouth.

In the first two cases were brand-spanking-new Kimber .45 semiautos, each with state-of-the-art Beamshot lasersights. He opened another case and started removing cartons of hydra-shok .40-caliber rounds. He hadn't planned on firing too many hollowpoints on this trip—his purpose wasn't really to cause any heavy-duty mayhem—but for some reason Digger was starting to get the feeling that he might run into more resistance from the boyfriend than he had first anticipated.

"Judas Priest, whattya packing all that heat for?" Rondo Hatton was perched on a carpeted wheel well, consuming an entire box of Dolly Madison miniature powdered sugar donuts while he watched Digger.

"The way that prick boyfriend came out blasting back at the psychic's place, I'm not taking any chances," Digger said, glancing toward the front of the van.

Lou St. Louis was calmly driving, his back erect, his

delicate hands wrapped around the wheel. He looked like a mild-mannered little bus driver for some backwoods Sunday school. Who would have guessed the agony that those delicate hands were capable of dealing out?

The van was tooling along I-80 toward Omaha, probably twenty miles or so away from town, and the landscape was starting to change. The wide open spaces were becoming dotted with condos, remote industrial parks, power plants, a big city on the horizon. The chiropractor was keeping the van down around seventy, and the sunlight was streaming through the windshield, illuminating dust motes and the haze of cigarette smoke. The interior was starting to reek of rotting smoked salmon and BO and the general closeness of the three men.

Digger couldn't wait to be done with this fucking job.

"Why haven't we heard from your guys?" he said suddenly to the fat man. "What the fuck are they doing out there?"

Rondo Hatton shrugged, licking his fingers. "Maybe the target's on a plane. I don't know."

"We got people at every fucking airport between here and the Pacific Ocean!" Digger angrily tossed his cigarette on the carpet and ground it in.

"We'll find them," the fat man said.

Digger turned back to his guns, pulled the bottom case out from under the shelving unit, and opened it. Inside was a Browning A-Bolt rifle, its black laminate stock tucked into a foam cavity. A finely tooled precision instrument, the rifle was best suited for long-range varmint hunting, off-season population control, small animal disposal. Today Digger had another type of critter in mind for the rifle. He reached down to the foam-padded case and pulled open a flap on one end.

Inside the cutout was a small metal vial.

Inside the vial was a matched pair of titanium .223-caliber Hornaday tranquilizer darts.

Across the back of the van came a spurt of radio crackle from the police scanner. A dispatcher was squawking something about a three-car accident on Highway 29.

"And what good's all that shit doing us?" Digger asked, gesturing toward the fat man's electronic gear in the back. It sat on a peach crate near the cargo doors. A stack of black components. The scanner was on top, hooked to a lithium battery, flickering, sputtering continuously with radio chatter.

Rondo gobbled another donut. "That scanner's an invaluable tool," he said, licking powdered sugar off his lips. "Allows us to hear what's going on across hundreds of square miles."

"Big fucking deal."

The fat man grunted: "I'm just saying, it could tip us off, lead us right to the target."

Digger wasn't listening anymore.

But he should have been. He should have been paying close attention.

The fat man was right about the scanner.

"This is nuts, Junie."

"I know it's nuts, believe me, I know."

"There's no way I'm going to do this."

"We don't have a choice, Ace—it's the best way to get you to Colorado."

"It'll never work."

"You got a better idea?"

There was a pause as Charlotte tried to come up with something.

She was sitting in the Geo's passenger bucket, holding a pair of scissors in her lap. Her shopworn jumper felt tight and hot all of a sudden, and her stomach was growling with tension. She wanted to start chewing the dashboard—she was so sick with anger—but she knew better than to let all that venom out. *Nice girls don't explode; nice girls keep their rage to themselves; nice girls keep quiet.* Who had taught her that? Her mother? Her father? The kids around the neighborhood?

Charlotte looked down at the scissors, which were gleaming dully in the sunlight, a pair of greasy all-purpose sheers that Junior had found in a tackle box under the back deck. It was a fluke that they had been in the Geo at all. Evidently Junior had gone smelt fishing a couple of months ago, and afterward he had simply forgotten about the tackle box. Now he was claiming that it was an act of God, but Charlotte thought it was more like an act of desperation. There was no way she was going to cut her hair with those things.

She licked her lips, swallowing acid, bracing herself for the coming storm.

They were skirting the edges of Omaha on Highway 34, and the barren terrain was starting to buckle and ripple like the folds of a vast blanket. Charlotte could feel it beneath her, the weight of all that endless acreage surrendering to the dips and twists of the Missouri River valley, the farmland giving way to regiments of Orwellian tract housing, the road banking wearily along the gorge. On the horizon, the great council bluffs rose like vast dark islands against the cornflower sky. These were the sacred places, the hills on which all the major tribes of the prairies communed together. These were the monoliths greeting Francisco Vasquez in the fifteenth century; they were explorers' first glimpses of the sprawling western plains, and on any other occasion, Charlotte would have found them gorgeous. But today, baking in the flat Midwestern sun, they were positively vibrating with danger, murmuring warnings like semaphore in the distant haze: *Stay* away, too many strangers, too many dark alleys, crowded buildings, curious gazes . . .

Charlotte started cutting the gauze bandage from her hand. She got it off and flexed her fingers. The stiffness was worse now; it was as though she had dipped her hand in papier-mâché; but the pain and the itching had subsided somewhat. The swelling had gone down, too.

"You okay?" Junior's voice was tuned up with nervous tension; Charlotte could tell he was as wired as she.

"I'm sorry, but I'm not doing this, Junie—I'm not."

"You have to."

She looked at him, a twinge of anger in her gut. "That's how it's gonna be? Huh? King Junie telling his woman what's what?"

He gave her a sidelong glance. "Yes, as a matter of fact, it is."

Charlotte rubbed her eyes. "Why are men such *assholes*?"

Junior smirked. "I resemble that remark."

"Go ahead and joke, Junie, go ahead, but this is really all about men, men playing with guns, men playing with people's lives, men!" Charlotte could feel the rage burning the back of her throat, a malignancy spreading. She could barely contain it, barely keep her voice from rising. "I don't care that a woman came to me first, it was men who started this thing, men and their dirty little games . . . and their fucking . . . damn it!" Charlotte threw the scissors to the floor, and they bounced across the hump onto Junior's mat. "I'm not cutting my hair for these bastards!"

Charlotte closed her eyes and tried to get her bearings.

After a moment, Junior said very softly, "You have to do this, sweetie, it's the only way you're gonna make it."

Charlotte looked at him, pondered his boyish face, his eyes lined in laugh lines and crow's feet. The way he said "*you're* gonna make it" . . . "*you're* gonna" . . . it was chilling. Then it occurred to Charlotte just exactly why she didn't want to do this insane stunt. She didn't want to do it because of Junior, because of the feelings that had radiated off his touch. And mostly because of his love. Junior had unlocked more than mere passion inside Charlotte; he had unlocked a hidden part of her soul. The problem was, along with the love came the pent-up angst, the long-repressed emotions, the searing rage.

After another moment, Charlotte sighed and said, "All right, hand me the darn scissors already . . ."

24

Tidal Wave of Iron

Trooper Gene Braaksma had been on the job for over nineteen years—in fact, his twentieth anniversary with the Nebraska State Police was coming up next summer, and he was *definitely* looking forward to locking in that pension—but in all those years, he had never seen a motorist so blatantly rubbing a 602 (speeding, 10 MPH or more over the posted limit) into the face of a law officer so clearly visible on the center median.

"Jiminy Christmas—!" Trooper Braaksma blurted, nearly dumping his Styrofoam cup of Hardees coffee as he glanced up at the highway.

The little Geo sedan had just zoomed by his cruiser, going like greased greyhounds, no regard for the double-nickel city limit zone it had just entered. As a matter of fact, Trooper Gene Braaksma could have sworn the Geo had actually *sped up* as it passed the cruiser, weaving precariously from lane to lane. A definite 601 (reckless driving), as well as a probable 002 (driving under the influence of liquor or drugs). Trooper Braaksma glanced over at his radar gun.

The LED screen was glowing, flickering as it tabulated the final speed.

It said *85 MPH.*

The trooper put the big Crown Victoria in drive and shot out onto the highway.

Less than a minute later, he was a quarter mile behind the Geo and gaining.

Trooper Gene Braaksma was doing his best not to smile—not even a little bit—as he flipped on his roof lights, hovering behind the Geo. The next few seconds were always the sweetest for Trooper Braaksma. This was the moment where the speeder suddenly sees that the jig is up, the tilt light is on, and the game is over. In other words, *Smile, Son, you're on Smokey Cam!* Their faces invariably snap up and see the bad news in the rearview, their shoulders slumping, their fallen expressions turning to each other in miserable chagrin. It was one of the only parts of Gene Braaksma's job that truly gave him pleasure. And right now, he was about to bask in it once again, watching another pair of assholes giving him that same kind of buzz.

Except they didn't.

Trooper Braaksma blinked, rubbing dust from his eyes, feeling as though he were hallucinating. The sons o' bitches were *not* slowing down. In fact, they weren't even reacting. In fact, it seemed as though they were even *speeding up* a little bit. Trooper Braaksma looked down at his speedometer and noticed the needle inching toward ninety, and he felt a ripple of nervous tension in his stomach. In nineteen years of dedicated service, this was another first.

He studied the couple in the green Geo. It was hard to get a look at their faces, but they seemed to be forty-somethings, the man behind the wheel a little older, dressed in a faded chambray work shirt. He had a stocky body and longish, curly gray hair, and he was hunched over the steering wheel with a weird sort of intensity. Next to him sat a big-boned woman in a cotton dress, some earth-mother type probably, some Janis Joplin wanna-be. She was also huddled in her seat with that weird intensity, leaning forward like somebody concentrating on a puzzle. Her big, full head of hair was fluttering and bobbing and flying every which way on the wind.

God, how Trooper Braaksma hated hippies.

He gave the Crown Victoria a little gas and inched closer to the Geo.

The Geo's taillights flickered on suddenly.

"Shit—!" Trooper Braaksma hollered involuntarily as the Geo braked hard in front of him.

The rear of the Geo loomed very large, very quickly, and Trooper Braaksma had no time to brake, and the cruiser suddenly thudded into the car's rear bumper, sending a dull, muffled shock wave back through the cruiser's undercarriage, tossing chinks of factory plastic into the wind. Trooper Braaksma fought with the wheel for a moment, the cruiser's front bumper caught on the Geo's molded rear end, and the sound of something scraping pavement rose like a knife edge on a whetstone, a faint fountain of sparks spewing off from the front quarter panel.

Then, all of a sudden—without warning—the Geo broke away, darting off like a rocket, its tiny one-liter engine screaming high falsetto. The driver had his hand thrust out his window, his middle finger raised in a crude salute.

"Son of a bitch!" Braaksma growled through clenched teeth, slamming the pedal to the floor.

The cruiser lurched, the g-forces hugging Braaksma to the seat, the engine thundering—three hundred and twenty-seven cubic inches of make-my-day—as the Crown Victoria gobbled up the space between Braaksma and Mister Curly-gray-hair. Within seconds the cruiser had caught up with the Geo and was nipping at the little car's bumper again, weaving madly, and the old gray-haired hippie had his middle finger raised in the wind, and Braaksma gripped his steering wheel so tightly his teeth felt as though they were cracking inside his skull, and he managed to grab the PA mike, flip the switch, and bark into it: "Green Geo—pull the hell over now or—!"

Suddenly the Geo veered.

"Hey—!"

Trooper Braaksma nearly swallowed his teeth, because the Geo had abruptly vaulted across the fast lane, and now was plunging down the grassy center median, dust and debris and gravel spraying a fifteen-foot wake behind it, and all of a sudden Trooper Braaksma was acting instinctively, without thinking, without hesitating, without yielding to any emotion other than anger: He yanked the steering wheel to his left.

The cruiser plummeted down the embankment.

Braaksma held on for dear life as the Crown Victoria rumbled over badger holes and boulders, engine roaring, chassis creaking, four tons of Detroit steel cutting through clouds of dust kicking up from the Geo, and the vibrations were spectacular, bone-rattling tremors that shook the undercarriage, jarring loose the Mossberg 12-gauge and the scratch pad and the cup of Hardees coffee and the maps from the map caddy, and everything was moving so fast now that Braaksma had little time to think or do anything other than grip the wheel and pursue those two assholes in that baby-shit green Geo as they fishtailed toward the opposite lanes.

"HOLY CHRI—!"

The trooper's voice was drowned by the noise of his undercarriage hitting the adjacent shoulder, the gravel sending spumes of sparks across the dust.

Up ahead, the Geo was weaving wildly toward oncoming traffic, the startled eastbound motorists slamming on their brakes, a chorus of horns rising up like wild animals. Trooper Braaksma tried to stay with the little green car, but it was like swimming upstream against a tidal wave of iron. The oncoming traffic was skidding off to the right, skidding off to the left, huge semis jackknifing, air trumpets shrieking, thunderheads of dust rising. Finally, without warning, the Geo turned sharply back to the right and clamored back across the median, and Trooper Braaksma let out a strangled, inarticulate cry of anger as he yanked the steering wheel.

The cruiser charged back across the wasted turf, then skidded to a stop on the inner shoulder.

The silence fell like a sledgehammer, and Trooper Braaksma sat there for several moments, catching his breath, trying to coax his heart back down his throat and into his chest cavity where it belonged. The fun part of his job was a distant memory now, the cacophony of horns still audible outside the sealed windows, a circus of angry travelers.

Braaksma glanced through his windshield and saw a faint green dot on the horizon; the Geo was vanishing into the heat waves.

"Damn shit birds," he muttered, scooping the radio mike off the floor.

He pressed the send button, called Dispatch, and started giving the gal on the other end an earful.

25

Three Rings

The cellular was chirping.

Connie Horgan fished the phone out of the detritus on the passenger seat, then thumbed the talk button. "Yeah, this is Horgan."

"We got 'em! We got the sons o' bitches!"

Horgan barely recognized the voice. "Rondo?"

The voice of the fat man was keening over the air: "Did you hear what I said, Horgan? We got those bastards! We got 'em nailed!"

"*Physically,* you mean? You got 'em with you now?"

"No, goddamnit, I didn't say we *had 'em,*" the voice crackled through the earpiece. "I mean we *located* 'em, ferChrissake—we located the locator—get it?"

"That's great, but—"

"Heard it on the scanner just minutes ago."

"Great, great, so where—"

"Heard the troopers jawing with each other about some crazy hippie couple in a green Geo."

Horgan sat up straighter, revved the Lincoln's engine. "So where are they?"

"Not far from you, if I'm not mistaken," the fat man replied, his voice taut with excitement.

"You got a mile marker?" Horgan asked. He was sitting at the junction of Interstate 80 and Business 680, not far from the outskirts of Omaha. He was smack-dab in corn country, an ocean of burnt sienna sutured by wasted ribbons of pavement, tattooed with truck rubber, sun-baked, cement as white as bleached bone. The air was heavy with manure and cottonwood. And the heat, and the waiting, and the nervous tension, were all adding to the edgy feeling deep down in Horgan's gut.

"Minute ago, he was heading the wrong way on 80," the voice replied. "Out near some little shit-hole burg called McClelland. You familiar with it?"

Horgan put the Lincoln in gear. "Hell, yes. I'm less than ten miles away."

"Get your ass moving; and we'll meet you there."

Horgan stomped on the foot-feed, and the Lincoln blasted off in a flurry of dust, gravel, and carbon monoxide.

Five hundred miles to the west, Paul Lattamore was cowering in the dim, musty light.

The closet was barely big enough for the vacuum cleaner and the overcoats and the winter boots, and the air was tight and smelled of mothballs. Paul had to press up against the pegboard wall just to have enough room to hold the receiver to his ear. A moment ago, he had pulled the phone inside the closet in order to insure that nobody would hear him. He didn't want Sandy to see him like this. He didn't want the kids to hear what he was about to do. He didn't want to alarm anyone. Swallowing back the fear and the shame, he squeezed his eyes closed as the connection clicked on the other end.

The first ring seemed to stretch forever.

Paul flinched suddenly at the jolt in his brain, a fragment of a voice, an aftershock, a clipped echo of some faulty transmission—

(—*oming!*—)

—and then nothing, nothing but a jagged throbb-

ing in the bridge of his nose, a wave of chills washing
down his back, making his scalp prickle. These jolts
had been going on like this for the last two days. Ran-
dom, incessant, excruciating, they would strike him
when he least expected them. And the pain would be
incredible. But what was it? Was it something he was
trying to remember? Was it a tumor? Or was it something inexplicable? Something psychic?

The second ring buzzed in his ear.

His mouth was going dry, his fingers tingling, his
eyes watering. He was losing his nerve again. He had
been trying to call the FBI Field Office in Denver for
the last twenty-four hours, but he just couldn't bring
himself to do it. After all, what in God's name was
he going to tell them? *Hello, this is Paul Stafford, and
I need to send the entire WITSEC witness protection
program into chaos because I'm having a series of psychic flashes?* It was ridiculous. As if the Feds were
going to allocate the funds required for a full-blown
relocation procedure because some twitchy witness
was getting messages from God in his goddamn
fillings.

Of course, there were other reasons why Paul was
reticent to call the feds. To have to go through the
relocation process all over again would be like reliving
the worse nightmare of his life. Uprooting the family,
pulling the kids out of school, throwing their lives into
turmoil . . . again. It was almost unthinkable to Paul.
And then there was the other, more intangible,
ephemeral reason. Maybe, just maybe, a move at this
point would plunge them into worse danger yet. If
only Paul could get up the nerve to talk it over with
Marshal Vincent or Special Agent Jenrette. Just get it
off his chest.

The woman's voice answered on the third ring:
"Federal Bureau of Investigation . . . how may I direct
your call?"

Paul hung up the phone.

Then he closed his eyes and stood there for a moment, trying not to think about the trouble coming his way.

26

Nerve

The butterscotch yellow Lincoln Town Car was gobbling up the blacktop, spitting it out the back, throwing a wake of dust that rose up into the overcast sunlight like a storm front. Inside the hermetically sealed interior, Horgan sat behind the wheel with the air-conditioning on. He held the cellular in the crook of his neck and spoke in low, hushed tones: "What I'm saying is, don't worry."

The voice of Rondo Hatton came crackling back over the air. "You found the goddamn Geo, and then you lost it?! And you're telling me not to worry?"

"A momentary problem around Bellevue, nothing to worry about."

"What do you mean, a momentary problem?"

"They must've got off the highway for a second."

"What you're saying is, you lost 'em."

"What I'm saying is, they only got two options, which is to go north or south—"

"Fuck this—"

"Wait a minute!" Horgan blurted. "Hold the phone, Rondo, I think we struck gold."

About a quarter mile in the distance, Horgan could see the two-lane blacktop cutting through a patchwork of scabrous cornfields like a scar. It was early in the season, and the corn stalks were still only ankle-high—it had been a very dry spring—and the wind was a sirocco, whipping up the dry, flaky soil, swirling clouds of dust through the air. But sure enough, out there in the brown haze, the little green Geo appeared like a phantom, fishtailing wildly along the two-lane.

"I got an eyeball on 'em—as we speak," Horgan said.

The fat man's voice: "You're kidding me."

"About a quarter mile ahead of me. Little baby-shit green Geo."

"You sure?"

"I'm telling you, it's them."

After a pause: "Gimme your coordinates."

Horgan glanced across the oncoming lane, saw a mile marker sign, did the math, then told the fat man.

Rondo's voice came back, a little tense, a little tickled: "Excellent, that's excellent, we're close, maybe five miles away. *Christ.*" For a moment there was a mumbling sound, as the fat man told the others in the van what was going down. Then his voice returned: "We'll be coming in from the north, Connie, down 34."

Horgan gripped the phone a little tighter. "What do you want me to do?"

"Try to cut them off from the south, box them in."

Horgan thought about it for a moment, thought about the heavy artillery he had on the backseat, wrapped in Howard Johnson towels. He had a cutdown 12-gauge, a Llama 9-millimeter, and six cartons of Hornaday hollowpoints. He said into the phone: "I get the chance, you want me to take 'em out?"

"No, no, no, for Chrissake—no. Listen. They want this bitch alive. You understand what I'm saying?"

Horgan told him that he understood.

"We just want to grab 'em and get the fuck outta here. All right?"

"Sure, whatever," Horgan said into the cellular.

"Keep the line open till we get there, and keep us informed, all right?"

"Sure," Horgan said, then set the phone down on the passenger seat.

He gazed into the haze ahead of him. He was gaining on the Geo; he had closed the distance to about a hundred yards, and now he could see the Geo's pocked rear bumper wagging furiously. He could also see the two figures inside it. Looked like the boyfriend was driving, his stocky shoulders hunched over the wheel, his long gray hair tossing in the wind. The figure next to him had to be the psychic gal, her long wavy locks flapping in the breeze. Horgan gave it a little more gas and started looking for a turnoff. He would have to pass them on an access road in order to cut them off. He glanced back at the Geo.

The boyfriend had rolled down the window, and he was now sticking his arm out.

"Fucking prick!" Horgan growled. The son of a bitch was giving Horgan the finger—the *finger,* for Christ's sake. The fucking *balls* on this little prick!

Horgan put the pedal to the metal.

Up ahead, the Geo made a sharp turn to the right, plunging into the adjacent cornfield.

And that's when things started happening very quickly.

27

Death Throes

The Geo was a bucking bronco, roaring through the corn, throwing a wake of dirt and dust, and Junior was riding the wild horse for all he was worth, white-knuckling the wheel, shoulders hunched, muscles tense with concentration, beads of sweat on his forehead. He was murmuring over the noise and the wind, murmuring more to himself than to Charlotte: "We're gonna be okay . . . gonna be fine . . . don't worry, don't worry . . ."

The ground beneath them was not what he had expected. He had expected soft, rich loam, but *this*—this was like driving over broken cinder blocks, the bone-rattling vibrations threatening to shatter the little Geo into a million pieces; but he kept going, kept barreling through the weeds and stalks. He kept his gaze focused on the far horizon, ignoring the butterscotch Lincoln—a mob car if ever there was one—careening through the weeds and corn behind him.

There was movement to his left.

He managed to throw a glance out his window and saw the horizon line—the endless high-line wires slashing a perfect sky, a storybook landscape of rolling hills, ancient cottonwoods, and endless brown farm fields quilted with early corn and winter wheat. The air was thick with the musk of old fertilizer, manure drying in the sun. It was almost postcard perfect. *Almost.* The bucolic lines were broken only by a distant thunderhead of dust. A second vehicle, coming this way, coming from the north, coming fast down an access road. Junior could just make it out in the hazy glare a half mile away.

A large, customized panel van.

"Wise guys are here!" Junior called out over the noise, his voice quavering from the vibrations.

No answer from Charlotte.

Junior pressed the accelerator to the floor, and felt the Geo's rear wheels biting into the turf, spewing dirt and corn and debris, shaking, shimmying, shrieking like a tormented animal. Its little sixteen-valve, four-cylinder engine was bellowing frantically, all of its seventy-five measly horses wailing their death throes, but it didn't matter anymore, it didn't matter, because Junior's plan was working. He could see the dust cloud closing in from the north, the butterscotch Lincoln behind him, gaining, and he felt like a rat in a maze, nowhere to turn, trapped.

"Here we go, here we go!" Junior was yelling, but it wasn't for Charlotte's benefit anymore. It was for *him,* it was his battle cry: *Phase Two of his plan.*

He turned sharply to the right.

And the Geo careened through a barbed wire fence.

The pickets exploded, shattering across the Geo's windshield, tumbling across the roof, and then the car was bouncing headlong down an embankment, and Junior managed to weave through a stand of hickories, the bark sideswiping the Geo, sending shards of debris and horrible keening noises through the air. Then the Geo landed in a dry creek bed, and Junior wrestled with the steering wheel. The car zigged, then zagged, then turned north. Junior slammed the accelerator to the floor, and the rear wheels gobbled the hard-pack.

The Geo took off.

The creek snaked around the edge of one farm's property and into another's, and Junior looked for an opening, a way out of the creek, but the Geo was vibrating so furiously now it was hard to focus on anything. Junior's teeth were rattling in his skull, and Charlotte had crumpled to the floor mat, and Junior tried to reach down and pull her up. But then he glanced up and saw a way out—a natural rampart of overgrown wild bush and thistle along the west side of the creek bank—and he abruptly turned the car directly into it.

The Geo leapt up the bank and pierced the foliage in a great paroxysm of dirt and debris.

Heading directly into the crosshairs.

28

Fireworks Display

"—shit!—SHIT!—THERE HE IS!!—" Digger Mussolino was leaning out the van's window, the Browning
rifle cradled in his lap as the van stuttered to an abrupt
stop in the dirt. Digger lurched forward, smacking his
forehead on the side mirror, stun drunk, blinking away
the shock and the haze. Fifty feet away, the Geo had
just burst through a wild hedgerow, skidding to a stop
in a fog bank of dust.

And now the two vehicles just sat there in the
weeds, frozen in a bizarre tableau.

Then the sound of an overheated car engine
snapped Digger out of his daze—

—because the Geo was revving its engine, its gears
sliding into reverse—

—and then it was slowly backing away through the
craggy soil and weeds.

"Fuckin' bastards, they're moving," Digger said,
slamming the Browning's bolt mechanism home, in-
jecting a .223-caliber tranq dart into the chamber. His
nerve endings were tingling now, tingling all over, and
goose bumps were crawling along his thick neck and
down his ham-hock arms. He was so tired of chasing
these goddamn mutts; he wanted to end this thing so
badly, he could taste the kill lust on his tongue. He
had the matched pair of Kimber .45 semiautos thrust
behind his belt on either side of his big belly, and he
would use them in a second if it meant ending this

thing. But right now, he had one goal and one goal only, and he knew it came down to how good he was with the Browning. "Go, Lou—GO!"

Lou St. Louis—who was no stunt driver, but still knew his way around a dashboard—put the van in gear without hesitation, then stepped on the gas. The van jolted out of the muddy, rutted trough it was sitting in, then lurched across the field. The contents in the back rattled and shifted as the van roared toward the Geo. The fat man was grappling for purchase among the road cases, trying to keep his balance, trying not to look as excited as he almost certainly was.

"You'd prefer to get as close as possible, I assume," the chiropractor was calling out over the noise and vibrations, the van's tires pistoning over rocky earth.

"That's right, Doc—get me into range, and I'll do the rest," Digger said.

It was like they were driving through a hurricane of dust and debris.

In front of them, the Geo refused to slow down, tearing backward through the dirt, its transmission wailing. Digger wedged the rifle between his knees for a moment, then pulled the Kimber .45s from his belt, snapping the slides on each, all ready to rock and roll. Fifty-five yards away, the Geo was still weaving wildly in reverse through the field. The van bore down on the little car—forty-five yards now, forty, thirty—and Digger snapped back the hammers. Twenty-five yards, twenty, ten: Digger leaned out the window, held his breath, aimed—

—and fired.

The barrage was deafening, the sudden fireworks display crackling around the Geo's front bumper as Digger emptied a half a dozen rounds. One of the bullets—either the fourth or fifth—struck the left front radial, and the tire popped and disintegrated, flopping on the wheel as the Geo kept screaming backward.

"Come to poppa," Digger whispered under his breath, dropping the hot .45s to the floor mat, then grabbing the rifle. He leaned out the window with the Browning raised and ready, pressing his left eye to the scope's eye-cup. The van was closing the distance down to inches, and the Geo was weaving and smoking furiously.

Digger looked through the lens at the Geo's passenger seat, which was now swimming back and forth across the scope's green field of vision. It took Digger a moment to center the psychic gal in his crosshairs.

Charlotte Vickers's face came into focus.

Digger's eye widened suddenly, growing to the size of a shiny silver dollar.

29

End of the Line

They were backing into oblivion, and there wasn't anything Junior could do about it.

The sound was excruciating—the Geo's overtaxed little four-cylinder engine shrieking and coughing, the air smelling chemical-hot like burning oil, and Junior could feel the car sliding out from under him, the steering wheel snagging. His ears were ringing unmercifully, and his head was clogged with panic. But the good news was, the big panel van was bearing down on them like a fire-breathing dragon, flares of high-caliber lightning flashing out its side window, sparks of ricochets chinking and whizzing about the dirt, and that was just fine with Junior.

His plan was working.

Now he had about a half a second to execute Phase Three, and he acted without hesitation, without speaking, without even taking a breath: Reaching across Charlotte, he pressed the glove box button. The glove box door flipped down, revealing a chrome SIG-Sauer .380 auto-load nestled in a hank of documents. Junior grabbed the gun, thumbing the safety off as he slammed back into his seat, keeping his left hand welded to the steering wheel, his gaze alternating between the cracked windshield and the field behind him (he did this very quickly, in a matter of split seconds). Then Junior took a deep breath, glancing back at his windshield.

The van was looming.

Junior aimed at the glass and started firing.

The SIG barked loud and harsh in the tight interior, the large-caliber holes blossoming in the windshield, a hot spittle of cordite and powdered glass snapping back at Junior's face, the gun kicking wildly in his hand. Junior didn't intend to hit anything; he simply wanted to create a diversion, fill the air with noisy fire while he got ready to execute the last maneuver. Now the gun was clicking dry—eight rounds gone, the auto slide opening—and it was time, it was time, and he dropped the gun because it was as hot as a branding iron and it was time.

He did two things simultaneously: He yanked the wheel and he slammed the shift lever into first.

Now the sequence of actions and reactions were coming very quickly, almost too quickly to even register in Junior's mind, because the Geo had suddenly gone into a spin, and for a single blind instant, the world turned liquid, the bright sunlight and the loud sound and the smell of cow shit melding into a kaleidoscope around the outside of the Geo, the gravity sucking Junior to the door. Then there was a bang like a pistol shot beneath the Geo, and the transmission blew, the gears tommy-gunning all of a sudden. And then the Geo skidded across the dirt, smashing through the wall of foliage and hickories and then down the embankment toward the creek bed, and Junior was frantically reaching across the seats, clawing at Charlotte—

—because the Geo was tipping over—

—and now it was starting to roll—

—down the rocky grade, turning end over end, and Junior was hollering garbled cries, the world turning upside down around him, the roof slamming hard-pack earth, then the wheels slamming violently, then the roof again, then the wheels, the vibrations jarring the puny frame, and thank God Junior was wearing his seat belt—

—but unfortunately Charlotte was *not,* and her door flopped open—

—and she was thrown—

—and finally the Geo came to rest upright in the weeds at the bottom of the creek bed.

And silence crashed down on Junior.

He felt as though elephants were standing on his chest as he lay across his bucket seat, the belt digging into his blood-soaked gut, the sudden silence like a fist in his face. His ears were ringing fiercely, and he could barely hear the van skidding to a halt somewhere in the distance, and the angry wind. He managed to unbuckle himself and get his door open.

He slid outside, then fell to his hands and knees in the weeds.

Where was she?

Junior crawled around the back of the crumpled Geo and saw her lying on the bank a few feet away. Face up, arms and legs splayed outward, she looked peaceful in her frozen stillness, Christ-like in the litter-strewn weeds, tangled in the thorny cattails and crabgrass. And Junior started to grin. His plan had worked, damn it; he had pretended just long enough to fool everybody. Over the last fifty miles of hard road, he had imagined that the hollow, brittle figure on the passenger seat next to him was Charlotte Vickers, and Charlotte Vickers she had become, sculpted in all her stiff, papery glory, complete with human hair, cotton jumper, and molded face.

He could hear noises coming from the field behind him, the van doors bursting open, the *snick-snick* of auto clips snapping shut, and he gazed one last time across the creek bed at the fake body. It was not Charlotte Vickers, and it never had been.

It was just a scarecrow, a scarecrow they had found next to an ancient maple.

A scarecrow with wing tips on its feet and a headful of glorious curly hair.

PART 111

THE STORM

"We cannot live, sorrow or die for
somebody else, for suffering is too
precious to be shared."
—EDWARD DAHLBERG
Because I Was Flesh

30

Gnawing Off the Foot

At about the same time Junior was plunging down the embankment in his crumpled Geo, Charlotte was running headlong down a narrow, cracked sidewalk that snaked along the banks of the Mosquito River a few miles south of Council Bluffs.

"Wait!—WAIT!" She was hollering at the top of her lungs, sheened in sweat, heart chugging, dodging a series of tree saplings planted along the river walk in cracked plaster pots as part of some forgotten suburban renewal program. She could see the intersection in the distance, simmering in heat waves like a mirage, the two access roads crisscrossing, the dusty little gas station, and the rows of low-slung brick professional buildings. The Greyhound office was there in the last brick building to the south, the bus station nothing more than a weathered wooden carrel out near the roadside.

The bus was starting to pull away.

"Wait!—please!—over here!" Charlotte was waving her bandaged hand now like a lunatic, rushing across a grassy lot, lugging Junior's greasy knapsack, which now felt like it weighed about a hundred pounds. Inside it were candy bars, a sweater, a flashlight, ammunition, and the Ruger .22-caliber semiautomatic that Junior had given her. Charlotte felt like a terrorist, and she probably looked like one, too—with her ragged, short-cropped hair, hastily chopped off, her face flushed and wild, her gaze filled with psychic noise and razor-edged panic. She was dressed in brand-new clothes—a V-neck blouse, a pleated skirt, cotton leggings, boots, and a denim windbreaker—all of which she had just hurriedly purchased with Junior's credit card at the Fashion Bug a block north of the bus depot. But unfortunately, she had taken too long trying on windbreakers, momentarily forgetting the departure time stamped on her bus ticket.

Now the bus was leaving without her.

"HEY!" Charlotte stumbled across an asphalt cul-de-sac, waving frantically as she approached the rear of the bus, carbon monoxide pluming out its rear end. The bus was pulling away toward the street, but Charlotte closed the distance fast, her knapsack bouncing and rattling against her hip, sweat tracking down the small of her back.

All at once, the bus's air brakes hissed.

Charlotte staggered around the side of the bus, lungs heaving for air, head pounding painfully. She dug her ticket out of her pocket, then hobbled up to the front door near the cab, waving the ticket sheepishly at the driver. The door folded inward suddenly, revealing the dark, cool interior. The driver was a string bean of a black man in a gray uniform and thick glasses. Didn't say a word. Just held his hand out for her ticket like he'd done it a million times.

"Thank you, thank you," Charlotte said breathlessly, climbing on board. String Bean took her ticket, nodded tersely, then closed the door behind her.

Charlotte made her way down the narrow aisle toward the last remaining open seat in back, as the bus rattled on its merry way, the muffled drone of the engine rising beneath the floor. Bracing herself on seat backs as she went along, Charlotte caught her breath, trying to adjust to the swaying, darkened interior. Her arm ached from lugging the knapsack, and her lower back smoldered with a dull pain. The bus was pretty crowded, filled with farm families, migrant workers, sailors on leave, and local types of every size, shape, and color. The air smelled of stale aftershave and stained upholstery, and the contents of the storage bins squeaked and shifted constantly.

Squeezing into an empty bench near the lavatory, Charlotte dropped the knapsack to the floor, then collapsed onto the threadbare seat.

It took her several moments to get her bearings back. She was a bundle of nerves, her mind churning with noise. Barely an hour had passed since Junior had dropped her off at the interstate oasis near Highway 29—where Charlotte had hired a cabdriver to take her to the nearest bus depot—but it seemed like an eternity ago. Since then Charlotte had closed down her psychic pathways, pulled the storm windows shut on her mind, boarded up the doorways, turned off the lights. It was as though she didn't exist anymore. It reminded her of animals who got their legs caught in traps, then gnawed off their feet in order to escape. Charlotte had gnawed off her foot the moment she left Junior.

At length, she managed to gaze out the window.

She barely noticed the bus crossing the state line and entering Nebraska.

"Here come the fucking boys in blue." Digger Mussolino was nodding at the distance. About a mile away, a cloud of dust was rising up over the blacktop road, the glint of blue and red flashing lights within it. Three, maybe four vehicles. A couple of state troopers, an E-unit, a paddy wagon maybe. The sirens were warbling on the wind. "Always a day late and a dollar short," Digger added wryly.

They were walking briskly back toward the van— not hurrying exactly, but moving with the kind of fuck-you brazenness that wise guys usually adopted in the commission of a crime. They had just retrieved the psychic's boyfriend from the dry creek bed, dragging him up the hill and through the trees like a sack of day-old shit propped between Horgan and the fat man. They had a Kimber .45 pressed into his back, and they were yanking him along like a drunk, paying very little attention to the oncoming authorities. A few of the local sodbusters must have heard the gunfire and called the state police, but it didn't matter. This was the way it worked for mafiosi. Mafiosi didn't hurry, they didn't hide their faces, they didn't look away—they were simply doing their job. They didn't care about lineups, they didn't care about civilian witnesses. Besides: No pig farmer in his right mind was going to be stupid enough to step into *this*.

"This is the part where I'm supposed to say you'll never get away with this," the stocky guy was murmuring, wheezing slightly. He seemed pretty shaken up, his shirt soaked in blood, his curly gray hair matted to his face. He didn't seem to have any major injuries, although he was limping pretty good as they dragged him along.

"I'd shut my mouth, I was you," Digger said, and he meant it. He was tired of fucking with this cocksucker and his crappy little Geo and his tricks with scarecrows.

"Just making conversation," Junior Parrick said, trying hard not to smile.

"You'll have plenty of time to get chatty," Digger told him.

"I can hardly wait."

They reached the van, which still sat idling in the dirt, its rear door gaping. Horgan and Rondo threw Junior inside, and Junior tumbled to the floor, tangling up in a plastic tarp that was spread across the floor, wincing at the pain in his side.

"That looks like a very nasty bump on your head," a voice said softly from the depths of the van.

Junior wrenched around until he could see the little man in the cheap suit.

"Don't you worry," the chiropractor said, his gold tooth glimmering. "Gonna make sure you forget all about that nasty old bump."

31

The Changing

Charlotte was sitting in the back of the giant metal sardine can with all the other sardines, engulfed in the close, peppery odors of humanity, stewing in a fog of confusion and regret as the interstate vibrated beneath her, the *clack-clack-clacking* of potholes marking time. Greyhound time. The kind of flat, colorless, interminable time that passes only on buses such as this. Shoulders slumped, face leaning against the smudged window, Charlotte gazed out at the passing oceans of corn without really seeing anything.

Concentrate on the place . . . Grand Lake, Colorado . . . Packard's Bar & Grill . . .

She was rubbing the ridges along the edge of the silver dollar, eyes closed, trying to catch an image on her flickering mindscreen. A clue, a road sign, a landmark—*anything*—amid the herky-jerky film strip unspooling in her midbrain. There were great, prehistoric granite cliffs rushing by her—was Paul driving again?—and the sensations of cold wind on Charlotte's phantom face. There were children. Two little boys running across the wooded lot in back of the cabin. There were blurry, indistinct glimpses of a woodshed, split logs being stacked in a dusty shack, the sunlight slanting through cracks in the walls. There were dinner smells, a woman leaning out the window, the sound of voices coming from the forest.

Nothing that would give away an address.

Charlotte sighed, and she let go of the circuit for a moment.

On the floor at her feet sat Junior's greasy knapsack, the gun nestled inside it, radiating heat like a beating heart. There was something strange going on with that gun. It was as though the very sound of it—that *whip-crack pop* in Charlotte's ears—had jostled something loose inside her. She still hated guns, was still terrified by them. But this one was different. Maybe it was because this one was owned by Junior. Maybe it had his goodness ingrained into its stock, into its very molecules.

(—snap!-CLANG!—)

Charlotte flinched, then looked away, looked out the window to clear her mind.

For a brief instant she caught a fleeting glimpse of her reflection in the glass. She looked horrible, absolutely horrible, her face drawn, her eyes rimmed in dark circles. She longed for some emergency eyeliner, a little blush-on, some light lipstick; then she silently cursed herself for thinking such things while Junior was probably dodging a hail of gunfire. What was wrong with her? She glared back at her reflection. Her impromptu haircut had been a disaster—not only had she been trembling through most of it, but the potholes and bumpy spots in the highway hadn't helped any—and now she looked like a mangy chemotherapy patient, her once luxuriant curls reduced to a close-cropped skullcap of irregular tufts and cowlicks. She knew deep down that she had sacrificed her hair for that scarecrow in the interests of survival, and maybe she would even look stylish—a little punky maybe, but stylish—but it did little to assuage her anguish. It was simply another instance of being violated, of being abused, of being toyed with.

There was something else, however, that was eating away at Charlotte like a cancer, and she couldn't put her finger on what it was. Perhaps it was the outrage at being forced to separate from Junior—the man with whom she was falling madly in love, and probably the only other person on earth whom she fully trusted. The odds were good he was in grave danger, probably already injured or dying. Or maybe it was the terror twisting inside her, telling her that she'd made a horrible mistake, the fear like a dreadful weight pressing down on her, the sick, venal mafiosi closing in on her, invading her head, forcing her on this fool's errand to protect the Lattamores—people she had never even met.

Or maybe, just maybe, it was something deeper, thornier, more complex and tangled in her psyche—

"Hi!"

The voice made Charlotte jump slightly. She turned toward the aisle and saw a little black girl standing by her seat. "Hello, sweetheart," Charlotte said. "How are you?"

"I'm seven and a half!" the little girl enthused. She was a little waif with pigtails, tattered blue ribbons in her hair, and dual tracks of snot running down her face. Her dress was tattered and soiled, and she had the subtle patina of low income in her eyes. She was holding a ratty brown Cabbage Patch doll under one arm.

"That's almost a grown-up," Charlotte said, smiling. "What's your name, honey?"

"Shauntay Waters."

"That's a pretty name, Shauntay. My name's Charlotte. Who's your friend?"

The little girl looked at the doll judiciously. "Her real name is Shanice, but my brother and his friend calls her Dumb-Bitch."

Charlotte felt an odd twinge in her solar plexus. "I like Shanice better, that's a lovely name."

The little girl looked at the floor, didn't say anything.

"Come here, sweetheart," Charlotte said, and the child took a step closer. Charlotte found a wad of gauze in her breast pocket—a leftover from a recent change of her bandage—and she used it to wipe the snot off the little girl's face. Charlotte noticed her own hands were trembling convulsively. Especially her bandaged hand. She tried to stop it from shaking, but it was going haywire. "There you go, Shauntay, all better," Charlotte said, wiping away the last dab of mucus.

The little girl nodded, clucking her tongue.

Then she scurried away.

Charlotte's gaze followed the little girl as she scampered up the aisle toward the front of the crowded bus. At the moment, most of the other passengers were dozing. Near the front, directly behind the driver, there was a large black woman in a brown uniform occupying a bench seat, and when the little girl approached, the woman reached out. "Where you been?" the woman said sternly, grabbing the little girl and gently pulling her onto the seat. The little girl started gibbering something about a lady in back and the bathroom and something else Charlotte couldn't hear, but the mother in the uniform just patted the child on the rump and said, "Don't you be running off like that without telling me where you're going."

Charlotte turned back to the window.

The bus was growling along I-80 at about sixty-five miles an hour, the vast, flat mosaic of farmland on either side of the highway unblemished by topography, a rippling ocean of wild goldenrod and wheat, rushing by on either side. The sameness was almost mesmerizing, especially now, in mid-summer, when everything was knee-high and verdant, the color of rich seawater, the endless rail fence bordering endless crops, the

high-tension wires overhead dancing and snaking and
fishtailing hypnotically. Charlotte had a hard time gazing at it. She was changing inside, and the passing
terrain was only magnifying the process. She was five
hours away from the Colorado state line, another four
or so to get into the Rockies.

She glanced back toward the front of the bus.

The little black girl was lying across her mother's
ample lap, mumbling nursery rhymes, and Charlotte
smiled to herself, thinking how nice it would have
been to have had a child. In another life, maybe.

Another universe.

The bus continued on, impassive and relentless.

There was a new vehicle waiting for them in an
unmarked garage adjacent to runway B at the Lincoln
Municipal Airport in Lincoln, Nebraska. It was
brought there by two *soldatos* from the Romani family, which ran the mountain states region, and it was a
beauty. A fully up-fitted Chevy G3500 RV with deluxe
camper kit, souped-up engine, and a high-performance
undercarriage. Inside, it had everything: fold-up beds
for six, a fully stocked sub-zero refrigerator, range,
dishwasher, microwave, computer, satellite TV, a
VCR with a library of porno tapes, and a liquor cabi-
net with everything from Chivas Regal to Dom Perig-
non. Plus there were cabinets full of complimentary
items such as jars of beluga caviar, expensive Italian
novelties, and even cartons of Digger's preferred
brand of European cigarettes. It was a tribute to Big
John Fabionne from the Romani bosses. It was also
the best way for them to blend into the normal ebb
and flow of the interstate.

They didn't make a big deal out of the switch.

They came up Highway 2 from the south, and they
slipped into the airport without fanfare. They pulled
around behind a row of warehouse buildings along the

far runway. There was a 727 taking off as they circled around the far edge of the tarmac, and the tremendous rush of noise added further cover. They wasted very little time. When they reached the unmarked garage adjacent to the last warehouse, they parked the van behind a Dumpster and then moved with the precision of a military drill team.

One of the Romani boys was waiting for them inside the garage. Digger and Rondo quickly ushered Junior out of the van at gunpoint while the chiropractor followed like a silent chaperon. The Romani boy handed Digger the keys to their new wheels, and nodded a good-bye. Then Digger ushered the other gentlemen inside the camper before rushing back around to the cab's driver-side door.

A moment later, Digger was firing the engine up and slamming it into gear.

The camper roared out of there.

All told, the entire switch encompassed the better part of five minutes.

32

Twilight

"You ain't taking no vacation, is ya?"

"Is it that obvious?"

The black woman pointed at the knapsack sitting on the floor at Charlotte's feet. "You ain't exactly packed for a vacation, and you been keeping your eye on that thing like it's gonna get up and run away. Not to mention the fact that you been wringing your hands and thinking about other things ever since you sat down."

Charlotte's eyes were burning all of a sudden, and it felt as though her chest were about to crack open.

Outside the windows the outskirts of Kearny were coming into view, obscured by the deepening shades of twilight. Another distant water tower with a happy face painted on it, another trailer park, another empty high school football field, its rows of empty bleachers throwing long shadows across the turf. Night was falling like a funeral pall, chilling the air, growing shadows. As far as the eye could see, the land seemed to be vulcanized, dotted with industry and asphalt, the echoes of Sioux warriors, covered wagons, and the Pony Express as long gone as the hoop skirt. And yet—cooped up inside the Greyhound—Charlotte felt as though she were in a time machine, the bus's stuffy, disinfected atmosphere and constant guttural drone transporting her back to a more primitive time, a time of big skies and vast places and life-or-death battles

among the whisker wheat. Maybe that was why she'd
been receiving all sorts of jolts off the coin, telegraph
signals from Lattamore's mind, paranoid flashes in fits
and bursts. And the farther west Charlotte rolled, the
sharper were her emotions, the edgier her mood. She
was positively vibrating with inertia, the strange cancer
inside her seething now, hotter than ever. She wanted
Junior here so badly. She needed a friend, she needed
help, she needed a miracle.

Maybe that was why she had wandered up the aisle
and taken a seat next to the little girl's mother.

"I'm in trouble, Mavis . . . I mean . . . I've done a
terrible thing."

"Take a breath, honey, it's okay."

"I'm going somewhere, trying to make some things
right."

"That's good."

"Maybe even save some lives, but it's . . . it's a
complete mess."

"Sounds pretty bad."

"You have no idea."

"Try me."

Charlotte swallowed bile. "People are in grave danger because of me, even the man I love, his life is in
danger, all because of me, all because of my . . .
stupidity!"

"Take it easy, honey," Mavis said after another
pause. "One thing I've learned, nobody's ever as stupid as they think they is . . . or as wise."

The big black woman started giggling then, and her
entire body started jiggling, and it was something to
behold. Stuffed into her Brinks Security uniform,
enormous breasts straining the buttons on the front of
her blouse, huge girth bulging at the hips, Mavis Waters was a mountain of motherhood, completely para-
doxical in her official-looking garb. Her little girl was
curled up in her lap, fast asleep, her tiny brown hands

clutching at Mavis's gun belt, which only added to the paradox. Mavis looked as though the last thing that would occur to her would be the .38 pistol holstered on her belt. If confronted with a criminal, she looked as though she might just choose instead to smother him to death, or spank his bottom for being a bad boy, or maybe just promise him a good home-cooked meal if he just straightened up and flew right.

Charlotte looked down at her own bandaged hand. How long had it been since she had thrust it into the furnace's pilot flames? A little over twenty-four hours ago? It seemed like years. Her fingers were still itching and tingling furiously, and she still had that silver dollar cupped tightly in her palm, the tarnished surface gleaming dully in the twilight.

Charlotte had been caressing the thing throughout her chat with Mavis, soaking up every last spark of psychic residue. But for the last hour, the signals had been intermittent, sketchy, weak. There was something happening to Lattamore—Charlotte could feel it vibrating off the edges of the coin—but she couldn't get a fix on anything, and she was starting to panic, starting to think the signals were fading. If Lattamore was getting paranoid and arming himself to the teeth, maybe he had already learned that the mobsters were coming for him. Maybe he had already fled. Maybe Charlotte had inadvertently sent him signals and driven him out of his home. It was a skill Charlotte had never mastered—sending her thoughts into someone else's mind. Charlotte was a receiver. She was a feeler, an absorber, a bloodhound. But maybe she had been sending feelings back into the minds of her targets and had never been aware of it.

Or maybe Lattamore was just naturally jumpy.

Charlotte closed her eyes. "I'm sorry—I just—I can't believe this is happening . . ."

Mavis must have sensed Charlotte's pain and disorientation, because the black woman leaned over and put an arm around Charlotte. "Just let it out, honey," the big woman said softly, squeezing Charlotte.

Charlotte began to cry.

It wasn't exactly a banshee wail—it wasn't even audible over the Greyhound's droning vibrations—but Charlotte let it all out, the knot in her chest coming undone, her shoulders rocking, her body quaking, and the tears tracked down her face and dropped to the cloth-and-vinyl upholstery like muffled drumbeats. Some of the other passengers were staring now. Charlotte could feel their gazes on the back of her head, but there was nothing she could do; she was trembling like a frightened sparrow now. And Mavis kept her arm around Charlotte, patting her, stroking her shoulder and her hair.

The coin slipped out of Charlotte's hand and bounced across her lap.

It landed on the floor with a clunk, and Mavis instinctively reached down for it.

"That's okay, I got it," Charlotte said, reaching down for the coin.

Both women clutched at the silver dollar at precisely the same moment.

Something sparked off the coin.

"What?" Mavis recoiled as though the coin had bitten her. She leaned back in her seat, rubbing her pudgy little hand, blinking, swallowing hard.

Her heart had just fluttered again, just like it had been doing—off and on—for the better part of her adult life. Her doctor had warned her about ignoring these little palpitations, warned her about heart disease, warned her about continuing to eat her sweet potato pie and fried steak and Philly cheese sandwiches, but Mavis would rather die young with a big smile on her plump face than worry about cholesterol and strokes and heart attacks. But just now—just as Mavis had touched this lady's coin—she had felt something more than a mere heart murmur. It was more like a jolt of something electrical, maybe even otherworldly, squirting through her mind for several seconds, a voice ringing in her ears as though it had been hollered through a public address system in her head—*ALL BECAUSE OF ME!*—and then—*MURDERED IN GRAND LAKE!*—and then something like—*LATTAMORE AND HIS WHOLE FAMILY!*—and then something garbled that Mavis couldn't make out.

"Excuse me?" The woman named Charlotte was drying her eyes now, putting the coin back in her blouse pocket, looking about as drawn and peaked as a rag that's been wrung out and hung on the line.

"You just said something," Mavis told her.

"When?"

"Just now."

The white gal looked shaken for a moment, sniffing back the emotion. "I don't understand—"

"I heard you," Mavis said. "Something about a lake? Grand Lake? Somebody named Lattamore?"

There was a pause.

The woman named Charlotte just stared, and Mavis felt so sorry for this poor creature. Eyes rimmed in red, close-cropped hair sticking up in tufts, chin quivering, she looked like a lost little girl. Whoever this Lattamore dude was, the mere mention of his name seemed to raise this poor gal's hackles. Mavis wanted to hug her some more and tell her it was okay and try to calm her down, but it was clear from the woman's haunted face that she was in no shape to be comforted. "I didn't say a thing," she uttered finally.

"I guess I must be hearing things again," Mavis said with a shrug.

"I swear to you I didn't say anything."

Mavis nodded. "I'm sorry, baby, I didn't mean to—"

"I have to go," she said suddenly, scooping her knapsack off the floor.

"You sure you're all right?" Mavis asked.

"It was very nice talking to you," she said, standing up on shaky knees, clutching her knapsack as though her life depended on it. Her eyes were hot with panic, and she started down the aisle with the slightly awkward, slightly herky-jerky motions of someone whose mind was racing. She bumped the sides of several seats as she stumbled along, apologizing, waking slumbering passengers on the way back to her seat. Mavis watched for another moment, then felt a tug on the front of her uniform.

"Mama—?" Little Shauntay had awakened and was gazing up at her mom.

"It's okay, baby," Mavis muttered softly. "Go back to sleep."

"Is that lady sad?"

"Is she what?"

"Is she sad?"

Mavis thought about it for a moment. She thought about the electric jolt she'd just received from that silver dollar, the voice in her head like a thunderclap echoing across a chasm. Mavis had heard the voice of Jesus once while singing hymns in church—at least, she *thought* she heard it—but she'd never experienced anything like this. This was about murder, and somebody named Lattamore, and Grand Lake—wherever the hell that was. Finally Mavis stroked her little girl's back and said, "She got herself in some trouble, baby. That's all. Now you go on back to sleep."

33

Trigger Point

"Relax, sir, please," the chiropractor said to the man on the massage table, the carpeted floor vibrating with road noise. "It won't help you to tense up, you can trust me on that."

"You oughtta listen to the doctor," Digger Mussolino said from a padded chair across the camper. Rondo was driving now so that Digger could watch the festivities.

"I'm listening to the doctor," the gray-haired man muttered, his face pressed into the head rest. "Believe me, I'm listening."

There was an awkward silence.

The camper was rocking gently as it cruised along the dark interstate, the occasional flicker of a sodium vapor lamp or passing headlight coming through the tiny porthole window. The space was fairly claustrophobic, albeit larger than the panel van. Maybe fifty or sixty square feet of carpeted floor, flanked by folded bunk beds and appliances. Everything had a rubbery smell to it, and the light was harsh from incandescent domes. The sound of the engine and double rear wheels whining on the pavement provided a constant buzzing drone.

The massage table was in the center of the camper, the gray-haired man strapped down on his belly.

Lou St. Louis detested working in such cramped quarters with such minimal equipment. His standards had risen far too high for such a primitive situation. Even back at the Southeastern School of Chiropractic Medicine in Kansas City, he had been a perfectionist; a trait which had pleased his strict, Mormon mother to no end. And even years later—after Lou was de-certified by the American Chiropractic Board for numerous harassment complaints from female patients—he had grown accustomed to working under much better conditions. If he had been back at his apartment—where he conducted many of these "sessions" for the mob—he would have had full benefit of his traction table, his galvanic current generator, even his acupuncture needles. But a professional works with the tools at hand, and so Lou was prepared to start another session. "Before we start," he said softly to the man on the table, "is there anything you'd like to say to Mr. Mussolino?"

"I told you already," the gray-haired man said. "She doesn't know where Lattamore is, she's scared, and she's on the run from you folks."

"I'm just not buying it, Parrick," Digger said.

"You can torture the shit outta me, it won't change the facts."

There was another long, tense silence.

Digger puffed his Dunhill. "You got one last chance to avoid some very unpleasant shit. All you gotta do is tell us where in Colorado this guy is living. You'll be doing yourself a big favor."

"I've told you everything, there's nothing more to tell," Junior said.

"All right, Parrick," Digger snubbed his cigarette out. "It really pains me to have to say this . . . but you're putting us in a difficult position here."

Digger nodded at Lou. "Go ahead, Doc."

Lou said, "Okay, let's start with a postural diagnosis." He squirted massage oil into each talented palm, rubbing it in as he spoke. "Watching you walk across the tarmac, I noticed you have a slight limp—it's very subtle but it's there—which leads me to believe that one leg is slightly shorter than the other. Is this correct? Sir?"

There was a pause.

Digger suddenly leapt out of his chair, lunged at the table, grabbed Junior by the neck. "ANSWER THE MAN!—ANSWER HIM, YOU COCKSUCKER!— YOU FUCKIN' PRICK!"

"Yes, yes, that's correct, yes, that's true," Junior said with a wince.

Digger let go, face flushed. He took a few moments to catch his breath, brushing himself off. Then he backed away and returned to his chair. There was a bottle of Chivas Regal sitting on the pull-down table next to him. He poured himself a couple of fingers in a paper cup and took a taste.

Lou nodded. "Okay . . . I suspected one leg was slightly shorter than the other, which can have a scoliosis-like effect." He set the bottle of oil on the counter next to him, then walked over to the massage table. The gray-haired man was a tough subject, heavily muscled, with lots of body fat. His chambray shirt had been removed, as well as his pants, and now he was naked from the waist up, clad only in boxer shorts. Lou gazed down at the freckled planes of his back as a symphony conductor might gaze upon his array of musicians. "This effect can cause trigger points," he went on. "Trigger points are pesky little bundles of nerves and muscles that ball up into pea-shaped masses and embed themselves in the deeper muscles. Drives a person crazy with pain."

Lou pressed a fingertip against the fleshy part of Junior's thigh.

Then he pressed harder.

"Aahhhh—AAHHHH—!" The gray-haired man bellowed, eyes slamming shut, mouth gaping. He looked so beautiful to Lou, like a first-chair violin just warming up, such gorgeous music yet to come. But at the moment, he was merely being tuned to the proper key.

Lou lifted his finger. "See what I mean? Very intense pain at that one point." He turned to the shelving unit behind him, put on a pair of rubber gloves, then found his T-bar. A varnished wooden stick with a rubber tip at one end and a T-shaped handle at the other, the T-bar was a commonly used tool of the physical therapy trade, designed to work out knotted muscles and sore backs. "Often a man of your size and age develops something called sciatica," Lou explained in his soft voice. "You see it with executives a lot, older men, weekend warriors who fancy themselves star athletes. Sciatica is caused when the sciatic nerve is compressed by the gluteus muscles." Lou rubbed his oily thumb down along the top of Junior's tailbone. "Right along here—see? Feel that?"

"Yes," the gray-haired man uttered meekly.

"One last question, sir, if you'll permit me," Lou whispered softly. "Can you tell us where the Lattamore family is living in Colorado?"

After a long pause, the gray-haired man finally caught his breath and said very softly, "Lemme ask *you* something . . . Do you know the difference between a porcupine and a camper full of wise guys?"

Lou shot a glance over at Digger.

"Give up?" Junior said almost cheerfully. "The answer is . . . the porcupine has the pricks on the *outside*."

"AAAAAAAAHHHHHHHHH—!!"

It burst out of Junior's lungs, a completely involuntary cry, sounding almost rhetorical, as though his central nervous system had just sent a bulletin to his vocal cords, and all he could do was let out the air like a pressure cooker releasing steam.

Something entered his rectum.

Junior bit down on his tongue, his eyes bugging, his mouth filling with salty, coppery blood, and he started to fight the urge to cry. He wanted to weep, he wanted to cry out, he wanted to tear the camper apart with his teeth. The hard rubber object was filling him now, and the pain was a searing, burning fire raging up his pelvis, roaring in his brain. He started to lose his nerve. He started to slip away, regressing back to the days he was in Catholic school and the nuns would take him down into the basement rectory where no light could get into the classrooms, and they would whip him with rubber hoses.

"We're going to make a little adjustment to your sacrum," said the nasty little man with the stick. "Wake up that femoral nerve where all the pain lives."

"Please . . ." Junior started to beg the nasty man to stop, please stop, but he couldn't get the words out.

The stick jabbed hard inside him.

"AAAAAAAHHHHHHHHHHHHHHHHHH—!!"

The fire erupted, and Junior caterwauled, his vision filling with bright Halloween-orange light. It felt as though a semi-truck had just driven over his midsection, like a Molotov cocktail had just exploded in his pelvis, and he cried now, he cried for the bad man with the stick to stop, but the stick kept moving, and the blast furnace spread down his legs, down his arms, around his neck, and up the back of his skull, and he cried like a little boy, and he tried to think about the good things, the candy corn and the Christmas turkey and his dog Gypsy and his little plastic Cox dune buggy and the Ohio State Fair and his brother's Yamaha and the steam from the corn dog vendors, and nothing could take the pain away.

The stick kept moving.

Now he tried to think about the only thing left, the last thing, the best thing, the sweet-curry smell of Charlotte's underarms, the medusa mane of her dark hair, the moist glow of her lips.

Junior's only hope for escape.

34

The Strike of a Dull Axe

The Greyhound skimmed across the Colorado state line shortly after midnight.

Charlotte sat in the back, chewing her fingernails, gazing out the tinted glass at the obsidian black prairies stretching off toward the horizon. The bus was barreling along Interstate 76, a barren section of four-lane which entered the state at the far northeastern corner, then looped down through Sterling, Fort Morgan, and eventually Denver. The terrain along the road was desolate scrub plain, sparsely strewn with an occasional cattle ranch or reservoir. The only lights were from distant refineries and radio towers, blinking forlornly in the vast night sky, the mountains still nothing more than distant cloud caps on the western horizon.

The Greyhound had made several stops over the last couple of hours, most of its passengers disembarking, and now the loneliness of the empty interior was blending with the darkness outside, the steady, droning chorus of the tires, and the relentless sound of night winds buffeting the roof. Charlotte had never felt this alone before. Never. She couldn't stop thinking about Junior. She couldn't stop thinking about losing him. She would never forgive herself for leaving him back there. She needed so badly to talk to somebody right now. Anybody. She even longed to have Mavis and the little girl back on board the bus. But that was out of the question now. They had disembarked at Ogallala, the little girl waving sadly as she trudged down the metal steps, the mother shooting worried glances back at Charlotte. Mavis Waters had absorbed something from the coin. Charlotte was sure of it now. The black gal probably possessed a little bit of the "gift" and didn't even know it, but a little bit had been enough. And now the name of the town—*Grand Lake*—was on a stranger's lips.

Sudden pain shot up the bridge of Charlotte's nose. The ice cream ache was back. Charlotte had gone through sixteen Tylenol caplets since purchasing the bottle at the Marathon mini-mart in Iowa, and yet the headaches had continued plaguing her. It was as though she were in a perpetual state of psychic overload, like a television caught between two stations, the horizontal and vertical holds slipping, the sound waves wowing and fluttering between the various signals. Images and sensations popped and crackled on her mindscreen. Mountain roads plunged into darkness, the trees black against the sky, and windows, windows, windows, windows everywhere, some cracked, some painted over, some old and rotted in their frames.

Why windows?

She looked out the bus's window and saw a green mileage sign looming in the wake of the bus's high beams. It said *Sterling 30, Fort Morgan 70.*

Charlotte quickly calculated the remaining distance—using information gleaned from the Rocky Mountain area map that she had purchased in the Ogallala depot—and she realized that she was at least three hours away from Estes Park, probably at least six from Grand Lake. That would put her arrival sometime around dawn. The plan was to rent a car in Estes, then drive around the rim of the park until she reached the little mountain town of Grand Lake. Then she would find the "Stafford" family by simply asking people at Packard's Bar & Grill. It all seemed so simple, so clean and easy. But Charlotte knew deep down it would turn out to be none of those things. And this knowledge made her pulse quicken and her mouth go dry. She needed sleep badly, but she knew it was probably out of the question. She had so much adrenaline cooking in her veins right now, she was finding it difficult to keep from clawing her nails through the seat back in front of her.

She reached down and unzipped the knapsack.

The gun was still there, still wrapped in the paper towels she had taken from the Marathon station. Charlotte reached down and unwrapped it, then she wrapped her fingers around the rough surface of the grip—

—and electric current jolted up Charlotte's tendons—

(—*flames*—)

—and Charlotte sucked in a breath, flinching as though cold water had splashed her face—

(—*two hundred meters in the distance, I watch napalm sucking the sky into its gaping maw, the F-100s peeling away over the chartreuse horizon*—)

—and Charlotte was finding it hard to breathe now as vision invaded her brain—

(—*on my belly in the shit soup, trembling like a wet rat, crying, snot running down my face, helpless, helpless, as I watch the hellish scene unfold through my nightscope, the little fireballs rolling across the clearing, and now I realize they're civvies, they're children, Goddamn this fucking nightmare party, the fireballs are South Vietnamese civvie children on fire, and they're dying, and we gotta do something, they're dying, they're dying, they're dying*—)

"Ahhhh—!" Charlotte gasped suddenly, dropping the gun to the floor.

The gun landed with a dull clank on the flashlight,

and Charlotte sat back with a jerk, the residue of terror still flickering in her mind, still cleaving her skull like the strike of a dull axe. Waves of emotion were pouring over her, feelings that she shouldn't be here, that she was doing the wrong thing, that violence was tearing the human race apart.

"Good Lord," she muttered under her breath as the feelings subsided.

She carefully picked up the gun again, and now the grip seemed drained of energy—no more current, no more sparks. Keeping it hidden behind the seat in front of her, Charlotte glanced up and saw the driver at the front of the bus—the string bean in the Greyhound uniform, his silhouette hunched over the wheel—lost in the hypnotic rush of the highway. She turned back to the gun and ejected one of the magazines into her bandaged palm. Then she checked the cartridge, making sure the .22-caliber bullets were seated properly. She snapped the magazine back into the butt and put the gun back in the knapsack.

Another bolt of pain struck the bridge of her nose, radiating down through her temples. It felt like an *echo* of something, maybe a scream. Was it a message from Junior? Another memory of Vietnam clinging to the gun?

Right then an idea occurred to Charlotte.

To send a message.

A message.

She closed her eyes, and she started taking slow, deep breaths. In through the nose, then out through the mouth, in through the nose, then out through the mouth. Then the imagery. She imagined the top of her scalp being warmed by the sun, then her face, then her neck, then her collarbone, then her chest, then her ribs. Down through her body, she imagined herself softening, warming, relaxing. She had learned these techniques years ago, when she had begun doing her missing persons work, but now she was about to use them for an entirely new purpose.

Charlotte had never tried to send a thought before. But now she was desperate, and she was willing to try anything. So she imagined herself transforming into something new. Something sleek, aerodynamic, and omnipotent.

She imagined herself as a guided missile.

Armed herself with a single message, as simple as it was foreboding.

She imagined the words.

And she fired them off toward the western horizon.

35

Puppet Strings

They were in the living room when the seizure came.

It was the middle of the night, and the wind had been rattling the power wires outside, and they had been fighting—the whole family—down in the living room, bathed in the harsh, incandescent glare of a fallen lamp. The boys were cowering at the bottom of the steps, watching their parents spar near the fireplace. Sandy had just slapped Paul for lying about purchasing contraband weapons, dumping over the lamp, and Paul had just screamed back at her, "I'M ONLY TRYING TO DO THE RIGHT THING—!!"

And that's when the seizure hit.

Sandy couldn't believe her eyes, the way her husband's head snapped back as though yanked by invisible puppet strings. "Paul? What is it?"

"I—d-don't—" He tried to speak, but it looked as though something had lodged in his throat, making him gasp for air, his arms rising up, reaching out at the nothingness, trying to grasp at nothing.

"What is it, Paul? You're scaring me!"

"I—d-d-don't—nn-nnn—" His eyes popped wide again, and he whiplashed back against the wall. A framed portrait of the family was jostled from its hook; it skidded to the hardwood and shattered noisily. A potted plant on a nearby end table tipped over. Paul cringed against the wall, teeth gnashing, eyes slamming shut as though current were jolting through him. He tried to speak but his facial muscles were twitching now, tensing furiously. It was horrible to watch.

"Daddy!" One of the boys shrieked across the room—Sandy couldn't tell which one—and the sound of it shocked her into action.

She rushed over to Paul and put her arm around his waist. He felt hot, like an engine revving.

"They're—c-c-commmm—commmmm—" He was trying to get the words out, face flushed deep scarlet, veins bulging in his neck and his temple.

"It's okay, honey, I'm here, I'm here," she murmured, trying to comfort him, wondering if it was a stroke or an aneurysm or maybe some other kind of seizure. Sandy was pretty familiar with her husband's health, and she often worried about high blood pressure. He oversalted his food, and he drank too much, and with all the stress of being in the WITSEC program, he was a walking time bomb. That's why Sandy had always pushed him to exercise, eat better, cut down on the drinking. But now, watching him writhe against the wall, all Sandy's anger was boiling away, replaced by terror. She didn't want to lose him. The sad truth was, Sandy still loved the scrawny little bastard.

Then, all at once, Paul sagged in her arms.

"Honey?" Sandy tried to shake him, but he slipped out of her grasp and collapsed to the floor as though cut loose from the puppet strings. "Paul!" Sandy knelt down by her husband and cradled his shoulders, holding up his lolling head.

The boys had gathered behind her now and were gawking at their father.

Paul looked as though a grand piano had just fallen on his head. "I know what it is now," he said, almost inaudibly.

"What?"

He looked up at her. The wind moaned outside. *"They're coming."*

"Who's coming?"

Paul struggled to rise. It took him a moment, but he finally managed to get his feet under him and stand up against the wall. He was still a bit wobbly, but he took deep breaths, his eyes glimmering now with emotion. "I can't explain it," he said finally. "But these are the words that have been crackling in my brain the last two days: *They're coming.* And I know who 'they' are now. They're the Fabionnes. I swear— I know this for a fact—the Fabionnes are coming."

"Paul, how in God's name—?"

He grabbed her by the shoulders. "You've got to leave right now, Sandy."

"But how—?"

"Don't argue with me anymore, Sandy, you've got to take the boys in the Suburban and you have to get outta here. Tonight. *Now.*"

She gaped at him, too flustered to make sense of anything anymore. "W-where?"

He licked his lips, eyes shifting busily. "Okay . . . you'll drive down to Marshal Vincent's place in Durango. I've got the address to his ranch."

"Wait—wait, Paul—hold on a second, calm down. We'll call him. He said to call him in emergencies. We'll call the WITSEC people."

Paul shook his head vehemently. "No, honey, no! You have to get the boys out of here, and you have to do it now!"

"But—"

"Listen to me—I can't explain how I know this, but I do, I know they're coming! Do you understand what I'm saying?"

Sandy's mind was swimming with contrary emotions, her chest tightening.

She felt movement next to her, the trembling shoulder of a little boy.

"What about you, Dad?" Darryl's voice was barely a croak in the windy silence.

Paul looked at his son, then looked across the room at the front window. The weather had turned chilly for July, a storm front moving in. The atmosphere inside the house was like a damp cave, the cool, dank mildew of Colorado taking its toll on the Lattamores. Paul walked over to the window, pushing aside ruffled gingham curtains and gazing out. Finally, he turned back to his family and said, "It's high time I finished this thing once and for all."

36

The Spoiler

The weather around the front range of the Colorado Rockies had always been as moody as an unbroken horse. Strong winds, frequent storms, and thin, pungent air that seemed to magnify the sun—all contributed to the ebb and flow. The natives who lived in the cool blue shadows of the Big Thompson Canyon— elevation 7,500 feet—were all too familiar with this ever-churning climate. Throughout the summer, the sun would rise sharp and bright over the great plains to the east, burning off the dew and sending long shadows down the gorge. The air would turn crystalline, perfumed with pine and wild columbine. But by mid-morning, the first wisps of clouds would drift over the summit of Long's Peak to the west. And by noon, the gray ceiling would push down on the meadows and towns like a shroud, the rain starting like clockwork. The locals could tell time by it. Every day it would come, always obliterating the sun.

Once in a great while, though, the microclimate would turn itself inside out.

The meteorologists called them summer storm fronts, but folks around here knew them by another name. They called them spoilers. They called them spoilers because they spoiled the tourist trade; they spoiled all the innkeepers' hopes for lucrative cabin rentals, trail rides, camping expeditions, and just plain old retail spending. They spoiled the summer, spoiled the economy. And they spoiled everybody's mood for months. They usually crept in from the northwest, from the glacial winds of British Columbia, and they brought freakishly cold temperatures, violent storms, fast-changing conditions, and general misery to the population. And there was no telling how long one might last. Sometimes days, sometimes weeks, sometimes the whole damned summer.

Estes Park was in the grip of one hell of a spoiler when Charlotte Vickers arrived at the Dollar-Discount Car Rental office sometime around dawn. She was bone-tired from the walk across the plaza from the bus depot, and her nerves were frayed and crackling from the tension. She asked the man behind the counter for a subcompact, and she quickly filled out her name, address, and license number on the standard lease form. Then she tried to pay for it with Junior's credit card.

"This is your husband's card?" The clerk, an officious little fop with a cranberry-colored cardigan and meticulously groomed silver hair, was gazing at Charlotte over the tops of his half glasses.

"Yes, that's right," Charlotte said, her heart racing. The wind was rattling the glass door behind her, a skinned cat shrieking in her ears. The rental car office was barely two hundred square feet of carpeted space, a couple of metal chairs, a vending machine, and a wall full of cutesy graphics and rate sheets. It smelled of smoky, day-old coffee, and some flowery fragrance the clerk was wearing to mask his sour, cigarette-cured clothing.

The clerk glanced back down at Junior's MasterCard and pursed his lips. "We usually require two forms of identification."

"It's just a rent-a-car, for God's sake." Charlotte felt the bile rising in her gorge, the rage turning in her gut. "I gave you my license number."

"Nevertheless, we must see a valid driver's license and some other form of identification."

"I don't have it."

He smiled condescendingly. "Then you don't have a rental car."

"I'm not applying for a loan!"

"Ma'am, it's company policy—"

"COMPANY POLICY?!" Charlotte bellowed suddenly, grabbing the stubble where her beautiful hair used to be. Her eyes were watering with anger, and the man behind the counter was rearing back as though he'd just encountered a poisonous snake.

"Ma'am—"

"Wait a minute!—Wait!—What happened to simple courtesy?! What happened to kindness?!—helping somebody else just because they're in a jam?! *WHAT HAPPENED!*"

She ran out of breath, her heart thumping in her chest, the sheer intensity of her outburst making her dizzy. The man behind the counter had turned stone-faced, and Charlotte swallowed hard, wishing she could take it all back. She had never thrown a tantrum in a place of business before—never in her life—and it was scaring her. It felt as though she were finally coming completely unglued.

After a long moment, Charlotte said, "Sir, I apologize . . . I'm a little upset right now."

"Yes," he said, and there was no warmth in his eyes.

Charlotte took a breath, steadied herself. "As I said earlier, my husband is stranded in Grand Lake, and I need to get there as soon as possible. Please, I'm asking you if you can find it in your heart to help me."

The clerk stared at her. It was obvious there was nothing in his heart but nicotine and chilled blood.

It was over.

"I'm sorry," he said finally. "There's nothing I can do."

Charlotte nodded, staring at the counter for a moment, catching her breath.

Then she gathered up her things, her knapsack and Junior's wallet.

And she walked out.

The old man was sitting out in front of his cabin on Fish Creek Road, perched on a lawn chair, fiddling with a small gas heater. Bundled up in layers of long underwear and ratty sweaters, he had a head full of wispy white hair that fluttered in the wind and a huge, leprous face. There was a clutter of metal parts spread out on a newspaper in front of him, and he was holding the parts steady with his foot, trying to keep the newspaper from blowing away.

He looked up as Charlotte approached. His eyes were milky and unfocused, but kind.

Don't look desperate . . . He'll suspect something if you look desperate . . . Just play it cool, casual.

Charlotte was trying to keep her racing thoughts under control as she strode up the narrow dirt drive, sidestepping the weeds and columbine, nodding a greeting at the old codger. For some reason, his dilapidated A-frame cabin in the background, and the window boxes overflowing with pink larkspur and wild lilies, all suggested a kindly soul.

"Hi there," Charlotte said as she walked up to the man.

"Afternoon," he said with a nod.

"Looks like a nasty storm blowing in."

"You bet," he said, cocking his head at her, squinting into the cold wind. His expression wasn't mean, and it wasn't inhospitable, and yet it had a certain "state-your-business-please" look to it.

"I'm sorry to bother you this morning," Charlotte said then. "But I'm in a real jam."

"That right?"

"Yes, sir. Yes. I'm in a jam, and I need to get my hands on a car as soon as possible." She gestured toward the driveway to their left. The Ford Escort was parked in front of the garage door. It was a two-door, late-eighties model, not a lot of rust. Looked as though the mountain air had preserved it pretty well.

The old man looked at her, blinking, wiping his grizzled chin. "You need a what?" he said at last.

"Your car. I'm willing to pay top dollar to rent your car. Just for tonight. It's an emergency. And I've tried the rental place, and they won't give me a car without a license—"

"You don't have no license?"

"It's a long story. I really need a car bad. You could say it's a matter of life and death, and I'm willing to pay top dollar."

He put his lantern down. "I'm sorry, honey, but that car ain't for rental, or sale, or anything like that."

She was losing him. She was blowing it. She had to do something quick. Pulling Junior's wallet from her knapsack, she counted out two fifties, and five twenties—nearly all the cash Junior had left—and her hands trembled as she handed the money over to the old man. Then she dug out Junior's credit card. Her hands were trembling so convulsively now that she dropped the credit card in the dirt.

The old man was watching. "Honey, I can't take your money."

Charlotte picked up the credit card and handed it to the codger. "Please, take the credit card as collateral, just for one day. I promise you I'll have the car back by tomorrow. Please. I'm begging you."

The old guy pursed his lips. "This here credit card's liable to be as worthless as this lantern."

"Look at the expiration date, call the bank, call the credit card company."

"Whoa, whoa, all right, all right now, I ain't saying

I don't believe ya." The old man looked at the money and credit card in his hand for a long time. Then he glanced over at the Escort. He was chewing on it now.

Charlotte could feel her pulse racing in her ears, her stomach tightening.

—*please, please, please*—

The old man sighed, nodding at the Escort. "The brakes stick a little bit, and she needs a tank of gas."

37

Phone Calls

"Jesus-Freakin'-Christ!" Digger Mussolino jerked away from the table, his big hands rising up in the air, the camper lurching slightly around a turn.

The asshole on the table had just puked his guts out down through the headrest, moaning like a frigging injured dog, writhing in agony, the vomit spraying down across the carpet beneath him, some of it spattering part of Digger's Italian boot and a good portion of his pant leg—all because the gray-haired cocksucker wouldn't stop being a hero. *The prick.* Even after they gave him a break last night, leaving him alone for a few hours to catch his breath, and even after they fed him this morning—a piece of toast and a couple gulps of Jack—he was still being a cocksucker, answering their questions with jokes, hollering out his name, rank, and serial number. The chiropractor had pulled out all the stops, too, yanking the man's back so far out of line, the bastard looked like a freaking car wreck. But still no mention of the town Lattamore was living in. Finally, around nine o'clock this morning, as the camper approached the outskirts of Denver—the camper's floor vibrating from all the potholes and rough road—Digger had gotten so pissed off he had told the chiropractor to go ahead and kill the guy, just go ahead and kill him, kill him slowly, kill him like a fucking insect.

But when the chiropractor had started wrenching

the guy's neck backward like a stubborn turkey leg, the guy had upchucked all over the place.

Now the vomit was clinging to Digger's double-buckle Armani boots, the pasty chunks of toast, bile, and liquor splattered across the front of his pin-striped Missoni slacks. Digger hated getting his threads dirty. It only served to remind him that he was still just a soldier, still just a mid-level button man working for a failing family, getting his hands dirty in the shit of everyday business. And now the anger was rising in Digger like a black tide of acid as he stared down at the particles of vomit on his pant leg. He reached inside his sharkskin jacket and pulled out one of the Kimber .45s from his belt. Snapping back the slide on the gun, he went over to the cocksucker on the table.

"Get away from him, Doc."

"But I think we're close to a breakthrough," the little doctor protested, catching his breath, wiping his hands on a towel, his eyebrows furrowed with concern as he stared at the gun. "If you'll just give me another—"

"Get away from him!" Digger aimed the gun down at Junior's head.

"But I'm certain—"

"GET THE FUCK AWAY FROM HIM!" Digger's voice was cracking with homicidal rage.

The doctor backed away.

"I'm through fucking with you," Digger said, pressing the barrel against Junior's skull. "Look at me, you stupid cocksucker—LOOK AT ME!"

Junior muttered something inaudible.

"What?" Digger snapped back the hammer, preparing to pull the trigger. "What did you say, you prick?!"

"Do it," Junior muttered softly with swollen lips and cottony mouth.

"Fuck you!"

"Do it."

"LOOK AT ME, YOU COCKSUCKER!" Digger reached down and yanked the man's face upward, stretching torn tendons and slipped vertebrae, and their gazes met, and the two men stared at each other for quite a long moment. And there was no fear in Junior's eyes. There was no fear at all. Only a soft glimmer of serenity—a sort of knowing—which Digger recognized immediately. Digger had seen that look only a couple of times in his long and checkered career as an enforcer for the Fabionne family. It was present in the gazes of two types of people—complete sociopaths and devout clergymen, both of whom had no fear of dying. Digger smiled knowingly, and then said, "You know, being tough is not all it's cracked up to be . . ."

The cellular phone started ringing across the room.

Digger wavered for a moment.

Then he closed the hammer down with his thumb, swinging the barrel up and away.

"Saved by the bell—huh, Parrick?" he said dryly, still shaking slightly from all the pent-up anger. He went over to the tiny Formica booth adjacent to the stove. The flip phone was lying on the tabletop amid a clutter of empty bottles, candy wrappers, overflowing ashtrays, and dirty paper plates. It was cooing noisily, and Digger felt a strange twinge in his gut. It was either somebody from the Romani family back in Omaha with more useless information, or it was the Queen Bitch herself calling from Denver.

Digger picked up the phone, pressed the send button, and said, "Yeah."

A shrill voice piercing the static: "Where the hell are you guys?"

"Miss Fortunato?"

"No, it's Mother Teresa—where the hell *are* you, Digger?"

Digger glanced across the camper's living area to the front fire wall, where a narrow strip of glass was letting in the overcast daylight. The cab was visible on the other side, Rondo Hatton's beefy shoulder, the back of his fat head, his roly-poly body hunched over the steering wheel. He was digging in a sack of caramel corn in his lap, munching compulsively like a fucking baboon. The camper was heading west on Highway 76, about ten miles outside of Denver, and Digger could see the surrounding landscape of industrial parks and rugged brown hills stretching off into the distant rock-cuts. He hated this area. Too much goddamn nature.

"We're almost to Denver," Digger said. "Are you calling from Chicago?"

"No, I'm not calling from Chicago," the voice chimed back over the line, sounding disgusted and excited in equal measures. "I'm in Denver. I couldn't stand waiting for you jokers one more second."

"You're in Denver?" Digger's stomach churned.

"We found her, Digger. No thanks to you and your genius doctor."

"You found her?" Digger blinked, adjusting his collar, not believing what he had just heard.

"That's what I said, Digger—blow the wax out of your ears, for Chrissake!"

Digger was speechless. His Versace shirt felt too tight all of a sudden, and his heart had started pumping a little faster. After all the bullshit he had been through tracking this psychic bitch and her boyfriend across hell and high waters, watching Lou St. Louis turn a man into ground hamburger, and finally—perhaps the worst indignity of them all—getting his Armani shoes covered in puke . . . he has to hear *this* from Natalie Fucking Fortunato. It was absolutely the worst fucking possible scenario. How was Digger supposed to impress the boss now? How was Big John

Fabionne going to feel when he learned that his best men couldn't track down a measly little psychic gal?

How the hell did this happen?

How in God's name did the Fortunato broad do it?

It had been so simple . . .

After all the frantic phone calls to the morons out on the highway, all the meetings with representatives from the eight western families, all the calls to Papa John down in Marion (where the old man was keeping track of the chase by putting stickpins in a map), all the cartons of Tarrytons and cans of Diet Rite and tabs of Valium and jiggers of Absolut vodka in her room at the Denver Four Seasons—after *all this*—it was amazing that a couple of simple phone calls could give the psychic away.

"Digger?" Natalie had the cell phone wedged against her shoulder as she dug in her purse for a cigarette. She was perched in the rear of a Sedan Deville, her whippet-thin body clad in a purple silk pantsuit, her bony ass nestled in the buttery leather throne as the car sped westward on Highway 70. The driver was a member of the Ciccioni crew out of Phoenix, a stone-deadly button man with a peroxide blond flattop and a magenta sunlamp tan. He drove like a machine, quiet and well oiled, which pleased Natalie immensely.

"Did you hear what I said?" Natalie barked into the phone. "Digger?"

After a moment of hissing silence, a terse voice: "Yes, ma'am."

Natalie rolled her eyes at the idiocy of her own men. With capos like these, it was no wonder her father had landed in jail. But *that* little problem was about to be reconciled in a big way. Natalie Fortunato was about to bring hell and damnation down on the fuck-heads who had set her dad up. She was about to restore the delicate balance. "I want you to meet us in a place called Grand Lake," she said into the phone, pulling a cigarette out of a sterling silver case and lighting it. "You got that?"

"Grand Lake, yeah, got it."

"It's about a hundred miles outta Denver, some of it mountain roads. Should take you about three hours."

"Got it."

"We'll meet at a little bar called Packard's."

"Mind if I ask you a question?"

"Make it quick, Digger."

"If you don't mind me asking, how did you find her?"

Natalie took a luxurious drag off her cigarette, exhaled, thinking about those simple phone calls.

In truth, it had been Judy Dandridge, Natalie's assistant, who had performed the first miracle.

Early this morning, Natalie had heard Judy's muffled footsteps in the adjoining suite, her voice yacking on the telephone with somebody, and it had given Natalie an A-number-one headache. But minutes later, Judy had come bursting into Natalie's room, throwing up the shades, babbling something about finding a needle in a haystack. Judy had been calling rental car offices in various tourist towns—Aspen, Telluride, Durango, Crested Butte, Winter Park—posing as a private detective's assistant, and had struck pay dirt at a Dollar-Discount franchise in Estes Park. The counterman described a woman who had come in just this morning, demanding a car without the proper identification, throwing a tantrum because she had to get to Grand Lake.

Upon hearing this, Natalie had sprung out of bed, throwing on a robe and kissing Judy on the lips. After ordering coffee from room service, Natalie decided to make a few calls herself before contacting Digger and Company. If the psychic had tried to rent a car in

Estes Park in order to get to Grand Lake, then she must have been seen by other locals. Natalie got on the phone, called the rental place back, and asked where the closest gas station was, and the counterman gave her two names: Clark's Conoco on 34, and the Chevron mini-mart on MacGragor Avenue. She called the stations, and a kid at the second place said he just gave directions to a gal in a Ford Escort.

Told her how to get to a place called Grand Lake, a place called Packard's.

"You want to know how I found her?" Natalie finally said, gazing out the tinted window of the sedan, sucking on her Tarryton with rose-lacquered lips.

"Yes, ma'am—I'm curious."

Natalie grinned. "It's because I'm psychic—now get your asses up there!"

Then she clicked off the phone.

38

The Green Cathedral

It took Charlotte about fifteen minutes to find her way across Estes Park using the thumbnail directions provided by the young man at the Chevron station. Shrouded in the miserable gray morning mist, the town had not yet awakened, its promenade of curio shops and boardwalks still quiet as museum exhibits: the Copper Penny five-and-dime, Ripley's Believe-It-Or-Not, Erewhon Outfitters, the Wheel Bar, the Salt-water Taffy Shoppe with its ancient stainless steel taffy puller turning lazily in the window. It all seemed like a dream, like a ghost-town diorama waiting for the doors to open. But when Charlotte reached the outskirts of town, the cheap tourist trappings were engulfed by the vast green waves of wilderness.

By this time, Charlotte was just getting used to the atmosphere inside the Escort. The vinyl was impregnated with the old man's odors, a mixture of Old Spice and coffee and stale tobacco and spent air fresheners. The defroster made intermittent whistling noises like a teakettle that just couldn't fully come to a boil, and loose coins rattled around beneath the seats. But the engine still ran smoothly and softly. And for a car with a hundred and fifty thousand plus miles on it, you couldn't ask for much more.

Clutching the steering wheel, Charlotte saw unbidden images from the old man's life flickering across her mindscreen—a string of desolate hotel rooms, a retired Fuller Brush salesman, a lonely widower trying to kick his alcoholism. There were old, yellowed newspapers on the backseat—the old man was trying to impress a neighbor lady by recycling—and Charlotte felt a wave of sadness washing over her, and she struggled to block the circuit. She needed to think about Paul right now. She needed to concentrate.

Without warning, a dark shape materialized on the edge of the forest.

The Fall River Ranger Station was situated at the northernmost entrance to the Rocky Mountain National Park. A modest little cabin with a rough-hewn roof, a few offices, and a roadside service window, the station had its blinds drawn across the front facade as Charlotte pulled up to the gate.

She rolled down her window and called out, "Hello—anybody home?"

There was no answer. Charlotte checked her watch and saw that it was 8:58 A.M. The sign above the service window said *Ranger Station Hours: 8:00 A.M. to 6:00 P.M.,* but the service window still had a shade drawn down across it, and there didn't seem to be a soul inside the place.

Charlotte honked the horn, chewing her lip nervously, fingers tingling under her bandage. Rain misted across the Escort's windshield, fogging the glass. Charlotte zipped up her windbreaker, then turned on the defroster. The fan rattled, and the compressor crooned high opera. Charlotte breathed in the Alpine air from outside the window, which was bracing. The rain had sharpened in the last few hours, and now there was a colder smell on the wind.

Maybe snow at the higher elevations.

Inside the ranger cabin something stirred, a shadowy figure approaching the window. The shade snapped up suddenly, revealing a young, stocky, athletic-looking woman with strawberry blond hair pulled back in a tight ponytail.

Charlotte managed a nervous smile. "Morning, hi, how are you?"

"Morning," the ranger girl said after sliding the window open. Even in her green park uniform she looked to be barely in her twenties. No makeup. No nonsense. She was holding a cup of coffee with the National Park seal on the side of the cup. "Can I help you, ma'am?" she said.

"Gotta get to Grand Lake as soon as possible," Charlotte told her.

The ranger girl nodded. "Okay, you have to turn around and take Highway 7 down to Raymond, then take 72 all the way around Central City, then take 40 up to Grand Lake. Should take you about five, six hours."

Charlotte felt the panic spurting through her stomach. "The kid at the Chevron station said I should go through the park—take the Trail Road, something like that?"

"Trail Ridge Road," the ranger girl corrected, taking a sip of coffee. "Takes you right over the Continental Divide, beautiful trip. Gets you to Grand Lake in less than two hours."

"That's what I want to do."

The ranger girl was shaking her head sadly. "No, ma'am, not today you don't. Believe me."

"But the kid said—"

"The kid would have been one hundred percent right, if the road was open. Trail Ridge Road is not open today. I'm totally sorry, ma'am. It's a gorgeous drive in August. Today, it's not so gorgeous."

Charlotte chewed on her lip some more, gazing through the windshield at the gate in front of her. It hung across the path, a twelve-foot length of rough pine. There was a little metal *STOP* sign tacked at the center, and one end was attached to a motorized housing. Charlotte felt gooseflesh crawling along the backs of her arms. It would be so easy to step on the gas and burst through that flimsy little gate—but *then* what? The rangers would probably catch her before she got halfway up the side of the mountain. Plus, by bursting through the gate, she would only be attracting attention to herself, which was the last thing she wanted to do.

"Okay, honey, fair enough," she finally said to the girl in the window. "Thanks for the directions."

"Sorry about the inconvenience," the ranger girl said, blowing on her coffee.

"Don't worry about it," Charlotte said, shifting the Escort into reverse.

She backed away from the ranger station, then took off across the lot toward the main road. But as she approached the *STOP* sign at the lot's exit, she noticed a small loop of blacktop snaking back down a hill adjacent to the ranger station. The road curled into a scenic little cul-de-sac bordered by columns of aspen trees. There were a few picnic tables and a couple of fire grates bolted to the ground.

On impulse, Charlotte turned down the road and pulled into the cul-de-sac.

She parked and sat there for several moments, not knowing exactly what to do.

Some time later—it seemed like hours, but in fact was probably more like five minutes—the ranger girl emerged from the cabin dressed in a rain poncho, carrying an armful of wooden trail marker signs. She vanished behind the cabin for a moment, doing something with the signs that Charlotte couldn't quite make out. The sound of Jeep doors opening and closing could be heard echoing through the mist. Charlotte glanced across the opposite side of the cul-de-sac and saw a window of opportunity open for just a split second. There was a rutted footpath that started at the edge of the cul-de-sac, running west along the park entrance, then vanishing into the woods. A shifty backpacker could creep along this path and avoid the ranger station completely. It was wide, too—just wide enough for a compact car to negotiate. Charlotte realized this in the space of an instant, and she acted without hesitation, putting the car in gear and giving it some gas.

The Escort jumped the curb, then started up the hill.

Charlotte held her breath the whole way, expecting the ranger girl to dart into view at any moment, waving madly, hollering warnings. But evidently the cabin was far enough in the distance, and the ranger girl was suitably occupied with her signs not to notice. The mist was coming down in sheets now, heavy enough to muffle the sound of the Escort's tires crunching gravel, snapping twigs, and thumping over stones.

Finally the Escort reached the pavement on the other side of the entrance gate.

Charlotte gave it a little more gas, and the car scooted up the macadam.

It was like driving into a dark green cathedral, the towers of ancient spruce trees blotting out the gray sky, the light dwindling abruptly, the air dropping several degrees. Charlotte flipped on her lights. She could hear her heartbeat thumping in her ears, barely drowned by the windy silence of the trees and the Escort's engine. She glanced up at the rearview mirror and saw the ranger shack receding into the distance behind her, shrinking into a tunnel of faint daylight.

Then she turned back to the road ahead . . .

. . . preparing herself to learn just why they would close a major artery like Trail Ridge Road in the middle of summer.

39

Ice

It took her a full hour to reach the ten-thousand-foot line, but it seemed like an eternity.

Charlotte was gripping the steering wheel so tightly, the knuckles on her left hand looked like icy white stones, the bandage on her right stretched as taught as a drum head. The car was climbing through the frozen sleet, inching along at just over twenty miles an hour, the radio sizzling with static, the sound of the sleet like firecrackers against the frosted glass of her windshield. Her body was a coiled knot of nervous tension and crackling, indistinct psychic signals. What month was it? What continent was she on? Antarctica? Iceland? She managed a fleeting glance out the side window and saw the world ending a mere five feet beyond the edge of the narrow pavement.

Beyond that was a half-mile drop down a rocky precipice into a sea of Englemann spruce.

Welcome to the roof of the world.

Up until now, the journey had taken her around dangerous switchbacks and suicide hairpins that jutted out over oblivion like a carnival ride, and she was still well below the tree line, still well over ten miles from the midway point. Along the way she had encountered a couple of deer poised on the shoulder at 9,000 feet, a badger scurrying across her path at 9,500 feet, and a chain across the road at 9,750 feet alerting her that this road was indeed closed—a chain which she had unceremoniously snapped in two with the Escort's dented front bumper. But she had yet to encounter another driver fool enough to be on this road. Probably the only saving grace was the fact that the sleet and fog had thickened to the point where she couldn't see a thing in front of her, in back of her, or along either side. She was enveloped in a cloud, and that was just fine with her.

The radio sputtered and sizzled, too high to pick up any stations.

Charlotte kept her gaze locked on the road ahead of her, a twenty-foot belt of white lines and wasted concrete that seemed to materialize out of the fog, then roll under the car. The Escort was whining in low gear, its oxygen-starved engine working overtime, climbing, climbing—the little engine that couldn't— and Charlotte felt her injured hand starting to tingle. Out her side window, she noticed the trees dwindling down to sickly little dwarfs and crooked scrubs, and she realized she was above the tree line—the land of tundra—a world so far above sea level that photosynthesis breaks down and only scattered varieties of flora and fauna still survive. It was an alien planet up here, and thank God Charlotte could only see the limited periphery offered by the gray tunnel of mist around her.

If she saw how high she was, she would wet herself.

She reached down and fiddled with the radio dials, making a futile attempt to tune in a station. For some reason, Charlotte had always been soothed by talk radio; no matter how rattled she was, no matter what she was doing, the modulated tones of professional broadcasters had always comforted her. And now she needed that comfort more than ever. She needed a safety line, an anchor, *something* to connect her to the civilized world. So she kept dialing, coaxing static out of the tiny speaker, dialing back and forth across the band, back and forth, back and—

—then she glanced up.

The sudden brightness shrieked at her, the mist parting like a curtain.

And Charlotte's heart stopped as she gaped at the breathtaking panorama materializing outside her puny little car—so much space, so vast, so infinite in the waves of silver sunlight, lashed by seventy-mile-per-hour winds—and the realization struck her all at once that she had risen through the top of the clouds—through the actual *top* of the clouds!—and now she was messing with God, and her eyes could barely absorb the monolithic, snowcapped peaks stretching off into the distance, their jagged glacier-carved slopes the color of frozen mercury, and she realized almost simultaneously that it was twelve thousand feet down on either side of the road. And right then she did what comes naturally, instinctively, innately to any creature of the late twentieth century—

—*she slammed on the brakes.*

The Escort went into a skid across a sheet of ice, skimming toward the edge of a hairpin curve. Charlotte felt her sphincter muscles contracting, her buttocks puckering, her tendons tightening into steel cables. She was paralyzed, helpless, she couldn't even scream. All she could do was gawk—bug-eyed—as the Escort slid sideways toward the edge of the cliff.

Then it went over the side.

40

Howl

The human mind can turn inward on itself like a turtle shrinking into its shell. Whether it's neurochemical evolution, innate reptile-brain muscle memory, or just plain old survival instinct, it usually happens in times of intense and sudden stress, and it often feels as though a hidden armor has suddenly snapped down over a person's psyche—like the bulletproof blinds on the windows of a military base.

Charlotte was hiding inside that fortress now, feeling her rental car careen backward down the side of the cliff, the world tilting on its axis, and all she could do was hold on, and cringe against the tidal wave of noise and feelings assaulting her mind, and then things were speeding up like an old motion picture traveling too fast through the projector, because the car was vibrating madly now, the sound of its tires scraping raw gravel and tundra, and Charlotte was screaming now but no sound was coming out of her, no air was coming out of her lungs.

Then the rear bumper slammed hard into rock.

Charlotte was sucked into the seats, taking most of the skull-rattling impact with her shoulder and her arm, fireworks filling her vision for a moment. Then there was nothing but silence, as abrupt and profound as the parting of the clouds. Charlotte collapsed across the seats in a fetal ball, wincing, holding her hands in front of her face in a totally involuntary gesture of self-preservation. And she lay there like that for several moments as the mist and fog cleared, the whipcord winds buffeting the side of the dented Escort.

Then she managed to sit up and look around.

Several moments passed before Charlotte realized what had happened.

The car had fallen down the *inside* bank of a switchback curve, its engine dying. The slope—although a steep seventy or eighty degrees—was barely over twenty feet long. After skidding down the embankment, the Escort had landed on the hard shoulder of the road coming back the *other* direction. And now it was taking Charlotte another few moments to realize how lucky she had been. Jacking the steering wheel a couple of centimeters in the wrong direction might have sent the Escort slipping off the opposite side of the hairpin, the side with the two-thousand-foot vertical drop. Charlotte shivered. Her body ached, her head dizzy with adrenaline.

The wind howled against the Escort's thin metal skin.

"WHAT AM I DOING!"

Charlotte's cry was shredded up with emotion, and she turned and slammed her bandaged fist against the window.

"WHAT AM I DOING WHAT AM I DOING WHAT AM I DOING—!!" She punched the glass again, and again, and again, until finally the window cracked, spider veins of fractures blooming across frosted glass. Charlotte sat back, breathing hard in the driver's seat, holding her wounded hand. She looked down at her bandage and saw the dark stain growing underneath the fabric, and she flexed her fingers a few times.

The pain helped. The pain was a smelling salt, bracing her, waking her up. She reached down, slammed the car into neutral, and turned the key. The engine whined, complaining loudly in the thin air. Then it kicked in, and Charlotte revved it for several moments, hands vise-clamping the steering wheel, nostrils stinging from the high altitude.

The wind roared at her again, making the Escort tremble, but Charlotte barely noticed it now. She was buzzing with .anger. Nothing was going to stop her now: not twelve thousand feet of storms, not hundred-mile-an-hour winds, not narrow switchbacks that jump out of nowhere like ghosts.

Not even the waves of primal dread surging through her like hot current.

She put the car into gear, then took off.

Toward the swirling storms on the western horizon . . .

. . . as unpredictable as Charlotte's future.

PART IV

THE BULLET

"In violence,
we forget who we are . . ."
—MARY MCCARTHY
On the Contrary

41

Chicken in a Foxhole

The Grand Lake Sheriff's Department was not exactly Fort Apache the Bronx. It was housed in a ramshackle annex of weathered gray clapboard and shingles tacked onto the back of the post office, the same building once used for storing dead letters. Inside the building, things were even less extraordinary. A single room of bare hardwood flooring and cheap fiberboard partitions, it featured three dented metal desks—each facing a wall—and one stained wooden counter facing the door. There was a pop machine in one corner which hadn't worked in years, a dusty rubber plant on one of the windowsills, and a faded portrait of Governor Roy Romer above the coffee machine. There was also a gun locker in the back by the rest room. The locker hadn't been opened since Reagan left office.

At the moment, Peggy Durmeyer was standing at the counter, sorting through complaint forms, filing the closed cases in green Pendaflex binders, the open cases in red binders. A gangly young woman with a shopping mall hairstyle that looked like a lopsided cheese soufflé and a pink sweatshirt that said *Party Hearty* in sequined script, Peggy was the department's secretary. She had seen it all, and she had done it all. And if knowledge was power, Peggy Durmeyer was Sheena, Queen of the Jungle, because Peggy knew everything there was to know about Grand County and its denizens. But at the moment, something was going on that Peggy Durmeyer just couldn't figure out. And it had something to do with the call that had come in early this morning.

That Brinks lady—the one from the bus—who said something bad was going to happen in Grand Lake.

"So whattya think that gal was talking about?" Peggy asked innocently, snapping her gum, not taking her eyes off the files in front of her, but all the while thinking that something really big was going down.

"Who the hell knows," the sheriff said from across the room, leaning against the bathroom door, chewing on a toothpick, watching his deputy squat down by the gun locker. Dressed in his brown county uniform, Sheriff Jay Flynn was a large, soft man with thick glasses and thinning blond hair combed back in strands. When he talked, he reminded Peggy of that big cartoon rooster—Foghorn Leghorn—but the things he said were usually pretty darned smart. Once upon a time Sheriff Flynn was a lean and mean Texas Ranger, but then his eyesight went bad, and his wife's chicken fried steak turned his muscles to mush. Now he was just a kindly old coot marking time in these little backwater barracks. The only problem was, ever since that phone call had come in, he seemed about as jumpy as a chicken in a foxhole.

"What are you two boys up to?" Peggy said, turning around and gazing back at them.

The deputy, Claude Templeton, was squatting down on the floor by the rest room, fiddling a key into the door of the gun locker. Templeton was a scrawny little guy with a Marine crew cut and a tattoo on his left forearm that said *Semper Fi,* even though he had never served in the military and the closest he had ever come to being a Marine was watching reruns of *Gomer Pyle.* Peggy liked Templeton nonetheless; he had always been polite and a perfect gentleman, and he worshipped the ground Sheriff Flynn walked on.

Templeton's father had died years ago, and Peggy always figured the deputy had sort of adopted Sheriff Flynn as his surrogate father. "Just trying to be prepared, Peggy," Claude Templeton murmured as he opened the door of the gun locker.

"What the hell you boys getting into *that* stuff for?"

"Don't you give us a hard time now, Peggy," the sheriff said, talking around his toothpick.

Peggy snapped her gum a couple of times. "You boys are liable to shoot your feet off."

The sheriff wasn't paying any attention to her; instead he was looking down at the blue steel racked inside the locker. "What do we got there, Claude?"

The deputy pulled out a shotgun. "Let's see, looks like a Mossberg, 12-gauge, pistol grip." He laid the weapon on the floor like a trophy fish.

"Got any magazines?"

"Yessir, coupla eight-rounders . . ." He pulled out a pair of black metal cartridges, set them on the floor. ". . . and another shotgun, looks like an Italian MAG 12." He pulled out another shotgun, laid it on the floor. This one was smaller, with a wooden stock and a larger bore.

"What about shells?" The sheriff kept nervously picking his teeth.

"Yessir, got plenty of buckshot—looks like double-ought."

The deputy pulled out several boxes of ammo and set them on the floor.

Peggy couldn't believe what she was seeing: a couple of overgrown little boys playing army. She walked over to where they were standing, then gazed down at the miniature arsenal spread out on the floor. The weapons and boxes of ammunition were neatly arrayed across the hardwood. They seemed so out of place in the dusty little office. Peggy was disgusted. Hands on her hips, Dentyne gum working busily in her mouth, she finally said, "Pity the poor fool who tries to speed in *this* county."

There was absolute silence.

Peggy looked up and saw that neither the sheriff nor the deputy was smiling.

Milner Pass was a vast glacial notch, strewn with prehistoric boulders and scabrous vegetation.

By the time Charlotte had reached the other side of the pass—and had started her descent down the western slope of Jackstraw Mountain—she was driving like a geriatric, creeping along the icy pavement at just over twenty miles an hour, tensing at every gust, every squall of sleet. The clouds had engulfed her again, and her entire body ached.

The trip was starting to take its toll.

By the time she reached Farview Curve, the light was swallowed by the shadows again, the sleet turning to rain—heavy mountain rain, the kind that could dent a tin roof. It filtered down through the dark primordial towers of bristlecone pines, making deafening noises across the Escort's thin molded roof, blinding Charlotte in the gelid wash across her windshield. She could smell the forest through her defroster. It smelled of cold stone and river rot and moose droppings, and it tightened her gut, and it made her all the more angry. Her brain was filled with hornets now.

A couple more miles of winding road, and then the pavement started to widen.

It might have been the change in the terrain, the denseness of the forest, the increasing number of directional signs, or the effects of the lower altitudes—Charlotte's ears had been popping for the last three thousand feet or so. It might have even been the psychic proximity of the Lattamore family working on Charlotte's fevered brain. But whatever the cause, Charlotte started breathing a little faster, her heart quickening slightly as she steered the Escort down the winding park road. A few moments later, a sign loomed out of the trees to her right.

It said *Kawuneechee Visitors Center—Grand Lake Entrance Station—¼ mile.*

Adrenaline spurted in her stomach, and she bit down on her lip, nearly breaking the skin. This was it. It was all boiling down to these next few moments. She tightened her grip on the wheel and felt her bandaged fingers tingling. What if Lattamore was already gone? What if he was already *dead*? She could barely swallow, her throat was so dry. She hadn't expected this part to be so difficult, so intimidating. But so many things could go wrong, so many variables. She felt as though she were driving into a trap. She wondered if Fortunato's men were waiting for her at this very moment.

Another ranger station materialized in the rain up ahead, a small pine cabin plopped right down on the center island bisecting the entrance and exit lanes. There was a gate lowered across the entrance. Charlotte roared toward the exit, without even glancing inside the shack.

A moment later, she came to a stop at a muddy four-way intersection.

Gazing out across the valley to the west, Charlotte licked her dry lips, heart racing. The intersection overlooked a muddy little tourist town a quarter of a mile away, nestled among the trees next to a crescent-shaped lake. And before Charlotte could draw another breath, she felt the machete-edge pain strike her nose—

(—*a sudden pistol shot cracking open the sky, the dark liquid spatter of blood looping out across the snow*—)

—and she slammed her eyes shut until the unbidden sensations went away.

Then she gave the car some gas and headed into the little town known as Grand Lake.

42

The 'Nam Light

Junior Parrick was engulfed in a haze of pain and disorientation, bright yellow flames clouding his bleary vision. His lower extremities were paralyzed, burned to a crisp from the fire, his spine like a flare that was sputtering out. And the camper was a ship on a stormy sea, winding up the narrow mountain roads, engine howling, the swaying motions and shifting g-forces threatening to topple the massage table. But Junior fought the urge to give up, the urge to flicker out like a candle flame. Basically, he had two choices: He could die, or he could pull off the greatest escape since Houdini did the water cell torture trick back in the 1920s.

Junior could sense the presence of the Bad Man with the Stick behind him, hovering . . . but now Junior was remembering something from long ago.

—*way down low in the valley behind Hill 56, a wooded knoll just off a nameless tributary of the Mekong River, and it's dusk, and the light is like no other light in the world, the light is the 'Nam light, that furry green-yellow glow, and you're hunkered down again. And this time it's just you. Just you and the weeds and the centipedes. And your Winchester Model-70. And the pain. Don't forget the pain. The pain is alive in your joints and your chest—*

—and just then, the camper shivered over a series of potholes, and Junior flinched, and he tried to keep his eyes closed, and he tried to let the memories of his military training carry him away again—

—*and you ignore the pain, you ignore it. In fact, you're beyond ignoring it. You don't even know it's there, because you're a combat sniper, and the combat sniper is a master of disengagement. Disengagement of fear, of feelings, of pain. You control your vitals. Slow down your breathing, your heart rate, your metabolism. You become a part of the landscape. Until there is only you and*—

—the Bad Man with the Stick saying something now in his low voice.

Junior was slowly drifting away. Junior was floating off into the vast green darkness of his memories. And all that was left was his fantasy.

A memory that had never occurred.

A secret revision of history—

—*in that place, that statue place, that cobra-calm stillness where you find that optimum performance level. Your body is so still now, a huge marsh beetle is crawling across your forehead, and you don't even need to bat it away. You're simply aware of it, and you're disengaged from it, as you are from every other external stimulus around you*—

—*except one*—

—*one last feeling before the night swallows you forever*—

—*you manage to reach into the pocket of your camo jacket and pull out a small object. About the size of a postage stamp. Dogeared and soggy from endless, repetitive rubbing. It's a small college photograph from some anonymous yearbook. A girl, her lovely cherubic face framed by lush, raven black curls. Stunning blue eyes. Your sweetheart. Your reason to get back to the World.*

Charlotte.

She smiles out at you, her gaze nourishing, full of

*secret intimacies. Her presence flows into you. Gives
you hope. You take one last look at the photograph,
then you close your fist around it and hold it tightly.
It's the closest thing you have now to a future.*

Hold her tight.

Don't ever forget her.

As the long, dark night closes in.

Charlotte twitched suddenly, grabbing the edge of
the bar to brace herself. Her mind was crackling again
with signals, noise, shapeless feelings. If she were a
cat, her back would be arching right now.

"You okay, ma'am?" the Marlboro Man asked suddenly, reaching out with his leathery hands to steady
her.

"I'm fine, I'm just fine—I'm okay," Charlotte gib-
bered, trying to catch her breath.

She was standing inside the fragrant darkness of
Packard's Bar & Grill, the cool odors of stale cigarette
smoke and rancid beer mingling with the overcooked
grease and ammonia-scented filth from the kitchen.
The rain was still coming down with a vengeance outside, pounding the roof, the muffled roar nearly
drowning the tinny squawk of country music from the
jukebox. The place was relatively slow for a weekday
lunch hour—probably due to the weather. A couple
of rednecks bellied up to the bar to Charlotte's immediate left, and a few vacationers and townspeople huddled in booths along the tinted front window. For the
last five minutes or so, Charlotte had been trying to
convince the Marlboro Man that she wasn't crazy, that
she had a legitimate reason to find out where the
Stafford family lived. But now her emotions were
starting to seep through like those staticky voices in-
terfering with the shortwave radio in her head. And
all the nervous tics and fidgeting were making Mr.
Marlboro Man very suspicious.

"Listen, Miss . . . ?"

"Smith," Charlotte said tersely, trying to smile, trying to appear at ease.

"Right, Miss Smith . . . the thing of it is, I sorta got a policy about telling strangers where to find people." He was fishing in his vest pocket for a crumpled pack of Luckies. "You know how it is."

Charlotte took a deep breath. "I understand what you're saying, I really do, and I think it's a lovely policy, but this is . . . an exceptional situation."

The Marlboro Man lit his last Lucky Strike, took a deep, lusty drag, then glanced around the bar, a smile creasing his tanned face. He was missing one of his eyeteeth. "Define *exceptional*," he said.

"It's very important."

"How important?"

"It's a family matter," Charlotte said after giving it some thought. She was ready to start spinning the lies—*anything* to get the information from this obnoxious, arms-dealing bully. "It's very personal," she added.

The Marlboro Man smiled again. "How personal?"

Charlotte felt the anger knifing up her belly, the static crackling in her head. What in God's name was going on here? Was this redneck flirting with her? The country music kept droning incessantly on in the background—Lee Greenwood singing something about being a good American—and it was barely audible above the rain and thunder echoing in the distance. Charlotte glanced at her watch: 12:30 P.M. *Already*. Time was getting away from her, the sense of impending disaster as palpable as her racing heartbeat.

She looked up at the Marlboro Man and finally realized what he was doing.

"I don't have any cash," Charlotte said suddenly.

"What?"

"All I have is a debit card."

"Congratulations."

"I'll be happy to give it to you, and you can call the bank and—"

"I don't want your money, lady," Marlboro Man said, flicking ashes on the floor.

Charlotte was burning her gaze into him. "Are you gonna tell me where the Staffords live or not?"

"I don't think I like your attitude," he said.

"Is that right?" Charlotte was clenching her sore fingers now, clenching and unclenching.

"Yeah . . . as a matter of fact, I think you just better turn that shapely ass of yours around and hightail it on out of here," he said, still grinning that rotted grin.

Charlotte stared at him for another moment, her stomach seething.

Then she turned and marched outside.

The noise and chill of the storm slapped her in the face as she emerged from the tavern, pausing on the wooden steps. The rain had leveled off to a steady downpour, but the wind had gotten colder, meaner, and now the rain was getting icier, threatening to turn into snow. It made everything raw and gray, the muddy roads exceedingly treacherous.

Charlotte hurried across the lot to the Escort, got inside, and slammed the door.

She sat there for a moment, the sound of the rain like corn kernels popping on the roof. She wiped the moisture off her face and looked at her bandaged hand. It was trembling furiously now. Both hands were trembling. Charlotte made fists and tried to breathe through the shaking, but it was no use. She was a nervous wreck. The fear and the anger had made quite a cocktail of adrenaline inside her. She could taste something bitter in the back of her throat. Her chest was tight.

Across the parking lot, something caught Charlotte's attention.

There was a face staring out the front porthole window embedded in Packard's entrance. An older woman in a rain scarf, a cigarette jutting out of her mouth. She was one of the people sitting along the window. Probably a local. At first it looked as though she were merely gazing out at the rain. But the more Charlotte looked at her, the more it became apparent that the woman was looking at Charlotte.

The entrance door opened suddenly, and the woman emerged and trotted across the lot toward the Escort.

Charlotte reached over and opened the passenger door.

The older woman slid inside the Escort without bothering to close the door. "You're looking for the Staffords, right?" she said, her cigarette bobbing as she talked. She had a bee's nest bouffant under her plastic rain scarf, and she wore a gray housedress, and judging from the lines on her face she had seen a lot of heartache in her life.

"That's right," Charlotte said, her heart racing.

"I shoulda said something inside." The older woman thrust an arthritic hand out for Charlotte to shake. "My name's Lorraine Erickson."

"Charlotte . . . Smith," Charlotte said, then shook the woman's hand.

"My grandson plays Little League baseball with the Stafford boy."

Charlotte felt gooseflesh break out across her back. "Really?"

"Yep. Nice young man. Saw him just a couple of days ago."

"You saw him?"

"That's right. Up ta Logan school. Playing baseball with the other kids. Name's Darryl."

"Darryl. Great." Charlotte was nervously rubbing

her bandaged right hand. "So you can tell me where he lives?"

"I should hope so. My grandson Ronnie and him are best friends. Only thing is . . ."

"Yes?" Charlotte swallowed hard. "Is there a problem?"

"Well, see, the thing is, I didn't want to say nothing in front of Harley in there." The woman motioned with her thumb back toward the tavern, presumably referring to the Marlboro Man. "It's just that, the Stafford boy's father—can't remember his name right now—he seems kinda troubled. And I was thinking you might be a social worker or something. You know. Checking into the possibility of abuse. Something like that?"

Charlotte looked at the woman and nodded. "It's something like that, yeah."

The older woman sighed wearily. "That's what I was afraid of."

"You think you can tell me where they live?"

"Of course, dear. You're a just a hop, skip, and a jump away."

And then the woman in the scarf started giving Charlotte explicit directions.

43

Candy Apple Red

He wasn't satisfied yet, not yet—there were still the windows in the rear of the house, across the back wall of the den. Three triple-pane Pella windows facing the woods in back. It was a west wall, and it offered a lot of wonderful mountain light filtering through the trees in the evenings, but now it was a liability. An assailant could sneak onto the property from the forest and get an eyeful through those three horrible windows.

Paul gathered another armful of cedar planks, then rushed through the kitchen to the den.

He was dressed in jeans, work boots, and a flannel shirt which was damp with his panic sweat. He had a carpenter's apron around his waist filled with sinkers, a hammer, a .38-caliber snub-nose, and a box of hollowpoints. He hadn't shaved for three days, and he had that musky smell of fear that alcoholics get when they lock themselves into detox. In some ways, Paul, too, was kicking an addiction. It was an addiction to lying, an addiction to hiding, an addiction to running away from his mistakes. Those days were over now.

He slammed a piece of cedar over the first window and started hammering it onto the frame. Then another, and another, and within minutes he had covered the rear windows with lumber, leaving only narrow slits through which he could peer outside. He leaned down and looked through one of the slits at the backyard, scanning the misty tree line.

.The home sat on a remote, three-acre wooded plot about a mile west of Grand Lake. The closest neighbor was five hundred yards to the south—a mechanic and his wife—and the rest of the locals lived across the highway to the east. The land around the Lattamore house was raw, undeveloped pine barrens, a carpet of decaying pine needles and deadfalls strewn here and there with the occasional wrecked car or fossilized snowmobile chassis buried in the humus. The view was incredible—it was one of the reasons Paul had chosen this place—with a scenic vista out the front picture window that was absolutely breathtaking. Plus, it allowed Paul plenty of time to see somebody coming; visitors were routed up the hill via a narrow access road that ran along the front creek.

But the backyard was another story. The backyard was much more problematic. Thick with knotty birch, Ponderosa pine, and towering blue spruce, the backyard sat at the threshold of the Arapaho National Forest, almost two hundred square miles of rugged wilderness, perhaps the wildest acreage in the entire continental United States. Virtually anything could crawl, slither, or creep out of that forest at any moment—without warning—and be clawing at the back door before Paul would have a chance to blink. But it wasn't a black bear or coyote that Paul was worried about right now. It was the species *homo erectus mafioso,* and that's why Paul was peering through the slat at the woods.

The rain had lifted somewhat, but the afternoon had turned colder, and now the vapors were rising off of the cooling ground like ghosts. Paul squinted to see beyond the tree line. The shadows answered him with more shadows, the wind playing in the treetops, making breathy noises, ebbing and flowing and swaying spastically—

A sudden noise came from the front of the house, muffled and indistinct.

Paul tensed, his scalp prickling. He wasn't ready yet, goddamnit, he wasn't ready. His mouth was dry all of a sudden, dry and pasty, and he reached down into his carpenter's apron with a trembling hand. He found the Taurus .38 and brought it out, checking the cylinder, hands still trembling, brain recycling Marshal Vincent's lessons about the "tripod posture" and keeping his elbows locked. He heard the noise again and acid squirted through his stomach. He hadn't imagined it. It was real, the noise was out there, and it was getting closer.

A car tire crunching over gravel.

Paul spun toward the kitchen, the gun pointing up at the ceiling. He shuffled through the kitchen sideways, his gaze everywhere at once, glancing over his shoulder at the back door—cedar planks across the jamb—then glancing over his other shoulder at the window by the sink, also boarded up. Paul felt nauseous all of a sudden, and he found himself wondering if he had the gonads to do what had to be done. Thank God he had finally convinced Sandy to leave with the kids. She had been calling him throughout the morning, begging him to leave, begging him to call the marshals, but he had refused to back down. After a while, he had even taken the phone off the hook. Whoever or whatever had entered his brain last night, the message was meant for him and him alone. A sign, a portent of death maybe—but if he was going to die in some kind of bloody showdown, it was going to be his *own* bloody showdown.

And he was going to go down fighting.

He glanced at the counter where several ammo magazines were lying in a neat little row on the Formica, the Heckler & Koch MP5 machine pistol perched on the windowsill like a black malignancy. He laid the Taurus down by the ammo clips, then scooped up the MP5. He snapped back the cocking mechanism, then crept out into the living room. There were a pair of mini-Uzis lying on the sofa under the front windows—also boarded—flanked by a row of twenty-round magazines.

The sound of a car door slamming could be heard outside, across the front yard.

Paul went over to the front windows and peered through the slat. At first he couldn't tell how many there were, only the make and model of their car: a Ford Escort parked at the base of the driveway. The driver was getting out, and Paul craned his neck to see better. The mist was obscuring the driver's face, and Paul felt his heart racing. The urge to open fire was like a fuse inside him—just spray the fucking bastard with nine-millimeter bullets and ask questions later—and he poked the MP5's short barrel through the slat and aimed just as the driver's face came into view.

A woman?

Paul pulled the trigger.

The MP5 barked, jiggling in his hands, the sparks blossoming in the gray light, popping like overheating fuses, sending hellfire arcing across the front lot, ricochets snapping like fireworks along the edge of the gravel drive—warning shots, mostly—and all at once the lady darted out of harm's way like a jittery gazelle, ducking behind the car. And then Paul let up on the trigger, crouching underneath the window. The silence was a sudden, jarring explosion. His ears were ringing. His hands were tingling—the MP5 warm in his sweaty grasp—and he couldn't move.

Then came the voice, straining to be heard above the winds: "I'm not armed! Please don't shoot!"

Paul could barely make out the words—his ears still ringing, the winds still tossing the trees—but something deep down inside him detected a contradiction.

The voice was hoarse with emotion, juiced up with adrenaline, but was also filled with *fear*. Paul could hear terror underneath the words, and it sounded very sincere. What in God's name would a hitter be afraid of?

Across the lot, the voice called out: "I'm not here to hurt you, Paul—I promise!"

Crouching in the silent house, Paul cringed at the pain in his knees and the pain in his chest. What kind of a goddamned hit woman was *this*—calling him *Paul*? His heart was beating so quickly now it felt as though it were about to crack open his sternum. He thumbed the release switch on the MP5, and the clip clattered to the carpet. Then he snatched another magazine off the couch, clicked it into the hot metal gun stock, and yanked the lever backward.

He peered out the window, aiming the barrel through the slat, finger poised on the trigger. He could see the woman's shadow crouched behind the car.

The sound of her tremulous voice: "You gotta believe me, I'm here to help!"

Paul called out: "Who says I need help?!"

"C'mon, Paul—you're in danger. That's why I'm here."

"I don't know what you're talking about! All I know is, you're trespassing, and this is my land, and the cops are on the way!"

"Paul, listen to me—"

"NO!" Paul roared suddenly, all the pent-up emotion bursting out of him. "I'M DONE RUNNING!— IT ALL ENDS TODAY!—RIGHT HERE!!"

Then he ran out of breath, heart racing, throat clogged with bile. He felt like an animal cornered in a cage, a monkey crouching in the harsh light of the lab. When he was a little boy, he once felt like this. He had stolen a can of Testors spray paint from an art supply shop, and the shop had called his father, and little Paulie had run out the back door and into the woods to his tree house fort. But his father had come and found him, cowering in that tree house.

Outside, there was another long, windy pause.

Paul closed his eyes. He didn't want to fire the gun anymore. He didn't want to fight anymore. But he was cornered. Cornered. And all he could see in his mind's eye was that little bottle of candy-apple red Testors paint. Gripped tightly in his ten-year-old palm while he cowered in his tree house. The little clear bottle was burned into his subconscious, and in his memory it seemed to pulsate with a fluorescent inner life, as though the paint were a cosmic test.

A message from God.

"Paul?!" The voice outside was sounding almost ghostly now, drifting on the wind. "Can you hear me?!"

Paul hollered, "Shut up or I'll fire another burst! You hear me?!"

"Paul, listen to me! I work with the police! I'm a psychic! You understand what I'm saying? I'm a psychic specializing in missing persons cases!"

Paul stared at the inside of the boarded window. All at once nothing looked real anymore. The factory-fresh plywood haphazardly nailed across the front picture window, the grape juice stain on the back of the sofa where Timmy had spilled—it was all taking on a surreal cast like spectral objects from a dream. Did she say psychic? She couldn't have said that. This was getting ridiculous.

"That's how I found you, Paul!" the voice called out. "I was fooled into locating you. I know it's a lot to swallow, but if you'll just—"

"SHUT UP!"

"—let me prove it to you!!"

"COPS'LL BE HEAR ANY SECOND!!"

Then there was a pause that seemed to press down on Paul's brain like a vise grip.

"Paul, I'm seeing something red! Did you hear what I said?! I can see something red! Metallic— No, wait!" There was another windy silence, and Paul's heart felt as though it were about to burst out of his chest. Then the voice called out: "Candy-apple red! A bottle of paint! Right?! It's a bottle of paint from your childhood?!"

Something shifted inside Paul. It felt as though his eyes were too big for their sockets now, the flesh on his scalp crawling. How could she know that? How could she know what he was just thinking? This kind of stuff just doesn't happen. It was a trick.

He couldn't breathe.

All he could do was stare at that stupid manufacturer's logo wood-burned into the plywood across the window: a cartoon panda bear.

The voice across the lawn called out: "I can see *Ash*! And *Land*! Ash Land?!"

Paul's breath froze in his throat. He couldn't move, couldn't answer.

The voice calling out: "Did you hear what I said?! I said Ash Land! Ash Land Mill!"

Paul couldn't budge, couldn't tear his gaze away from that stupid panda bear logo on the back side of the wood, or the three words printed below the symbol in flowery cursive script: *Ashland Mills Incorporated.*

Paul dropped the MP5 to the carpet.

44

Fun House Mirror

Charlotte's mind was a riot of sights and sounds.

Crouched behind the Escort's rear bumper, soaked to the bone, heart palpitating, flesh crawling, head swimming with sensations, she could sense all sorts of danger closing in on them like a black shade being drawn over the sky, the signals crackling hotly in her brain, the ice ache throbbing behind the bridge of her nose. She wanted to run; she wanted to cry out for help; but didn't; she didn't budge. She was trying to stay locked on to Paul's eye line. What was he seeing? How did it feel?

The coin was still enclosed in Charlotte's white-knuckled fist, her other hand pressed against the gravel of the driveway like a divining rod, absorbing residual electrical energy. She refused to give up. No matter how much he shot at her, no matter how terrified she became, she refused to locate another dead person.

She was going to save this one.

"Paul!" she called out through the spitting sleet. "Did you hear what I said? Paul?! Do you believe me now?!" No answer. "Paul! Please!"

Only the wind swirling through the tops of the ancient yellow pines.

Charlotte slammed her eyes shut—

(—*peering through the slat between makeshift plywood—*)

—and she gasped—

(—*seeing the figure out there, crouched behind the car in the driveway*—)

—and she flinched backward, nearly toppling down the sloped gravel drive.

She gasped for breath, steadying herself against the Escort's slippery bumper, her heart racing. She swallowed a mouthful of terror, the wind buffeting her, flapping her windbreaker. She shivered. In all her days, she had never seen through the eyes of a person looking back at *her* before. Looking right at Charlotte. It was the strangest sensation Charlotte had ever felt. Like sticking a wet finger in a light socket. She saw her own image, filtered through the noise of someone else's perception. She felt the fear, the suspicion, the mistrust, the rage.

It was like staring into a fun house mirror.

"Paul!" she cried. "I'm not here to kill you! Think about it! Would I drive up and park in your driveway?! Come on! Those flashes you've been feeling! Who do you think's been sending them! Let me help you!"

There was an excruciating stretch of silence then, and Charlotte cringed at the throbbing ache behind her eyes. Her knees were on fire from the awkward crouching position, but she didn't dare move, she didn't dare step into view of those windows yet. There was no telling whether Lattamore was convinced yet, and no amount of talking was going to get Charlotte to step into the line of fire.

A strangled voice from inside the boarded windows pierced the windy silence: "Who are you?!"

Charlotte wiped her face, took a deep breath. "I'm Charlotte Vickers!"

"Why are you here!?"

"I'm here to help you!"

"WHY!?!"

After a long pause, Charlotte licked her lips. "Because I think I helped the Fabionnes find you!"

"You're insane!"

"No, Paul, I'm not insane! A little naive, maybe, but not insane!"

"I'm serious about the police!"

"The police aren't coming, Paul! You know that as well as I do!"

There was another pause.

Somewhere behind Charlotte—maybe a mile or so away—there was a sound.

Charlotte glanced over her shoulder.

In the distance she could see the highway snaking down the side of the mountain and into a boulder-strewn valley known to geologists as an alluvial plane. A repository of glacial silt, wild scrub, and garbage, the alluvial plane was a barren, brown wasteland, broken only by the gray ribbon of pavement. And right now, under nasty skies and rapidly falling temperatures, the road looked like a mirage, like something from a dream, completely deserted.

Except for the single, beige-colored Chevy camper coming this way.

Charlotte turned back to the house, her pulse accelerating, her brain crackling. The dreadful feelings echoing across the valley from that camper were unmistakable. This was no middle-class family on vacation. "Paul, listen to me!" Charlotte hollered. "They're coming!"

"Who?"

"Fabionne's men—they're coming up the side of the mountain!"

"Put your hands up where I can see them!" the man called from the house. He sounded different somehow, more resolved, steadier. And that was a good sign.

Charlotte swallowed hard, girding herself. Then she rose up, her hands thrust up into the air, her heart a sledgehammer in her chest. "We're outta time, Paul," she said. "We gotta get outta here!"

"Turn around!"

Charlotte obliged, turning a complete circle, showing him she wasn't armed.

"Okay, stay there for a second!" The man in the house backed away from the boarded window, then vanished. A moment later, the front door slowly cracked open. Paul Lattamore was standing there, peering out. "Hurry up, get in here!"

Charlotte glanced over her shoulder and saw the camper, maybe a quarter mile away, coming up the winding road. It was hauling ass, its tires singing around the turns. It would be here in a matter of minutes.

Charlotte grabbed her knapsack, then scurried quickly up the gravel drive toward the front door.

Paul was waiting for her. "Drop the bag!" he yelled, pointing the machine pistol at her.

Charlotte froze, dropping the bag.

She raised her hands in the air. "Paul, listen to me," she said. "They're coming. I need the bag. Yes, there's a gun in it. I'm going to use it on them. Not you. Them."

Paul looked at her.

Then he quickly grabbed her sack and ushered her inside, slamming the door behind them.

45

Dark Glass

Charlotte was breathing hard now, glancing around the cabin, trying to get her bearings back.

The house was exactly how she had intuited it, right down to the threadbare pleated drapes on the front windows, the big ratty sofa on the east wall, the doilies on the secondhand side tables, even the kids' pictures over the couch—most of them new, hastily shot Polaroids of recent picnics and school functions—the feeble attempts to rebuild a shattered family history. The place smelled of burnt toast and mildew, and something hot and metallic—probably from the gunfire— and Charlotte saw the ammo clips and weapons spread across the sofa cushions. She also saw the makeshift carpentry across the front windows. She stared at the tiny panda logo on the wood, the cursive script burned under the symbol: *Ashland Mills Incorporated*.

Gooseflesh rippled down Charlotte's back.

She turned and looked at Paul. His face was flush and moist, and he seemed a lot smaller than she had imagined. Small and pale and freckled in his denim jeans and flannel, like an overgrown child, a child fighting to survive.

"How do you know it's them?" he asked, cocking the MP5 with a wince.

"Like I said, I'm a psychic." She glanced around the living room. "Although there's plenty I *don't* know—like where's the rest of the family?"

"They're gone, they're safe."

"Because of the—?"

Paul nodded. "I thought I was losing my mind; your 'messages' were driving me crazy."

Charlotte glanced over her shoulder. "Is there a back way out of here?"

"I'm not sure that's the best approach."

"Why?"

"It's pretty rough back there, pretty rugged."

She looked at him. "So are these guys, honey, believe me."

"We might have a better chance fighting them off from in here."

"Did you call the police?"

Paul shook his head. "No, no, you can't trust them, you can't risk blowing your cover—that's one of the first things they teach you."

"Is there anybody you can call from the Program? Anybody you trust?"

Paul looked at her, licking his lips, swallowing air. "I decided to face this alone—whatever it was—I wanted to face it alone."

Charlotte nodded, understanding perfectly what he was saying, understanding it so well she felt connected to him on a deeper level now. She knelt down by the knapsack—Paul had dropped it by the window—and unzipped it. She pulled out the Ruger, found one of the magazines, and slid it into the stock, slamming it home with her bandaged palm. Then she looked up at him. "You're not alone anymore."

Paul stared down at her for a moment, his eyes shimmering with emotion. Then he nodded, not saying a word, and that was all it took.

They trusted each other now.

They both went over to the front window, Paul with his MP5, Charlotte with her .22 semi-automatic, and they peered out at the icy gray mist. Charlotte pointed to the north. "See the beige camper coming up the hill?"

"I see it," Paul said.

"That's them."

Paul nodded, licking his lips. "No offense, Charlotte, but your timing is pretty shitty—you realize that, don't you?"

"I tried my best to get here sooner," she said. "Believe me, Paul, I tried."

In the distance, through the trees, the mountain road was barely visible, the camper still a good way off, maybe a couple hundred yards now, but closing fast. It was obvious the wise guys were not concerned about sneaking up on the Lattamores—barreling full steam ahead toward the house—and Charlotte wondered what they would do when they saw her rental car. Would they realize it belonged to an outsider? Would they think it belonged to the Lattamores? All at once, a stitch of panic ran through Charlotte's gut: What if she was wrong about this camper?

"I say we start shooting the minute they approach," Paul said.

Charlotte chewed on her lip for a moment. "We gotta be sure they're the right guys."

"I'm not expecting anybody else, are you?"

"We can't just shoot blind."

"We'll go for their tires."

"Why their tires?"

Paul shrugged. "It'll show them we mean business—I don't know."

"What if we fire warning shots over their heads?"

"Then what?"

Charlotte chewed her lip some more. "I don't know, I don't know, I really didn't think this part through."

"Well, you better start thinking it through."

"Won't the police come eventually?" Charlotte asked.

"What do you mean?"

"Somebody's bound to call the sheriff, right? All the gunfire?"

Paul shrugged again. "This is the boonies, Charlotte—by the time they show up, it'll all be over."

Charlotte nodded, looking down at the pistol gripped in her sweaty, bandaged hand. The feelings had stopped crackling off it, and now it was just a cold, dead slab of metal in her hand. A tool. A really noisy, dangerous tool, as Junior would say—but nothing more, nothing less. And Charlotte wondered if she had the guts to use it.

She glanced back out the slat.

The camper was less than a hundred yards away now, coming around the final bend in the road, approaching a series of small, roadside reflectors that marked the Stafford driveway. There were plumes of black vapor shooting out the camper's rear—probably engine fatigue from the high altitudes—and the big wipers in front were oscillating hypnotically across the tinted windshield. The glass was too dark to see anybody on the other side.

"Wait a minute," Paul said suddenly, his voice taut. He was gazing out at the camper.

"What? What is it?"

"Look—"

"What?"

"They're not slowing down—look!"

Charlotte glanced back out at the camper, and sure enough, it was roaring past the Stafford homestead, a cloud of exhaust and wet vapor trailing behind it. It vanished around the bend to the south. And then there was an awkward stillness, a pause where nothing seemed to move—no sound, no wind, and time itself seemed to halt. Charlotte could not take her eyes off the tree line to the south. Had she been mistaken about the camper? Had her feelings been wrong?

"I don't believe it," Paul said incredulously, like a man awakening from a dream.

"It wasn't them," Charlotte said softly.

"I'll be damned."

Almost simultaneously their gun barrels lowered, moving away from the slat.

"I don't get it," Charlotte uttered.

"You don't think—"

"Wait!" Charlotte grabbed his arm, squeezing hard, her gaze locked on that distant tree line to the south where the aspens and pines swallowed up the road. Something was moving behind those trees. At first it looked like a big, amorphous shadow weaving behind the deadfalls, but then it loomed closer.

Soon Charlotte could make out the shapes, becoming clearer and clearer in the frozen, steel gray drizzle.

Two beefy men with automatic assault rifles walking steadily this way.

46

Unexpected Guest

"Okay . . . let's just take this one step at a time."
Charlotte's voice was nerve-racked, almost a hoarse
whisper.

She was gently urging Paul away from the window,
and she found herself trying to remember what Junior
had told her about shooting, about relaxing, about
breathing through the shot and not trying to compensate for the "kick" when the gun fires. Her body felt
hot all of a sudden, flush, moist with perspiration. Her
fight-or-flight instinct was kicking in, and oh God, how
she wanted to fly away from there, but instead she
aimed the Ruger out at the gloomy light and drew a
bead on the two killers approaching the property from
the south.

They were a hundred yards away now, coming
round the curve at the southern edge of Paul's lot line,
moving with steady, purposeful strides. Dressed in
identical plastic gray raincoats, walking side by side,
heavy artillery cradled in their arms, they looked like
journeymen plumbers coming to fix a leaky faucet.
The one on the left was younger, burlier, meaner-
looking. Charlotte recognized him from the showdown
in her living room—a battle which had occurred only
a couple of days ago, but which seemed like several
lifetimes ago. The one on the right was obese, stuffed
into his gray rain slicker like a plump sausage, an
angry gleam in his eyes.

Paul said, "You ready?"

Charlotte aimed at the ground around their feet and said, "Honey, I'm as ready as I'll ever be."

Then Charlotte started breathing steadily, trying to recall Junior's instruction. She gripped the gun a tad tighter with her bandaged hand. "I'm gonna fire some warning shots first," she said.

"I'm with you," Paul said.

The two killers were coming across the front lot now, creeping along the tree line.

Charlotte squeezed off three quick shots, and Paul followed suit.

The sound was much bigger than Charlotte remembered, the noise reverberating off the walls, the sparks arcing out the gap in the wood, the hot spit of blowback, splintered wood, and heat in Charlotte's face. She was jerking at the recoil, wincing at the sound of Paul's MP5 barking next to her. The noise was making her deaf, making her barely cognizant of the commotion outside. The two wise guys had each flopped to the ground, and now were crawling for cover. Charlotte clutched at Paul's arm, and he immediately ceased firing.

The silence landed like a load of bricks.

"Shit—look out!" Paul grabbed Charlotte by the waist, then yanked her to the floor.

The answer came immediately.

The front windows vaporized, the dragon's roar of large-caliber gunfire gobbling the front of the house, the glass and wood shards hurling across the living room, plaster dust blossoming, filling the air with angry buzzing shrapnel, and it went on and on, much longer than Charlotte thought possible. Her face was pressed down into a moldy braided rug, the rain of splinters on the back of her head, the heat and noise engulfing her. She could feel Paul's body next to her, also facedown and twitching at every blast, and Charlotte closed her eyes and cringed at the sound of hurri-

cane lamps exploding all around her, picture frames
erupting, drywall puncturing.

Charlotte started screaming.

The barrage halted.

Charlotte heard her own scream in her ears—a teakettle whistling—and then she fell silent. She turned
to Paul. He was saying something; his mouth was moving, his eyes bright and hot with panic, but no sound
was coming out. Then Charlotte realized her own ears
were ringing so profoundly now, she couldn't hear a
thing. Paul grabbed at her and motioned toward the
south wall, and she heard him say, "I WON!"

I won?

Charlotte was dazed, stun-drunk, woozy; she had no
idea what the hell Paul was talking about—*I won?*
She turned her body so she could see the south wall,
the single window offering a view of the creek, the
aspens swaying in the wind, and the woodpile stacked
high with cords of pine. Charlotte's ears were still ringing fiercely, but she was starting to hear other things
now. A tiny, shrill voice coming from outside the
house, maybe behind the woodpile—it was hard to tell
in this weather. It sounded like a cat squalling in pain.

Then a tiny figure rose out of the shadows behind
the woodpile.

And the realization struck Charlotte instantly, sending icy chills down her spine, making her scalp crawl:
The little figure had been hiding behind the woodpile
all along, waiting for the right time to step into the
battle, and now he was stumbling across the front lot,
heading directly into the line of fire, hauling something
square and bulky in his arms like an old peach crate,
screaming at the top of his tiny lungs, and Charlotte
recognized him from the sad little framed photographs
across the living room.

Paul had not cried *I won.*

He had hollered *My son.*

47

Whirlwind

Digger was huddling behind a tree, ejecting a spent ammo magazine from his AK-47, when the kid first appeared around the corner of the house.

At first Digger thought he was seeing things—a little snot-nosed kid in dungarees and clod-hopper boots, stumbling across the front lot, screaming some garbled gobbledygook like some retarded little mongoloid— but it was real, and it was happening just as sure as Digger was standing there. The kid was carrying a small wooden box with faded decals on the side, and his little freckled face was all screwed up with piss and vinegar as he staggered across the lot toward the front tree line. It took Digger a moment to realize that the kid was heading straight toward *him*. Digger plucked another ammo clip from behind his belt, then plugged it into the AK's stock.

A strangled cry from the house: *"DARRYL— NO!!"*

Everything seemed to shatter to a halt; even time itself seemed to freeze.

Digger glanced over at the fat man. Crouched behind a deadfall stump about thirty feet away, sheened in sweat and cold moisture, shaking convulsively, Rondo Hatton was trying to reload his own AK. His pudgy face was as pale as uncooked dough. His trembling was partially from the cold, partially from the excitement, and partially from low blood sugar.

For the last couple of hours, Digger had been starving the fat man, forbidding him to stuff a thing into his fat pie hole. The reason was simple: Digger wanted Rondo sharp and mean, and maybe a little crazy. Like a junk yard dog. A big, fat, junk yard dog. But now Digger was starting to regret his decision. The fat man was becoming psychotic. Shoving a new ammo magazine into his gun, Rondo started fiddling with the breech lever, blinking the sweat from his beady little eyes, putting the gun to his shoulder, and taking aim at the tyke.

"Hatton! Hold it!" Digger hissed loudly over the wind and the racket coming from the kid, waving off the fat man's easy shot, because now a thought was occurring to Digger, a realization sparking his synapses: The kid belonged to Lattamore, and that meant that the kid could be used as currency.

Digger glanced back at the youngster, who was coming this way, stumbling over rain-slick leaves.

"IT WAS ME!—I STOLE 'EM!—IT'S MY FAULT—!" the kid was croaking in his trembly, prepubescent voice. He was halfway across the front lot now, approaching the aspens, maybe twenty-five feet or so from Digger's position behind one of the bigger trees. At this distance a single hollowpoint would shatter the kid's skull in a blink. A full auto-burst would take the boy's head off. Digger felt his trigger finger tingling, his eyes watering from the wind and the sleet. He had never zapped a kid before—it seemed like a sin—but hey, there's a first time for everything.

"Come here, kid!" Digger called out to him. "Before you get hurt!"

Another cry from the house: *"DARRYL—PLEASE!!"*

The kid kept marching along, his face hot with fury, his boots uncertain on the icy-wet ground. "My dad had nothing to do with it!" he shouted.

Then his footing slid out from under him, and he

toppled backward, landing hard on his ass, the wooden box flying out of his hands. The box flipped end-over-end behind him, spilling its contents—a bunch of cards, greeting cards maybe, playing cards, something like that. The boy started crawling back toward the cards.

"What the hell you doing, kid?" Digger yelled, getting a little frustrated with this stupid demonstration. What the fuck was going on?

"I don't want 'em anymore!" the kid cried, crawling toward the cards.

"Don't want *what*?!"

The kid started frantically scooping up the cards now, crying and scooping them up: "The baseball cards!—It was me!—I stole 'em!—"

"C'mere, kid—!"

Again from the house: *"DARRRYLLLL—!!"*

"You can have them back!" Darryl cried.

"C'mere, kid—before you get hurt!"

"TAKE 'EM BACK!!" the kid screeched, rising up on wobbly legs, clutching the baseball cards against his little chest. He spun toward Digger's tree, his little face contorted with emotion. *"TAKE 'EM!!"*

Then the kid flung the cards as hard as he could toward Digger.

For one bizarre instant the air seem to fill with baseball cards, spinning magically on the whirlwind before Digger's very eyes, all the cherished faces and numbers and uniforms swirling around on cold gusts—all the Roger Marises and Roberto Clementes and Mickey Mantles and Ernie Bankses—until finally everything started to happen very quickly . . .

. . . like a tinderbox catching fire.

48

Mad Carousel

"Steal this, you little pecker!" The frenzied rasp of the fat man's voice pierced the winds.

Then Digger heard the dry-match strike of the fat man's AK-47 a few feet away—

—and the fat man started firing at the cards.

The kid dove away from the noise, the air filling with high-voltage pops, arc-lightning sparks like anti-aircraft tracers whizzing sideways across the lot, shredding baseball cards, pinging off the side of the Escort, spreading dimples across the quarter panels, pulverizing the glass, and Digger was ducking behind the tree now, wincing at the noise, his ears whistling, his rage boiling over, thinking, *Hatton, you fucking tub of lard, you fat, fucking idiot—*

Then the fat man's clip ran dry.

The house answered immediately.

Twin barrels roared from the boarded windows, blossoms of flame and noise tommy-gunning, punching holes in the ground around Digger's tree, in the branches overhead—these people were lousy marksmen, but dangerous nonetheless—their bullets chewing divots in the bark, spitting chinks of shrapnel all around Digger, a mad carousel of chaos, and all Digger could do was cringe and watch the kid scurrying back across the yard toward the woods in the rear. No more hostage, no more bargaining chip, no more easy money—

The gunfire ceased.

"DARRRRYL!!" The accountant was screaming for his boy again.

Digger peered around the edge of the tree and saw the kid about thirty yards away, making a beeline toward the woods behind the house. The little brat was sprinting like a race dog after a rabbit. Looked like he knew exactly where he was going, like he knew this fucking forest like the back of his hand. Digger looked back over at Rondo and saw the fat man slamming another clip into his AK, his eyes all hot with kill-lust, and Digger started to say something, when all of a sudden there were noises coming from the house—a door squeaking on its hinges, the sound of thunder overhead—

—and Digger glanced back at the house just in time to see two figures emerging from the south side; the little prick accountant and his psychic gal-pal—

—and the first barrage came from the accountant's automatic, a ring of flame flickering around the barrel as he darted toward the woodpile, the psychic close behind him, aiming her own little .22 semiauto. Gunfire filled the air again, puffs of dirt zigzagging around the ground at Digger's feet. Digger huddled behind the tree for a moment, until the firing stopped, and then he peered back around the edge of the trunk. The accountant and the psychic were ducking behind the woodpile now, staying low, moving toward the woods.

Twenty yards to the south, the boy had vanished down a narrow trailhead.

"Lattamore!" Digger's voice was surprisingly calm, considering the pure, unadulterated rage flowing through him.

There was no answer. Digger turned toward the fat man, who was aiming his AK, and he gave the detective a withering glance. The fat man froze as if he were a dog with his tail between his legs, trembling furiously, wiping his face with pudgy fingers. Digger didn't have to say a word. The message was very clear: Lattamore was *his* and his alone. Digger had come too far, had eaten too much shit, to let the fat man do the honors.

"Lattamore!" Digger shouted again, with all the benevolence he could muster. "You listening?!"

No answer.

"You're not being a team player here, buddy!"

Still no answer.

"You want to keep your kid out of this thing?!"

Once again, no answer.

"All you gotta do is come out, sit down, have a little pow-pow!"

Again, there was no answer (not that Digger expected one), and Digger could sense the fat man going nuts behind the deadfall. The detective was radiating blood lust like a musky smell, hyperventilating like a rabid dog, dying to fire some more of those high-velocity, seven-six-two-millimeter rounds.

Another barrage suddenly erupted from the woodpile, spraying the matted leaves at the base of Digger's tree.

Then there was silence.

"They're getting away!" the fat man hollered behind the deadfall in his raspy voice.

Digger mumbled, "Bullshit . . . not in this weather, and not in those woods."

49

Nosedive

In the gray, rainy distance, the accountant and the psychic were vanishing down the same trailhead the boy had taken. It was starting to sleet hard again, and the wind was howling, and the distant forest was swaying and undulating now like a gargantuan creature that had swallowed the kid.

Digger turned and started back toward the road, his plastic rain poncho billowing in the gusts.

The fat man followed him. "Wait a minute—hold it! What's the plan?"

Walking with his head down like an angry bull, his AK-47 at his side, Digger muttered, "The plan is, I'm going to make that fucking bean counter dead—*that's* the plan."

"Aren't we gonna follow them?"

"First things first," Digger said, heading back down the street toward the camper, which sat on the other side of the bend. The wind was a machete across his back, the sleet spitting in his face. He could hear a car coming up the hill behind him, coming very fast, but he paid little attention to it.

He knew who it was, and quite frankly he was in no mood to deal with it right now.

Digger reached the camper and opened the side door, ignoring the smell of human misery that wafted out at him—that oily, cheesy smell—and the sounds of the gray-haired guy's shallow, ragged breathing.

Digger grabbed one of the road cases and slid it out-side onto the pavement.

"What exactly is the game plan here?" the fat man was saying, shivering behind Digger, looking more than ever like a homicidal Humpty Dumpty in his cheap raincoat.

"Grab some extra clips for that AK," Digger said, pulling supplies from the case, stuffing the pockets of his raincoat with boxes of Winchester 52-grain soft-points and small incendiary canisters.

A car was approaching.

Digger glanced over his shoulder and saw the gray metallic Sedan Deville roaring past the accountant's house. It squealed around the curve, then pulled up behind the camper, skidding to a violent halt on the gravel. The rear window was lowering. Digger turned his attention back to his work, pursing his lips as though he had a bad taste in his mouth. He knew what was coming, and he was in no mood.

Natalie Fortunato stuck her face out the Cadillac's window, squinting into the sleet. "You said you were gonna signal me on the cellular when the thing was done; I've been waiting down there for over a half an hour!"

"It's not done yet," Digger said, not taking his eyes off the road case.

"What do you mean, it's not done?"

"It'll take another couple of minutes—tops," Digger said. "And then it'll be done."

"What the fuck are you talking about?!"

Digger didn't answer.

Natalie's nostrils were flaring now, her eyes bright with anger. She thrust her pink, lacquered fingernail at him. "Goddamnit, Mussolino, I swear to God, you're not gonna fuck this up again."

Again, Digger didn't answer. Gut churning with anger, head throbbing, he was busy unsnapping the latches of a long anvil case. He flipped up the lid and revealed a brand-new Browning A-Bolt nestled in the velvet cutout. Compliments of the Romani family, it was similar to the one Digger had left in the panel van, only *this* rifle was the deluxe model, chambered to a .22 Hornet with a state-of-the-art Pentax 16-X scope. It was the kind of big-game rig that also proved extremely useful for rodent control, and today it would prove invaluable for hunting down a *human* varmint named Paul Lattamore.

"I'm sending Carl with you this time," Natalie said through her open window, tapping her driver on the shoulder.

The driver's door opened and out came the blond behemoth in the polyester safari jacket. His bulging biceps crimped the fabric of his sleeves, his vacant, babyish face topped by a geometric flattop so well groomed it looked as though it were made of varnished pine. He was holding a pump-action 12-gauge with a pistol grip. His icy blue eyes were dead little buttons, the eyes of a shark.

"Maybe Carl can finish the job the rest of you so-called professionals keep screwing up," Natalie growled.

"Sure, whatever . . . ," Digger mumbled, scooping up the varmint gun by its strap, slinging it over his shoulder. Then he grabbed his Kimber .45 and thrust it into his belt. He rose and started marching back into the direction he had come.

Natalie called after him: "We'll meet you at the rendezvous point!"

Digger gave her a cursory wave, then strode around the bend in the road toward the Staffords' lot.

The other two men followed silently like a pair of hulking guard dogs.

Digger crossed the property line, marched across the lot, approached the house, then tossed a small metal canister inside the front screen door. Then he walked around to the bushes beneath the windows and put two more canisters down by the cinder-block foundation. The other two men were looking on with only vague interest. It was a risky venture, torching the house of a witness, especially *this* particular house. The flames would only add to the pandemonium that was about to break out any minute now, bringing more police, more firefighters, and more overall attention to the area, but that was precisely what the Fabionne family wanted: *attention.* It was pure mafia, and it was the best way to send a clear and forceful message to future potential witnesses: Rat on the Fabionnes and you will be annihilated from the face of the earth with extreme prejudice—amen. Plus, the fire just might have an added benefit of creating a diversion, keeping the cops out of the woods while Digger hunted down the accountant.

Finally, Digger took an unmarked bottle of clear liquid that he found in the road case and poured its contents around the base of the foundation, sloshing some up the side of the clapboard. Then he fished around in his pocket, found a book of matches, lit one, and tossed it onto the damp ground. The flame licked up the side of the house.

Digger nodded at his comrades, then strode off toward the woods to do a little last-minute rodent control . . .

. . . completely oblivious to the nosediving temperatures already under way.

50

Revelations

The explosion echoed over the treetops behind them—an enormous, muffled, subsonic *FFFOOOMP,* followed by another, then another—and Charlotte nearly tripped and fell on her face. Staggering sideways, dropping her Ruger in the dirt, bracing herself against a crooked phalanx of aspens, she glanced over her shoulder and saw Armageddon rising up into the dark sky a quarter mile away. It looked as though the storm had cracked open right down the middle, and now fire was pouring out of the trees. The bastards had set the Lattamores' house ablaze. Distant flames were swirling up into the mist, sparking stubbornly, then dissipating in the wet sleet, and Charlotte found herself flashing back to snippets of scripture from her seventh-grade catechism classes, snippets out of Revelations—*and the sky vanished like a scroll that is rolled up*—and Charlotte sucked in a breath of cold air for a moment, shaking her head, trying to get her bearings.

"DARRRYLLLLLL—!!"

The sound of Paul's voice snapped her back to the here and now.

The accountant was about thirty paces ahead of her, stumbling along the trail, his leather carpenter's apron bouncing wildly. He had been wailing his son's name ever since they had entered the woods—not a good idea with wise guys on your tail—and now his voice was beginning to fail in the wind and the cold. Unfortunately, the boy had vanished without a trace. Charlotte scooped up her gun and started after the accountant. She didn't want him to get too far ahead of her; the storm was worsening, and if they lost each other, their chances for survival would be severely diminished.

"DARRRRRRYLLLLLLLLL—!!"

Charlotte started running as fast as she could up the winding dirt path.

For a woman who occasionally shopped at Chadwick's Full Figured Boutique, Charlotte Vickers was a pretty darned efficient runner. Although she rarely jogged—the home treadmill that she bought herself for Christmas five years ago was still in mothballs in the basement—she still possessed a natural sort of gait. A distance runner's grace. Back in high school she used to win second- and third-place ribbons in track and field—usually the 100-yard dash and the 440 relay—and for some reason, the skills had simply remained embedded in her muscle memory all these years. And now she was drawing on every ounce of energy she had left to make it up the steep grade and catch up with the accountant.

The trail was a monster, a narrow ribbon of hardpack snaking up the side of White Mountain. Ascending the steep grade, chugging furiously in the thinning air, Charlotte dodged the rutted steps, the crags of stones embedded in the dirt—as slick as ice sculptures—and the wall of swaying junipers and yellow aspens on either flank, tearing at her, scraping her shoulders, clawing at her face. Daggers were thrusting into the bridge of her nose as she ran, harsh signals crackling in her brain.

The wise guys were coming. Charlotte could sense them gaining on her like a toxic rain on her neck. All that black, venomous adrenaline squirting—blood lust shrieking in her head—*here they come, here they come, buzzing with rage, hungry*. The wind was picking up, the gusts lashing icy hail down through the towering pines. The storm was rolling in almost imperceptibly, the sleet turning to hail, and the higher Charlotte climbed, the colder it got, the meaner the winds, the sharper the gusts.

It took her another five minutes to catch up with the accountant.

"DARRYLLLLL!" His voice was faltering now, breaking up like a staticky broadcast as he stumbled upward.

Charlotte caught up with him, grabbing his shoulder. "Paul—PAUL!"

The accountant jumped at her touch, his legs tangling. He tumbled and went sprawling to the ground, slamming hard against a boulder half-buried in the earth. His automatic went skidding across the trail into the weeds.

Charlotte helped him up. "They're coming, honey," Charlotte said, breathing hard. "I don't think it's a good idea to keep screaming."

"We gotta find my boy," Paul said, huffing and puffing, gazing back at the black smoke rising up into the churning sky a mile away.

"They burned the house," Charlotte told him.

Paul looked at her, his face flushed red from the cold and exertion. "Fucking animals."

"They're desperate now," Charlotte said.

"We gotta find Darryl."

"We will, Paul."

"Come on—" The accountant went over to the weeds and scooped up his weapon. The dark blue steel was shiny with moisture.

"Wait!" Charlotte rushed over to him, grabbing his arm. "Let me take the lead, Paul, please—"

"But what if—?"

"This is what I do—"

"But—"

"Please," Charlotte said, her gaze locking on to his watery eyes.

After another brief moment, Paul nodded. "Okay go—go!"

Charlotte turned and led him up another series of narrow hairpins.

Within minutes it seemed as though the entire world had changed. The temperature had plummeted, and the sleet had turned to a mixture of hail and snow— the tiny white granules as hard as BBs from a BB gun shooting down through the pine boughs—and the sound was like a vast jet engine, the surging snow virtually blinding Charlotte in its silvery blur. Her damp jacket and leggings felt as though they were freezing to her skin, her joints starting to stiffen, her feet frostbitten in her lightweight boots, her bandaged fingers like icicles curled around the gun, and she started flashing back to Revelations again, Chapter 16, Verse 21: *And the great hailstones, heavy as hundredweight, dropped on men from heaven, till men cursed God for the plague of hail*—and Charlotte felt the molten-hot rage in her belly again, driving her up the path, turning inside her like a chemical reaction, her anger, her hatred for these beasts on her tail. She kept scanning the forest.

Where are you, Darryl?

Eventually the trail narrowed even further, the snow starting to accumulate.

They were at least nine thousand feet above sea level now, and the air tasted like aluminum, like ice crystals, every breath, every gasp of vapor aching deep in their lungs. Charlotte sensed the wise guys still on their tail, still just out of sight—every now and then the distant sound of a twig snapping or the echo of a voice raised gooseflesh on Charlotte's neck—but she kept struggling onward and upward, through the wind and the snow, her gaze jumping from tree to tree, sniffing for the child.

Speak to me, Darryl, show me where you're hiding, honey, it's okay.

Somewhere around 9,300 feet the first vision came. And it hit Charlotte hard.

51

Pieces of Meat

The object was up in the pine boughs, twenty feet above the ground, and Charlotte saw it just as she was hopping over a tangle of roots poking out of the snow.

She flinched backward, nearly tripping, glancing up at the tiny frozen cherub impaled on the spindles of a massive fir twenty feet above the trail. The snow had dusted the dead infant, making it look like white powdered marble in the bluish light: *The baby from the car wreck.*

"No!" Charlotte clenched her chattery teeth, hard enough to crack her molars, blinking away the vision. The wind was sharp enough to cut diamonds now, and the light was failing under the weight of the storm— all of which was wreaking havoc with visibility. It was difficult to tell whether it was day or night, and exceedingly difficult to see smaller objects. But Charlotte could see the baby all right; Charlotte could see it as plainly as a glowing ember, its head luminous, like a tiny light bulb with eyes.

"What is it?" Paul joined her, puffs of vapor shooting out of his open mouth.

"It's nothing—"

"What did you—?"

"Come on, Paul, we're getting close, come on!" Charlotte tore herself away from the ghostly baby, blinking it away as though it were a bad dream.

She continued trudging up the trail, lifting the collar

of her denim jacket, buttoning it tight against her
throat. She was shivering convulsively, and she was
starting to worry about hypothermia. The storm was
a steady flurry now, the trees bending with the weight
of the wind. She tried to not think about the baby.

The baby had haunted her dreams for years. The
sight of its dead china-doll face nestled in that tree,
those tiny blue lips, so helpless. Charlotte had never
talked to anybody about it, had never seen a therapist,
had never even told Junior. It was simply something
that she lived with. Like an emotional allergy. Every
few months she would see a child, and then the
dreams would start again. It wore her down. The sadness of it. The bone-deep, cancerous sadness.

But now, as she struggled through the storm, inching up the side of the mountain pass, the sadness was
galvanizing into something else.

Something uglier, more volatile.

A few minutes later Charlotte had another vision.
She jerked back, shielding her face from it, the psychic
static sizzling in her brain. The torso lying in the dry
creek bed to her left had been dead for several
weeks—most likely a teenage girl—her flesh as pale
as alabaster, her arms and legs ending in ragged
stumps, her head missing, the neck sprouting slimy
viscera like a dying bouquet. The girl's ghostly moaning rose in the back of Charlotte's memory—*he raped
me, left me out here, cold and torn apart like a piece
of meat*—and Charlotte staggered, nearly tripping on
a tangle of roots.

"What—?" Paul was clutching her arm.

"It's nothing, nothing," Charlotte uttered, trying to
get her bearings.

"You feel something? Is it Darryl?"

Charlotte was gnashing her teeth now, grinding
them, wiping the icy sleet from her eyes, scanning the
woods. "Be quiet, Paul, please."

They climbed another series of hairpins.

The storm raged, and the trail narrowed to a strip of dirty, granular snow—the kind of mountain snow that never really goes away—and Charlotte could feel the cold fire in her belly again, the anger, the pent-up bile that had been rising up her gorge over the last few hours. And the realization washed through her like a fast-acting poison.

All the sadness she had weathered over the years, all the grief, all the forlorn loved ones, the bereaved, the devastated parents of lost children—all of it—curdling into pure, unadulterated, liquid rage flowing through her veins.

Moving slowly upward, she could sense more bodies in the wet, icy blur in her peripheral vision. The poor old man with Alzheimer's who had wandered off and died of exposure; the brokerage firm executive who was kidnapped and died of a heart attack in a warehouse basement; the nurse who was raped and murdered and left in a ditch along Interstate 94 still dressed in her sad little crepe-soled shoes that she wore because her feet would ache at night when she got off the second shift—all these pitiful human remains with which Charlotte had connected, empathized, sympathized—they were back, haunting her, making her sick, making her crazy, the snow flickering in her face like a strobe light, like the flashbulb glare of the forensic technician's camera, recording one tragic loss after another, leaving Charlotte scoured out and numbed by all the evil. How could men do this to each other? How could God let this happen? *How?*

Charlotte's foot tangled in a root, and she went careening to her hands and knees in the snow.

"Charlotte!" Paul rushed over to her side, nervously wiping moisture from his face.

"Where are you?" Charlotte muttered into the snow, her breath coming out in white vapor.

"Charlotte?"

"Where are you? Where? *WHERE?!*" Charlotte was slamming her bandaged fist down on the icy hardpack now, her vision clouding, her tears freezing on her cheeks. The wind bullwhipped across the trail, shivering the trees, sending another barrage of snow across her face.

"Charlotte, what's wrong?" Paul was nervously glancing over his shoulder at the whiteout behind them.

"WHERE! ARE! YOU!" Charlotte kept slamming her fist in the snow.

"They're coming, Charlotte," Paul said over the wind, holding his gun up like a crucifix meant to ward off vampires. "They're getting closer—"

"*—you're alive, honey, you're alive, you're gonna make it, just tell me where you are—*" She was gibbering now, crawling through the grainy snow, the wind convulsing in the trees, the jet engine sounds rising. Signals were crackling in her brain again, the feelings sputtering. Something nearby, something significant on the ground. Her hands were numb now, one step away from frostbite, but she kept crawling and mumbling and wiping away the snow as though there were gold nuggets underneath. Over an icy boulder, across a deadfall stump, through a matted stretch of weeds.

Finally she stopped.

"What *is* that?" Paul was standing behind her, several feet away, craning his neck.

Charlotte reached down and picked up a tiny object that had fluttered to the ground only moments ago, its face dusted with snow.

A baseball card.

52

Deadfall

Noises coming through the deep woods, twigs snapping, the click of a cocking mechanism piercing the rush of the storm, and even the labored breathing of the fat man—

—as Paul crouched beside Charlotte, pointing his gun back at the curtain of powder billowing up on the wind, while Charlotte rose to her knees, squeezing the baseball card, slamming her eyes closed, struggling to open a circuit between the frightened little boy and her cerebellum—

—as the electrical charge hopped through her—

(—*peeking out of a tunnel, no, wait, not a tunnel, not exactly, it only looks like a tunnel, because, because—*)

"Charlotte! For God's sake!" Paul's hand was on Charlotte's shoulder now, radiating fear, making the images crackle and break up on her mindscreen. His strangled whisper was an awful thing to hear. Half-terror, half-madness. "They're right behind us! We gotta move!"

"Wait—!"

Charlotte rose up on her haunches, the wind spitting in her face, nearly knocking her over. She squeezed the card, and she opened the circuit into Darryl's brain—

(—*because I'm inside a huge deadfall log that's been hollowed out, and the dim light is filtering in one end, and the air smells like rotten, wet fur and raccoon turds, and I'm so scared, I pissed my pants, and I can hear something like crazy whispering—)*

"It's him!" Charlotte's hushed cry was almost swallowed up by the wind.

"Where?! Where?!" Paul was swinging the gun every which way now.

"This way!" Charlotte rose to a crouch and started moving—creeping, really—through the snowy undergrowth, squinting against the cold spit in her face, trying to simultaneously see where she was going and still maintain the contact between the card and her mindscreen. She could smell strange odors, and she could taste the coppery taste of fear in her mouth.

She was getting close.

"Darryl!" Charlotte's frenzied whisper warbled on the winds.

No answer.

She kept moving, clutching the card, her mind like a homing beacon in the storm. She was dimly aware of the sound of footsteps in the trees behind them. Was it an ambush? Were the bad guys surrounding them? The storm was like a train approaching, the Doppler-effect roar swirling through the trees. The sleet was a razor on Charlotte's face. But Charlotte kept moving along. She wasn't going to lose this boy. Not this one. Not ever again. She was the Locator. She had a job to do, and she was going to do it right this time.

Clutching the card.

(—a shadow coming, just outside the end of the log, so scared, it's getting closer—)

"Darryl!!" Charlotte raised the card and started waving it back and forth.

On Charlotte's fractured mindscreen she could see her own shadow moving across the snowy ground outside the log.

"There!" Charlotte pointed straight ahead, directly at a huge rotted-out log.

It was half-buried in a drift, the rotted bark like old, blackened leather. There was a good two feet of snow drifted on the top, and most of its length—at least twenty-five feet of it—was slumped under the extra weight. There were slashes of footprints leading into its gaping mouth.

"Darryl?!" Paul's voice was stretched to the breaking point as he started toward the log. He tripped and fell face-first into the powder.

Charlotte made it to the log first. "Honey, it's okay." She knelt down in front of the mouth, peering into the fetid darkness. "My name is Charlotte, and I'm here with your father, and we're gonna get you out of here."

No answer from the darkness, only the faint sound of moaning and a shifting of fabric.

"Darryl, can you hear me?!" Paul had made it to the mouth of the log, and now he was peering over Charlotte's shoulder. "Come out of there, son, please!"

Charlotte could hear movement in the woods behind them, closer now, maybe fifty, sixty yards away; it was hard to tell for sure in the storm and the thick trees. Charlotte turned back to the log and pleaded with the boy: "Darryl, listen to me, please, you've got to come out now. We don't have much time!"

Paul howled at the darkness inside the log: "DARRYL YOU COME OUT OF THERE THIS INSTANT!!"

Charlotte had started to say something . . . when she heard the dry-husk sound of gunmetal snapping behind her.

"Get down!" she cried, barely managing to grab a piece of Paul's shoulder and yanking him to the ground—

—as the woods ignited behind them.

53

Slugs

Automatic gunfire flickered and crackled in the forest, bullets chewing through the soft bark of the log, splinters erupting in all directions, showering Charlotte and Paul in scalding hot powder and noise and confusion, and Paul screamed a primal scream, and Charlotte slammed her eyes closed and covered her head, and the barrage seemed to go on forever, the sound of slugs cracking and pinging through the trees, and the hot-flash sparkles glittering across Charlotte's mind-screen, and her ears ringing again—

—and then it stopped.

For several moments Charlotte forgot to breathe. Hunkered down in front of the log, her heart hammering painfully, she could feel the static electricity on her face. It was as though the storm had been galvanized by the gunfire, as though the particles of snow had been negatively charged, and now the air seemed to sizzle with tension.

"Animals!—Animals!—ANIMALS!!" Paul's voice was barely audible through the storm as he raised the machine pistol, impotently aiming it at the shadows of trees.

Then he fired.

The mouth of his gun barked, strobe-light bright in the storm, silver sparks flickering, three bursts, tracers arcing out into the dark, the hot kickback sending tremors down Paul's arm, shaking his whole skinny body, the bullets going high and wild and useless and pathetic, but at least the noise and light provided some kind of an answer.

When he ceased firing, the silence was like a clarion bell in Charlotte's brain.

She turned back to the log and, in one quick movement, stuck her head into the darkness.

Her senses were bombarded with musky odors and fractured impressions—inarticulate fear; hot, moist, skunky terror. She scanned the darkness, and she finally found the boy, his huddled form about six feet inside the log. He was shivering, his face barely visible in the dim light. He had his hands over his ears, and there were tears and snot on his face.

"I wet my pants," he murmured, his voice full of profound shame.

"It's all right, sweetheart, it's okay, take my hand, we're gonna make it, you and your dad and me."

"I can't move."

"It's okay, honey, take my hand, come on—"

"I'm scared!"

"I'm scared, too, honey, but we're gonna do this together, you and me, all you gotta do is take my hand." Charlotte reached out with her bandaged hand, and she saw the little boy's hand flutter in midair for a moment like a wounded bird trying to fly, and then she felt his hand clamp over hers—

—which is precisely when the next barrage came.

"DOWN!" Charlotte cried, almost to herself more than the boy or Paul.

And the fireworks display erupted outside the mouth of the log.

It lasted only a second, but the noise and light and heat made the air inside the log almost unbearable, and Charlotte shielded Darryl's head with her arms, and she pressed the boy's body down against the icy-moist floor of the log, and she closed her eyes, and she prayed that Paul was okay outside the log.

A moment later, the windy silence returned.

"C'mon, honey, let's go!" Charlotte clutched at the boy's collar and pulled him out.

The snow gusted in Charlotte's face, the icy wind smelling of cordite and burning metal.

Paul was a few feet away, crouching behind a boulder. "Stay down! Stay down!"

He aimed at the woods and fired off another chaotic burst of heat lightning.

Charlotte was on her hands and knees now, dragging the boy toward the other side of the clearing. Her ears were ringing so badly now, she was nearly deaf. She had one arm around Darryl and the other clawing through the snow, her frozen fingers gripped around the Ruger pistol. "Paul!" she whisper-yelled. "Come on! Forget it!—Come on!"

Paul was right behind her now, also on his hands and knees, crabbing through the snow.

The wind screamed.

The sound of something metallic clanging out there in the darkness behind them.

Something flashing across Charlotte's mindscreen, just for a moment.

"Down!" she cried, and the three of them slammed to the ground just as another burst of auto-fire discharged in the darkness forty yards away.

Charlotte felt hot spit on her ear, and she saw a couple of aspen trees shivering ahead of her—this was getting too close for comfort!—and something sparked suddenly in Charlotte's brain, something important.

"C'mon!—C'mon!—C'mon!—" Paul was clutching at Charlotte's jacket, trying to pull her and Darryl toward a narrow backwoods trail.

"You two go on!" Charlotte whispered loudly.

"But—"

"I'll catch up in a second, just go—GO!" Charlotte shoved the boy and his father toward the trail.

They scuttled away.

And Charlotte quickly crawled back toward the slender trunks of aspens shivering in the wind.

She started madly scanning the bone-white bark of the first one, trying to find something very small, very specific—a needle in a haystack—and she found a gouge in the bark, a small notch, and she frantically crawled over to the next tree, ignoring the sounds of footsteps coming behind her, thumping through the snow, thirty yards away now and closing.

Charlotte's heart was racing now, her ears ringing, her mouth dry. Where was it? Where the hell was it? She ran her frostbitten fingers along the trunk of the third aspen, the bark like curled paper.

Then she found it, embedded in the trunk.

A long shot, to be sure, but very possibly her last chance for survival.

Blood Lust

It hardly even looked like a bullet anymore; the casing had collapsed on impact with the first tree, and the rest of the thing had flattened and torn as it penetrated the second and the third trunks. Now it was merely a slug of crumpled, brass-colored metal, a piece of fool's gold embedded in a snow-dusted aspen. It was also a key to her survival.

Charlotte frantically tried to dig it out of the tree. She tried doing it with her bare hands at first, but that was hopeless; her fingers were practically numb. Footsteps were approaching behind her, the sounds of ragged, heavy breathing unmistakable above the winds. She dug in the pockets of her windbreaker, but all she had were the gun—which she had slipped behind her belt—a spare ammo magazine, and Paul's coin.

The wise guys were getting closer. Charlotte's heart started beating faster.

Paul's coin!

She plucked it out of her pocket and jabbed it into the bark, grinding it into the notch above the slug. It was like trying to chisel frozen concrete. The footsteps were closing in behind her, twenty-five yards now, maybe closer. Charlotte's scalp was crawling. She felt woozy all of a sudden, hot-cold flashes shuddering through her, but she kept rooting at that slug, madly picking at it.

The bullet finally popped out of the tree and flipped off into the snow.

Jesus-God-don't-lose-it-in-the-snow!!

Charlotte spun around on her hands and knees and crawled through three inches of dirty snow and ice crystals, searching for the slug, the wind lashing her face, tossing her icy curls into her eyes. A twig snapped about twenty yards off to her right, the sound of a metal bolt clanging. Charlotte was panting now, wallowing around in the slush, panicking, thinking it was hopeless, and she was about to give up . . . when her left hand suddenly fell on something warm.

The bullet.

She scooped it out of the snow.

Sharp, hot pain sang out of her left hand, and she flinched and dropped the bullet. It was branding-iron hot. She grabbed it again and blew on it. It was hot enough to leave a slug-shaped blotch on her palm. But Charlotte ignored the pain and the dizziness, and she took a quick breath, and she braced herself, and she brought her right hand up to her mouth and tore the bandage off with her teeth.

Behind her, something shifted in the storm, something in the foliage, a rustling. Charlotte rose to a crouching position and started creeping away from the sounds. There was another loud click behind her above the wind.

Charlotte paused near a boulder, shifted the slug over to her right hand.

Opening the circuit.

Into the eyes of her pursuers.

(—I see her! I see her! Goddamnit I can see that motherfucking cunt over there by that boulder, and she's ten, maybe fifteen yards away, and I gotta clean shot! The fat man's going to do it, the fat man's going to blow that bitch away—)

—and Charlotte reached around, grasped the shank of her pistol, and yanked it out of her belt.

She did this in one quick motion—within a fraction of a second—without even looking over her shoulder. It was as though she had forgotten who she was, or what she believed in, and now she was working through some lower form of behavior, some kind of reptile-brain, mother-lizard survival instinct, and all she cared about was eliminating the threat to her brood. Her brain was fragmented now, like a split screen in a motion picture, and she saw her own killer—

(—*drawing a bead on that bitch with my AK, aiming directly at her brain*—)

—and Charlotte pointed her gun over her shoulder without looking.

And she fired five times.

It was like a fuse igniting a powderkeg behind her, the storm cracking open with light and sound, the first two shots missing the fat man by a mile, scaring him though, scaring him enough to send his auto-bursts skyward, a brilliant fountain of flickering light into the storm above him, and then the third, fourth, and fifth shots from Charlotte's gun striking the detective in the torso, shoulder, and arm, sending him spinning through the foliage, tossing blood threads and powder outward in every direction.

His automatic was still barking and flickering as he landed in the weeds.

Charlotte didn't wait around to see if she had finished him off.

She could hear the other two pursuers coming now, closing in on her from either side. One of them was about twenty-five yards to the north, coming fast, huffing and puffing. The other one was coming up from the south, about forty yards away, a gigantic presence roaring toward her. Both men were breathing hard and thick, like predators, sending bright tendrils of phosphorescent psychic energy.

Blood lust.

Charlotte rose and started running eastward, through the veil of snowy undergrowth.

Hoping they would shoot at her.

Hoping they would miss.

55

Eyes in the Back of Her Head

The wind was shrieking in Digger's face as he stumbled across the clearing, his Italian shoe-boots slipping and sliding on the granular snow, his .45 in one gloved hand, his hunting rifle in the other. The storm had swallowed all the light now, and the woods had faded to a deep purple color, which was why Digger didn't see the fat man writhing on the ground until it was too late.

Digger's foot caught the edge of the fat man's shoulder, and Digger went careening to the ground.

His guns slid off in either direction, and Digger landed hard against an aspen, his shoulder absorbing most of the impact, his weight nearly shaking all the snow off the tree. His mind swam for a moment, the pain buzzing up his spine, until he heard the fat man moaning inarticulately next to him. Digger managed to rise to his knees.

The fat man stirred. "Mussolino—that you?—Digger?" The fat man's voice was choked in blood. His breathing was labored, his throat whistling faintly.

Digger looked down at the detective. It was clear the fat man was dying. He was soaked in his own cholesterol-rich blood. "Goddamnit, Hatton, what the fuck happened?"

"It's that witch."

"What? What the fuck are you talking about?"

"The psychic lady—I can't explain it—she's got—"

The fat man coughed, a spattering of blood on his chin. It looked like tar in the dim twilight. Then he managed: "—eyes in the back of her head."

Digger felt the rage burning in the back of his throat, the heat in his groin. Yeah, right. She was Wonder Woman. He rose to his feet, then went over and scooped up his guns. He went back to the fat man. "Hatton, you listen to me—"

Fifty yards or so to the east came the sound of gunfire—an enormous blast from a 12-gauge.

The dry silver flash ignited the flurries.

"Fuck! That fucking mutt!" Digger wiped the moisture from his face, gazing out across the curtains of snow, realizing this was turning into a no-win situation: If the blond asshole Carl turned out to be the one to bag the accountant, Digger was in the doghouse. If the accountant managed to get away . . . well, Digger didn't even want to think about that right now.

He turned to say something else to the detective but it was too late; Rondo Hatton had already either passed out or expired. Digger didn't give a shit which it was.

Digger turned and started toward the east, toward the sound of the gunfire.

He didn't hurry. It wasn't in him to hurry. And besides, this was turning into a simple coon hunt, just like the ones his pop used to take him on down in Muscatine. They would get up early—before dawn—and take a cooler full of beer and submarine sandwiches down to the river, and they would hunt the little bastards in the gloomy, green morning light.

This was no better, no worse.

He crossed the clearing and saw movement ahead of him, so he ducked down behind a ridge of snow-dusted boulders. The wind raged in his face, and he squinted to see better. In the distance, he could barely make out two dark shapes sliding through the haze of snow, one ahead of the other. It looked like the psychic lady was a few paces ahead of Blond Carl, but not for long. The big asshole was closing in on her fast with his pistol-grip shotgun, and Digger could smell the tang of cordite and smoke on the winds.

He hopped over a phalanx of rotting logs, then crept down a narrow, rudimentary trail.

Eyes in the back of her head.

"My ass," Digger muttered to himself as he shoved the .45 behind his belt.

He cocked the bolt mechanism on the high-powered rifle and prepared to finish this thing once and for all.

56

.22-Caliber Message

Breathing hard, brain crackling, heart hammering in her chest, Charlotte found one of the pellets embedded in an ancient, gnarled pine about twenty yards east of the trail. She frantically picked at it with the frozen coin, with her numbed hands, with her bloody fingernails. She had the pistol stuffed inside her jeans again, and she could hear the *snap!-CLANG!* of the shotgun behind her, making the flesh on her neck prickle and tingle. The blond bodybuilder had missed her the first time, but he was closing in now for a better angle, and the sonic boom would be coming any second now, vaporizing the back of Charlotte's skull.

She made one last frenzied attempt to dig the buckshot pellet out of the tree, and she finally got it, she got it out and into her palm—

—and then darted toward the deeper woods.

Blond Carl was right behind her, coming through the mist. Charlotte could hear his breath, the vicious pace of his heavy boot steps over the wind. She ducked behind a copse of enormous pines, and she concentrated on that hot little buckshot pellet in her hand. She squeezed it, and she slammed her eyes shut, and she tried to open the circuit.

Her mindscreen crackled with static.

(*—I see her now, I see her shadow behind those trees, and I'm gonna hurt her bad, I'm gonna make*

*her be all dead cuz I'm a real big bad boy with a real
big gun—)*

Charlotte ducked behind the tree, her heart jitter-
bugging in her chest. Several things were flickering
through her mind at once, momentarily sucking the
breath out of her lungs: The blond behemoth had the
intellect of a child, a deranged child, and he was coming to blow her head off right this instant, and he
could see her shadow, and she was trapped, *trapped!*

She glanced to her left, and then to her right, and
she realized she was a goner no matter which direction
she ran. As soon as she crossed the open gap between
this tree and the next, she was dead.

The wind howled.

She clenched the pellet as she inched toward the
south edge of the copse.

*(—that sound, that scratching, shuffling sound, she's
moving, she's moving toward the far side of the tree,
and hey-hey-hey, I'm gonna blow her away-ay-ay—)*

All at once Charlotte got an idea.

She pulled the Ruger from her pants, then reached
down and scooped up a stray stick.

She tossed the stick at the opposite side of the
copse, and the sound it made when it landed in the
weeds startled Blond Carl, and the big man instinctively spun toward the sound, and he fired a single
shell at the stick—a wet depth charge that cracked
open the air—and in the brilliant flare of silver light
that accompanied the blast Charlotte darted out the
opposite side with her Ruger pointed blindly back at
the bodybuilder.

She aimed through her fractured mindscreen.

*(—she's pointing a finger at me—no, no, wait!—
that's not a finger!—)*

Charlotte squeezed off a single shot.

The .22-caliber message struck home, penetrating the
left hemisphere of the bodybuilder's brain, jerking him

off his feet in a paroxysm of blood mist and garbled grunting. His shotgun went off again into the air—another bone-rattler that flashed in the treetops—and the big man tumbled backward, collapsing to the snowy turf with a resounding thump.

And that was the end of Blond Carl.

And Charlotte scurried away.

She found the narrow trail down which Paul and the boy had fled only a few moments ago, and she moved down it as quickly as possible in the swirling winds and sleet. She didn't have time to think about the fact that she had just killed two men, or that the rage was turning her inside out. She didn't have time to think about her frozen fingers, or her frozen toes, or her dwindling ammunition. She had to find Paul and the boy and get them to safety.

The storm was spiking now, and Charlotte could barely see ten feet in front of her. She kept her Ruger raised and readied out in front of her—what did Junior call it?—the tripod posture? She was doing the frantic mental arithmetic as she stumbled along the path: eight rounds in a single magazine, and she had fired seven—one outside the house, five at the fat man, and one at the blond.

She hopped over a deadfall, then started around a hairpin turn—

—and ran directly into Digger Mussolino.

He was fighting his way out of the foliage, and it happened so quickly, neither of them was fully prepared for it, and Charlotte did an almost comical skid across the icy hard-pack, her gun raised and trembling convulsively.

She came to a stop just as Digger was raising his .45 and aiming at her, his eyes big and hot with panic, the top of his head and shoulders covered with snow. There was a crazy beat of silence, a kind of insane tableau where neither moved or said a word or blinked.

The wind screamed.

The two of them just stood there with their guns trained at each other.

Then Digger said, "Wonder Woman, my ass!"

And they both fired.

57

Cold Thunder

Their weapons discharged at the same time—at least, it *seemed* like precisely the same time—because there was a single flash of dry strobe light that lit up the storm, and a thunderous boom that shook the heavens, and Charlotte felt something cold and sharp in her side, just above her hip, like a dog bite—

(—*taste the fear, watch the motherfucker hurt, cut his heart out*—)

—as Charlotte was whiplashed backward with such startling inertia it felt as though she had been shot backward out of a cannon.

She landed on the path and slid several feet across the icy mud.

She came to rest against the base of an aspen, her breath knocked out of her lungs, her numb, frost-bitten fingers still clutching her gun. There was snow on her face, and she couldn't breathe, and she saw stars, and her ears were ringing furiously now. The wind was a jet engine above her, making the trees undulate and creak, and she gasped instinctively for breath. She finally caught her breath in a coughing spasm and managed to look down at the sharp dagger in her side—

(—*tightening the garrote wire around his neck, yeah, watching his eyes bug out, his tongue getting swollen, yeah, watch his bladder cut loose*—)

—and Charlotte gasped at the unsolicited signals crackling across her mindscreen.

She took deep breaths and tried to get her bearings. What had happened? How had she fallen down on the ground? She tried to take deep breaths and move, but it was hard. She was so cold, and she was so confused. She looked back down at her side and saw the jagged tear in her windbreaker, the dark wet spot spreading. She felt her side. It burned fiercely. She had been shot. That's right. She remembered now. But thank God, it seemed that the bullet and passed through clean.

But it had left a trace of itself.

A trace of a hit man's scrambled, homicidal thoughts.

(—*fuck Big John, I'm gonna drink these motherfuckers' blood, I'm gonna rip their heads off, and fuck the five families, I'm gonna stick my iron up that bitch's cunt, blow her a new hole, shit down her throat, fuck her eye sockets, no mercy, ever-ever-ever*—)

And Charlotte bit down hard on her tongue, her mouth filling with warm copper.

Her mindscreen was crackling with noise, sputtering with half-formed thoughts and sensations, flickering with ugly, fractured images. Questions buzzing in her forebrain: What was happening to her? Why wasn't the big man shooting at her? What were these horrible, ugly sensations radiating out from her wound? Was it the bullet? Was it Digger's bullet? Had he infected Charlotte with his poison?

She managed to sit up and gaze out beyond the hazy middle distance.

The big man was lying in a heap, half-buried in the dirty snow, a corona of dark red spreading off each shoulder like huge, dark angel wings. Blood. He'd been hit in the chest, perhaps in the heart. His arms were moving lazily, reaching out at the air as though trying to grab hold of something. His mouth was moving, but it was hard to tell over the noisy winds whether he was actually making any sounds. He looked like an enormous upturned sea turtle.

All at once, the sequence of events came rushing back to Charlotte.

The two gun blasts must have *not* happened at precisely the same time. Charlotte's must have happened a split second sooner, throwing off the big man's aim. Charlotte's bullet took Digger right in the sternum, while Digger's went wide enough that it merely grazed her side.

Charlotte managed to stand on wobbly knees, her side throbbing.

She walked over to the big man.

She stood there in the wind for a moment, gazing down at him. She could see that he was not as badly wounded as she had first thought. The bullet must have caught him high, probably shattering his collarbone. The dark, scarlet button of an entry wound was situated just below his shoulder. The impact—along with the rapid loss of blood—must have merely stunned him. But it was certainly not fatal.

(*—no mercy, ever, ever—*)

Charlotte thumbed the button to the left of her pistol's grip.

The empty magazine tumbled out.

She found the last ammo clip in her back pocket, and she shoved it in the gun—keeping her eyes on the big man all the while—and she snapped back the slide with a *snick-snick!* The sound must have registered in Digger's ears, because his eyes suddenly focused on Charlotte.

She pointed the gun at him.

(*—no mercy—*)

Digger started to say something.

Charlotte fired eight times in a row, until the Ruger clicked empty, the sound of the gunfire echoing up into the sky like cold thunder.

And then there was only the sound of the winds.

And Charlotte felt nothing . . . not even the ghastly vibrations from her wound.

Her mindscreen was blank . . .

. . . as silent and cold as the forest around her.

PART V

THE RENDEZVOUS

"However broken-down is the
spirit's shrine, the spirit is there
all the same."
—NIGERIAN PROVERB

58

Smoke on the Water

The black-and-white was coming down Halifax Road, approaching a secluded clearing just off Shadow Mountain Lake, when the Cadillac and camper came into view.

Officer Carla Strobe pumped the breaks, careful not to send the cruiser into a skid on the ice-slick pavement. A rail-thin German gal with a deeply lined face, Officer Strobe was a veteran policewoman from the Grandby Police Department, and she could smell trouble a hundred miles away. And that's why she put on her roof flashers immediately, opting not to take any chances with this silver Sedan Deville, which sat idling next to a beige Chevy camper. With all the hoopla going on up north—all the shooting and arson and whatnot—it was always better to be safe than sorry.

"You mind running that Caddy's license for me, Bobby?" Carla said, pulling into the turnoff lot, then coming to a stop behind the Cadillac. Twenty feet to the north, the camper was dark and cold, the side door flapping open.

Officer Roberto "Bobby" Garcia was sitting next to Carla in the shotgun seat, nodding amiably. A second-year rookie, the young Latino was a real eager beaver, always trying to win Brownie points. "No problema," he said, chewing on a pencil.

He gazed down at the little laptop computer mounted

to the cruiser's dashboard, and started typing in the appropriate letters and digits.

Officer Strobe put the cruiser in park, grabbed her hat, zipped up her leather jacket, and climbed out. The wind howled at her.

On her way across the clearing, she unbuckled the top of the holster on her Charter Arms .357 Bulldog service revolver—standard procedure—and lowered the brim of her hat against the pounding sleet. As she approached the Caddy, she started getting a tight feeling in her stomach. Something wasn't right, something about the way the Sedan was angled haphazardly next to a garbage Dumpster, engine running, exhaust spewing up into the hectic, stormy night sky. And what about the camper next to it? Its door wide open, not a soul stirring inside, and fresh footprints tracking out its side door, across the lot and into the forest. Officer Strobe could not, for the life of her, figure out what was going on here.

She walked up to the Caddy's driver-side window and tapped on the tinted glass.

The window buzzed down, revealing a mousey little bottle-blonde in a purple pantsuit. "How ya doing, Officer?" the woman said with a sugary smile. "Booger of a night out tonight, huh?"

"Yes, ma'am," Officer Strobe said evenly. "I need to see your driver's license and registration."

"You bet," the woman said, and started digging through the purse in her lap.

A moment later, the woman handed over a license and a temporary vehicle registration for the Cadillac. Officer Strobe plucked a flashlight from her coat pocket, then shone the light down on the documents. It was an Illinois driver's license—issued to one Natalie Marie Fortunato. The car was registered to another person. Someone named Thurston Ciccione. Officer

Strobe pondered the documents. "This vehicle is registered to a Mr. Ciccione," the officer finally said.

"My uncle," the blond woman said, the twinkle fading out of her eyes.

"Uncle?"

"Yes, Officer, the car belongs to my uncle. Uncle
Thurston. I drive it all the time. Is there a problem?"

Officer Strobe kept staring at the registration. "Can
you show me the proof of insurance please?"

The blond woman blinked, and something sparked
behind her dark eyes. Thinly concealed anger. She
leaned over and started rooting through the glove box.
"What's with the third degree?" she started mumbling. "I mean, since *when* is sitting in a parked car
illegal in this state—"

Right then, Officer Strobe heard a noise behind her,
a car door bursting open.

She glanced over her shoulder and saw Officer
Bobby Garcia climbing out of the cruiser, his eyes
wide and panicky, his right hand on his holster, and
Officer Strobe knew immediately what it meant. It
meant that Garcia had found something on the computer, and from the look on his face—the way he was
fumbling for his gun—it was big. Very big. Stumbling
toward the Cadillac, Garcia finally gave Carla a sign
that said everything, a sign that made it all clear: the
international symbol for organized crime.

He reached up to his nose and bent it sideways.

Officer Strobe whirled toward the Cadillac, drawing
her gun and aiming it at the blond woman. "Don't
move!"

The woman had her hands in the glove box, but
now she froze stiff.

"Put your hands on your head! NOW!"

The blond woman sighed, then put her hands on
her head.

"Out of the car! Slowly!" Officer Strobe opened the

door with her free hand, the stainless steel revolver still aimed directly at the blonde. Officer Garcia was approaching, coming around the other side of the car with his own gun drawn and raised, a flashlight in his free hand, sweeping across the tinted windows.

"On the ground! On your stomach!" Officer Strobe hollered at the blonde.

"Oh for Chrissake," the blonde grumbled, kneeling down, then dropping to her tummy on the icy pavement. "All you gotta do is give my fucking attorney a call—his name is Albert Ander—"

"SHUT UP!" Officer Strobe barked angrily, then shot a glance over at Garcia, who was holding his gun on the blonde. "Bobby! Stay with her! Call for backup on the wireless while I check the camper!"

Officer Garcia nodded.

Then Officer Strobe turned and hustled over to the camper, her gun raised, the flashlight gripped against its barrel. She approached the camper's cab and shone the light through the passenger window. The cab was empty. Then she moved over to the side door cautiously, the wind gusting, banging the lightweight aluminum door against the jamb. She aimed the light inside the dark living space.

The first thing that struck her was the smell—a horrible stench, human waste and stale liquor—and then her light played across the floor. The place was a shambles, chairs overturned, broken bottles, dark shiny stains, still wet and putrid. And finally the beam landed on a body. Curled into a fetal position against the front fire wall, naked except for the damp boxer shorts pulled down around his ankles, the man was in his late forties, gray curly hair, stocky. His eyes were open, pupils fixed and dilated. He was drooling.

He looked to be in a coma.

"Bobby!" Officer Strobe called out. "Ask Dispatch to send an ambulance!"

* * *

She found them through sheer luck.

She had been descending a steep, icy slope—almost completely blind—her boots unsteady against the frozen rock and hard-pack, her extremities burning with frostbite. Every breath was a chore, every inhalation burning her lungs. Her feet felt like cinder blocks, her flesh wound still throbbing. She was pretty sure she was moving north, but she could have been wrong; the darkness and the blizzard had pummeled her senseless. The only thing that was keeping her sane was the song.

It was a song from her childhood, the one about smoke on the water.

It had been running through her mind for the last twenty minutes or so like a mantra, the incessant, repetitive melody of heavy-metal power chords like a churning heartbeat in her head, urging her on, a drill sergeant's voice chanting about fire being on the water, and smoke being in the skies. Or was it the other way around? Charlotte had a vague idea the name of the group was Deep Purple, but she wasn't sure about that either. She only knew that the song was embedded in her auditory muscle memory from countless summer nights of smoking cigarettes and brooding in her bedroom about some boy she had a crush on or some drama at school . . . and tonight it was saving her life.

Right up until the moment she slipped on the ice.

Her legs flew out from under her and she went down hard on her ass.

She grunted on impact and slid down the hill, kicking up a clod of snow and rock as she careened. She caught herself on a clump of wild brush, which prevented her from sliding the rest of the way down to the next switchback—fifty or sixty feet down. She gasped for breath, her arms tangling in the scrub. She could hear the tiny avalanche of rock that she had kicked up tumbling down the rest of the slope beneath her. Then she heard it land on the trail.

She couldn't see that far down, but she heard a shuffling noise then, and a few twigs snapping. There was somebody down there, and the falling rock must have startled them. Charlotte tried to move.

A voice called out from below.

"Charlotte?!—that you?!" The voice was tense, wary, and exhausted.

It was Paul.

"Paul!?!" Charlotte tried to holler but it was more of a croak. She rose up to her knees and squinted to see through the flurries.

The voice yelled, "Yes! It's us!"

"Thank God!"

"Are you all right?"

"Yeah, I think so," she said, managing to stand up in the wind. She still couldn't see them. "How about you two? You okay?"

"Yes!" the voice called. "We're a little lost . . . but we're okay!"

Charlotte started making her way down the slope, grasping low-hanging branches for support, following the sound of Paul's voice. The powder swirled around her, and she squinted to see. "Talk to me, Paul!"

"Those wise guys—are they still—?"

"They're gone, Paul." She was nearing the bottom of the slope, and she was just starting to make out the blurry, indistinct shapes of two figures standing in the storm. A skinny man holding a little boy's hand.

"What do you mean by 'gone'?" Paul asked.

Charlotte reached the switchback, then limped over to the accountant and the boy.

They were standing on the trail, both of them shivering, their faces raw with fear and cold. The boy's Oshkosh overalls were coated with snow and he was staring at Charlotte, his eyes haunted. Paul was still in his flannel shirt—which looked soaked with either sleet or sweat or both—and he still had his carpenter's apron on. Both of them were flirting with pneumonia . . . but they were alive. And that was good enough.

"Don't worry about those guys," Charlotte said softly. "They won't be bothering you anymore."

59

The Pit

He lay at the bottom of the pit of despair, the lowest point in the seventh circle of hell, and as his lifeblood seeped out of him, he found himself thinking of his mother. *So cold, Mama, so much blood.* He couldn't feel anything anymore. All he had were his final, pathetic memories of Mother. He wasn't sure, but he had a vague memory of hearing her reading aloud from a nature book, something about these bear pits. Ten feet wide, twenty feet deep, rigged with sharp-pointed stakes and camouflaged with leaves and detritus, the pit was meant to surprise a black bear, sending it down through the false ground and impaling it on one of the stakes. But once in a great while, it happened to a man. Usually a foolish, arrogant man.

A man like Lou St. Louis.

What would his mother say? If she could see him now, writhing in the darkness of this moldering pit, going into shock, the razor edge of a stake piercing his Sunday school suit, skewering his kidney, another one embedded in the meat of his skinny thigh? How had this terrible thing happened? How would Lou explain this to Mother? It was all the curly haired man's fault.

Lou shuddered in the darkness.

The events of the last few hours had been playing over and over in Lou's failing mind: the way the curly haired man had triumphed over the pain. Somehow,

the curly haired man had gone inward, heartbeat slowing down, eyes fixed on some imaginary point in the
distance, his dry, chapped, bleeding lips mumbling to
some imaginary person named Ace. Somehow he had
managed to completely disconnect his own central
nervous system, disengaging the link between his brain
and his body, and this unexpected phenomenon had
driven Lou insane. Lou had lost control for the first
time in his long and strange career. He tore the
camper apart, heaving the curly haired man's limp
body across the room like a sack of rancid potatoes.
And when the flashing blue lights of police cars had
finally appeared on the horizon, Lou had fled the
camper in a frenzy of panic. Unfortunately, he had
misjudged the strength of the storm—as well as his
ability to find his way through the forest—and before
long, he'd become hopelessly lost. From that point on,
it had been only a matter of time before Lou stumbled
into the bear pit.

Now he was dying, the darkness pouring over him
like a subterranean tide rising inside the pit. Had
things been different, he might have started praying
at this point. But Lou was an atheist, and right now
he was as numb and empty as a cold black stone. He
blinked, and he tried to take in a deep breath, but it
was becoming more and more difficult to draw air into
his wounded lungs. He glanced up at the top of the
pit, the dim light from the sky barely illuminating
the opening.

Footsteps were approaching in the darkness. But
they weren't real footsteps. Delicate and dry, they
echoed like tap shoes on cobblestones: the footsteps
of a ghost. Lou stared up at the opening. A shadowy
figure was peering over the edge of the pit, her slender
form silhouetted against the brooding black clouds.
The whisper of a woman's voice.

"Mother?" Lou gazed up at the figure. "Mother, is that you?"

"For goodness' sake, Louis." The woman frowned, her flesh like frozen porcelain. "What have you been up to?"

"I'm dying, Mother."

"You should be ashamed of yourself," the ghost said.

"I'm sorry," Lou uttered in a strangled, watery voice.

"Good-bye, Louis," she said. And then she wasn't there anymore.

"Mother?" Lou strained to see through the rising darkness. "Where am I going?"

But there was no answer from the darkness.

And in a while, there were no more questions from the pit.

60

Return to Sender

"Over here . . . HERE!"

Charlotte had fallen to her knees, the blinding sleet in her eyes as she strained to see the source of the light ahead of her—the shaft of thin, white light dancing to and fro, slicing through the mist. Her voice was almost gone, her body cast in granite from the exposure and frostbite, her flesh wound completely numb, her fingers and toes on fire. She had been hallucinating for over a half an hour now, the whipcord flurries flickering from white to gray like photo negatives, the inky black spots swimming through her field of vision. But she was certain about these three figures emerging from the snowstorm ahead of her like milky phantoms: They were real.

Their flashlight beam glimmered behind an aspen for a moment, then swept toward Charlotte.

"—OVER HERE!—"

Charlotte's voice was weakening, cracking, the ringing still incessant in her right ear. She waved her hands, moving in slow motion. Behind her, Paul and Darryl Lattamore were huddled inside a natural shelter of gigantic, upright deadfall logs, shivering, trying to keep each other alert, awake, and alive. The snow was clinging to their clothes, their faces, their hair, their eyebrows. They had stopped yelling ten minutes ago, close to exhaustion, and now they probably figured Charlotte was seeing things again.

Little Darryl called out suddenly: "Look! Dad! It's the sheriff! It's Sheriff Flynn!"

Charlotte's eyes welled with tears, which instantly dried in the cutting wind.

Thirty yards ahead of them, a big, pear-shaped man in a snow-crusted Stetson and down parka was emerging from the trees, wielding a big industrial-sized flashlight. Sheriff Jay Flynn walked with a huge, deliberate gait—like an old cowboy gone to seed—and he had a big, mean-looking shotgun under one arm. He was flanked by two other men. The one on the left was younger, also wearing a sheriff's uniform, and a ratty down vest and a stocking cap—he looked like a deputy. The other one was middle-aged, leathery and tough-looking, dressed in a green federal marshal's jacket.

"Marshal Vincent!" Paul's voice pierced the wind behind Charlotte. "It's Paul! Paul Stafford!"

"Judas Priest!" Sheriff Flynn exclaimed as he approached, scanning his flashlight across Paul and the boy, and then across Charlotte. The light burst in Charlotte's face, and she squinted, putting her hands up to shield her eyes.

"Everybody get their hands where we can see them!" the deputy hollered.

Charlotte thrust her hands up in the air, squinting, still on her knees in the snow, and Paul and the boy joined her, hands raised, eyes watering, blinking at the harsh light. The lawmen approached cautiously, guns raised, still sorting things out. Sheriff Flynn held the flashlight against the barrel of his 12-gauge, sucking thoughtfully on his teeth. He was the first one to break the ice. "I'll be goddamned," he said. "If it ain't the hole-in-the-wall gang."

The marshal stepped forward. "Is everybody all right?"

Paul still had his hands raised. "Other than a possible case of frostbite—we're still in one piece. Right, Darryl?"

The boy nodded, hands still up in the air. "Yeah, Dad, we're still in one piece."

There was a bizarre pause, as though nobody really knew what to do next.

The wind yowled through the treetops.

"You can put your hands down, folks," Marshal Vincent said, shaking his head in disbelief, putting his .44 back in his holster. He fished in his pocket for a cigarette, grinning at the situation, his head still shaking.

"Give your vest to the boy, Claude," Sheriff Flynn said, and then he rested his shotgun against a boulder. The deputy gave his goose-down vest to Darryl, and Darryl quickly put it on, and then Sheriff Flynn took off his own parka. "Ma'am . . . ?" The sheriff turned to Charlotte, offering his big gloved hand. "Can you stand up?"

Charlotte managed to rise to her feet, her ears ringing, her head still swimming, completely disoriented. The sheriff wrapped his parka around her, and it helped her focus a little bit. "Thank you," she said. "How in God's name did you fellas find us?"

"Ask Claude," the sheriff said.

The deputy shrugged. "I grew up on this mountain. When they couldn't find no bodies in the house, and then they found those boys up on Puma Hill, I figured you folks must've climbed across Bowen Gulch."

Marshal Vincent was cupping his leathery hands around a Camel, trying to spark it in the wind. He finally got it lit and said, "I gotta be honest with ya, Paul, you screwed things up nice and good. Minute your wife shows up on our doorstep in Durango, we know there's gonna be hell to pay back here. And when the boy vanished in the middle of the night, things just went from bad to worse."

Paul looked at him. "Is Sandy okay? Timmy?"

The marshal nodded. "They're fine, they're both waiting for you at a new safe site."

There was another pause, and then Charlotte spoke up: "This whole thing is my fault." Her head was throbbing, the dizziness threatening to wash over her. She needed to get inside soon, or she was going to pass out, or maybe even die of exposure. "Everything," she added. "All my fault."

"We're gonna sort all that out back at the office," Sheriff Flynn said.

"The sheriff's right," Marshal Vincent said, taking one last drag, then dropping the butt in the snow and stomping it out. "Hate to break up this little party, but we gotta get a move-on. Paul, Darryl—you two boys come with me. We're heading west. Miss, you can head back east with the sheriff."

Paul and Darryl walked over and joined the marshal, then paused and gazed back at Charlotte.

Charlotte felt sick, woozy, her head buzzing, her arms and legs burning-cold. Her feet were completely numb; they felt like two blocks of lead. But she couldn't collapse just yet. She had one more item on the agenda tonight. She looked at Paul and managed a smile. "I'm sorry about all this, Paul," she said.

Paul nodded, smiling wanly. "I don't know whether to thank you or . . ." He shrugged.

"You don't have to thank me." She felt her knees wobbling, threatening to buckle. She looked at the boy. "Good luck, honey," she said. "And stay away from the baseball cards for a while."

The boy nodded. "Yes, ma'am, I will."

Marshal Vincent said, "Time to saddle up and ride, boys, come on."

Charlotte glanced back up at Paul, reaching into her jacket pocket. "Before you go, Paul," she said. "I've got something of yours." She plucked the coin out of her pocket and held it up for all to see. The dull finish glimmered in the beam of the flashlight.

Paul frowned. "What the hell is that?"

"Your lucky coin," she said, and then she took a couple of steps toward him. She felt drunk, her ears whistling, gooseflesh surging hot and cold down her spine. Her vision was starting to go, starting to waver in and out of focus. She handed him the coin.

His fingers sparked faintly as he grasped it, and Charlotte felt a jolt of shapeless emotion in her mid-brain, threatening to topple her. She wavered for a moment, struggling to remain upright.

"Make sure you hold on to that thing, Paul," she said finally, and then she kissed his cheek.

"Let's go, boys," the marshal said, and put his big hand on Darryl's shoulder.

The threesome started toward the tree line to the west.

Charlotte watched them for a moment.

Then she collapsed.

PART VI

THE OHIO STATE FAIR

"Human blood is heavy; the man who
has shed it can not run away."
—AFRICAN PROVERB

61

One Last Transaction

The day after the amputations, the staff at Boulder General told Charlotte she could see Junior just for a minute.

She spent the better part of a half an hour at a bedside table the nurses had set up for her, trying to make herself beautiful. It wasn't an easy task. Slumped in a cheap particleboard chair, her shopworn terry-cloth robe wrapped around her hideous cotton gown, staring at herself in the makeshift mirror the nurses had canted against a radiator, she felt like a freak, like the elephant woman the day after a major bender. The tally on her body was measured in yellow, stained bandages across her ribs, and on each of her hands and feet. The bullet wound in her side was superficial . . . but frostbite had turned her extremities into darkened, festering claws. She lost two fingers on her left hand, the index finger on her right, and a total of four toes—three on her right foot, one on her left.

At least her eardrum was not permanently damaged.

Gazing at her frost-burned face in the mirror, she felt oddly buoyant, floating on a cushion of Darvon and Valium, as though she had been disconnected from her physical body. Yesterday's surgery had capped a twenty-four-hour nightmare of relentless interrogation from the FBI, the Federal Marshal Service, the Cook County Sheriff's Police, and the state police from Colorado, Nebraska, and Iowa. Charlotte told them all the truth, every last detail, and the funny thing was, they all believed her. Almost every last one of them had come into contact with psychic detectives like Charlotte, and they were all believers. But none of that had mattered to Charlotte. She was far more concerned with the medical procedure: They were going to take pieces of her livelihood—*her hands*. They were going to take her gift away.

The operation had been relatively easy. They wheeled her into the O.R. yesterday afternoon at two o'clock, put her under general anesthetic, put some microstitches in her side, and then lopped off her infected appendages about as unceremoniously as pruning a shrub. Most of the fingers had been removed at the first knuckle, a flap of muscle and skin folded over to cover the bone. And then the bandages had gone on and they wheeled her out. By three o'clock she was lying in Recovery, feeling her phantom fingertips starting to throb. And that's how she had been measuring time ever since—the ubiquitous throbbing, the inexorable clock inside her. But before they disposed of her severed pieces—which strangely reminded her of lucky coins; lucky charms; talismans—she made one final request to the surgical assistant.

She asked that they save her right index finger.

She had plans for it.

Now she set about to make herself pretty for dear, sweet Junie. Glancing back up at her reflection, she fished through the contents of a shoebox the nurses had brought in, fumbling through the tiny products with her mittenlike bandage. She found some Cover Girl liquid foundation and put that on first, then a little under-eye concealer. She used a blusher to give her cheeks a little color, and a very minimal amount of eyeliner—Maybelline Smoke—just to help her puffy eyes a little bit. And then a mascara on her lashes, waterproof just in case she started bawling when she saw Junie. She finished things off with some lipstick—Crushed Cranberry—and some liner to define the outer contours of her lips.

Then she was ready . . . as ready as she was ever going to be.

She limped out of her room using crutches, then shuffled down the hall to the ICU ward.

Junior's room was the last one on the left, and Charlotte paused outside it for a moment to gird herself. Her heart was starting to beat a little faster, and the throbbing was now like a timpani drum. She reached out, opened the door with her gauzy mitt, and went inside.

The first thing that struck her was the light. The room was a nimbus of white light, the overcast sun streaming through the drawn venetian blinds, glaring off the white tile and the white sheets and the white panels on the walls. The air smelled faintly of disinfectant and urine. The bed was in the center of the room, and Junior was lying prostrate on it, mummified in white, his head lolling to one side, his eyes open, his face like a waxen dummy. The stillness was breathtaking, the dusty silence broken only by the pulse of vital-sign monitors and IV drip bags. And there was a psychic silence as well, as dead and cold as a stagnant black pool in Charlotte's head. Was it because Junie was gone? Or was it because Charlotte had lost some vital part of her own skill along with her ruined fingers?

She went over to the bed, pulled up a chair, and sat down.

"How goes it, Junie?" she said, and then she reached her bandaged left hand over the metal railing and squeezed Junior's hand, and she felt nothing but cold gauze and a faint throbbing. Charlotte began to cry, softly, her tears tracking down her face and pattering against the railing.

So much for the makeup job.

Earlier in the day, the doctors had given Charlotte the lowdown on Junior's condition. He had sustained severe damage to his spine, rectum, and bladder, but chances were good that he would recover—at least physically. His mental condition was another matter altogether. Technically, Junior was in a full-blown coma, and there was no way to predict whether he would ever come out of it. They used a measurement known as the Glascow Scale, which involved three factors: eye movement, verbal response, and muscle response. Junior scored low on all three. The sad fact was, he was in such a vegetative state, it was impossible to provide a prognosis.

Eventually, Charlotte stopped weeping and sat there for quite some time, thinking.

Junior was part of her now, connected in ways that were beyond even Charlotte's understanding. He had come to her in her darkest moments and had saved her life, had given his sanity so that she could live. Charlotte would never forget what he had done. She would never abandon him, even if it meant being his caretaker for the rest of her life.

Charlotte gazed at his placid, empty face. There was a trail of saliva along his chin, and Charlotte reached up and wiped it away with her bandage. She swallowed hard and remembered there was one last thing she could try, one last possibility—a way to wake him up.

But she wasn't ready to try that yet.

Not yet.

Two days later, Charlotte was released.

She took a cab to the nearest shopping center and bought a new skirt and lightweight blouse—the lower elevations were going through a hot spell and she wanted to be comfortable in her bandages. Then she took another cab across town to the Federal Courthouse building in downtown Boulder. She walked with a crutch, and she carried a small nylon backpack with her. The backpack had a single item inside it.

She arrived at the underground holding facility—a vast subterranean labyrinth of carpeted corridors, offices, and minimum security cells—at about four o'clock that afternoon. She went inside the main reception area and was greeted by a beaming Sheriff Jay Flynn and a couple of senior field agents from the local FBI office. Sheriff Flynn's deputy, Claude Templeton, was also there, dressed in a starched white shirt and tie, and he made Charlotte a cup of herbal tea while she chatted with Sheriff Flynn and answered a few questions from the FBI agents.

Then they let her do the one thing that Sheriff Flynn had promised she could do.

They let her spend five minutes alone with Natalie Fortunato.

The feisty little blonde was in the lower level. She had been a "guest" of the facility for three days now, undergoing rigorous interviews, being shuffled from the main facility during the daytime to the women's facility across the street during nights. Natalie's attorney had been bellyaching constantly about the injustice of keeping his client under arrest without charging her with anything, but it was only a matter of time until the state and federal district attorneys came back with a major list of charges on her. This time, they had a witness. And that witness was currently heading down a narrow corridor in the bowels of the complex, approaching the last holding cell on the left.

Charlotte walked up to the front of the cell.

"What in God's name do *you* want?" Natalie growled from the corner of the cell, glancing up from her crossword puzzle. She was sitting in a folding chair next to a card table, wearing a leopard jumper and half-glasses, and she had a cigarette perched off one corner of her mouth, her deep scarlet lipstick staining the butt. The cell was two hundred square feet of pea green tile and bare walls.

"Afternoon, Natalie," Charlotte said, stepping up to the iron mesh. There was a small metal drawer embedded in the mesh about waist high—designed for passing documents. Charlotte glanced down at the drawer, then looked back up at Natalie. "How they treating you?"

"Can't complain too much," Natalie said. There was an odd, sheepish quality to her voice, as though she couldn't figure out how to play this particular situation.

"I've got something for you," Charlotte said.

"You what?"

"A gift, a present." Charlotte shrugged off the backpack, unzipped it, and took out its contents. "I hope there's no hard feelings."

Natalie was getting nervous, glancing across the corridor. "What the hell are you doing, Vickers? The guards are right outside the hallway."

"It's nothing to be afraid of, Natalie." Charlotte was unwrapping the wad of Kleenex, revealing the slender little object nestled inside. "I just thought you'd appreciate some closure."

Charlotte opened the pass-through drawer and dropped the severed finger into it.

Then she slammed the drawer shut, flipping open the lid on the other side. Across the cell, Natalie jumped slightly, unnerved by this whole unexpected visit, too far away to tell what was in the drawer. She set her crossword puzzle down, took off her glasses, and rose to her feet, her face all screwed up with fear and confusion, and maybe even a little curiosity.

Then Natalie walked over to the drawer, reached inside and picked up the severed finger.

Charlotte closed her eyes and opened the floodgates.

Natalie stiffened suddenly, as though a million volts of electricity were pouring into her from the amputated finger, and she shivered convulsively, her eyes rolling back into her skull, and she couldn't let go of the blackened little finger because the psychic current that was emanating from it was welding her hand around it, and Charlotte kept concentrating on the phantom appendage, and all the pain she had lived through, all the rage, all the broken bodies in shallow graves, all the cruelty visited on innocent men in the name of greed and hubris and arrogance and fear and evil, and Natalie's mouth was gaping wide open now, ruby red lips all crooked and deformed as though she were having an epileptic fit, a grand mal seizure, the drool oozing, and she shuddered and moaned like that for several more agonizing moments, her mouth opening wider and wider, the silent scream coming out on a thin wisp of noxious breath.

Then Charlotte turned and walked away, leaving all her black rage and pain in that cell.

Several minutes later, long after Charlotte was gone, the scream started echoing down the empty corridors.

She stood beside his bed, gazing down at his empty, waxen face.

A week had passed since the debacle in Grand Lake, and now Charlotte was walking almost normally with a special prosthetic left shoe. Her hands had healed nicely as well. The sutures had dissolved, and the infection had dried up, and early this morning they had taken her bandages off. Now she was standing in Junior's room, dressed in a new yellow peasant dress, surrounded by the silent dust motes, softly beeping equipment, and Junior's blank face. She gazed down at her hands. They looked alien to her, a pale pink color, the color of a salmon's underbelly, and they itched, and they looked half-finished, their shapes absurd, like combs with broken teeth.

But Charlotte was alive, and her remaining fingers and toes worked just fine, thank you very much.

If only she had the nerve to make her last-ditch attempt to awaken Junior.

She pulled a chair beside his bed and sat down, and all at once she realized that she hadn't touched him— *really* touched him—since they had parted company on that lonely interstate back in Nebraska. But now the prospect of touching him with her damaged flesh was almost unbearable. What if it didn't work? What if her last chance to revive him failed? The prospects were so unsettling that she was almost paralyzed right there in her cheap hospital side chair.

But she had to try.

She reached out and touched his hand.

It was like grasping a chunk of dead cold meat, the shortwave radio in Charlotte's head hissing with a steady drone of white noise. Nothing stirring, no feeling, no images, no sound. His body as cold as a rock, his face just as ashen and empty as ever. A totally dead channel. And the vacuous feeling reached down into Charlotte's guts and twisted, the horrible emptiness of it making gooseflesh crawl along her spine, and she wanted to cry, she wanted to break down right there and wail for her poor lost Junie. But she didn't weep, not yet, not just yet.

There was still one last trick up her sleeve.

She squeezed Junior's hand even tighter, her missing index finger tingling with ghostly sensations, almost as if *it* were squeezing as well, and then Charlotte slammed her eyes closed, and she started concentrating her thoughts harder than she had ever concentrated them before, focusing with laser intensity, aligning every last brain cell on the sights and sounds and smells that Junior had once fed into her own soul like nectar. The steam from the corn dog vender, the girls in halter tops, the yammer of the freak show barker, the shrill keening roar of the thrill ride, the smell of cow shit and tap beer and bratwurst, the taste of cotton candy and cinnamon apples and lemonade shakeups—

—and then something sparked off Junior's flesh.

Charlotte opened her eyes. "Junie—?"

His head moved, ever so slightly, maybe a single centimeter to the left.

Charlotte squeezed his hand tighter, focusing the sensations like light through a magnifying glass. "Come back to me, sweetheart."

His head moved a second time.

"Junie—? Can you hear me?"

Now Junior's eyelids started fluttering, his lips moving as though he were searching for words.

"Junie—omigod—can you hear me?" Charlotte was stunned, paralyzed.

He stared up at her, frowning, moving his lips.

Charlotte's eyes were welling up. "Can you understand me, sweetheart?"

Again he tried to speak, but his brain was still unable to send the words to his mouth. His body was trembling faintly under the blankets, and his eyes were bright with confusion. Finally he managed to squeeze her hand and smile wanly.

"Welcome back, stranger," Charlotte said with a tearful grin, lurching forward into his arms, embracing him desperately. She started to weep softly. "Welcome back . . . welcome back . . . welcome back . . ."

The sound of his voice was hoarse and weak in her ear. "Is . . . it . . . smell . . . ?"

She reared back suddenly, wiping the moist saliva

off his chin, drying her own tears. "What did you say, honey? I didn't hear you."

He looked up at her, blinking a few times, then uttering, "Is it me . . . or do you smell . . . corn dogs?"